Nedjma

Caraf Books
Caribbean and African Literature
Translated from French

Serious writing in French in the Caribbean and Africa has developed unique characteristics in this century. Colonialism was its crucible; African independence in the 1960s its liberating force. The struggles of nation-building and even the constraints of neocolonialism have marked the coming of age of literatures that now gradually distance themselves from the common matrix.

CARAF BOOKS is a collection of novels, plays, poetry, and essays from the regions of the Caribbean and the African continent that have shared this linguistic, cultural, and political heritage while working out their new identity against a background of conflict.

An original feature of the CARAF BOOKS collection is the substantial critical introduction in which a scholar who knows the literature well sets each book in its cultural context and makes it accessible to the student and the general reader.

Most of the books selected for the CARAF collection are being published in English for the first time; some are important books that have been out of print in English or were first issued in editions with a limited distribution. In all cases CARAF books offers the discerning reader new wine in new bottles.

The Editorial Board of CARAF BOOKS consists of A. James Arnold, University of Virginia, General Editor; Kandioura Dramé, University of Virginia, Associate Editor; and three Consulting Editors, Abiola Irele of the University of Ibadan, Nigeria, J. Michael Dash of the University of the West Indies in Mona, Jamaica, and Henry Louis Gates, Jr., of Harvard University.

Caraf Books

Caribbean and African Literature
Translated from French

Guillaume Oyônô-Mbia and Seydou Badian, *Faces of African Independence: Three Plays*

Olympe Bhêly-Quénum, *Snares without End*

Bertène Juminer, *The Bastards*

Tchicaya U Tam'Si, *The Madman and the Medusa*

Alioum Fantouré, *Tropical Circle*

Edouard Glissant, *Caribbean Discourse: Selected Essays*

Daniel Maximin, *Lone Sun*

Aimé Césaire, *Lyric and Dramatic Poetry, 1946–82*

René Depestre, *The Festival of the Greasy Pole*

Kateb Yacine, *Nedjma*

Léopold Sédar Senghor, *The Collected Poetry*

Nedjma

Kateb Yacine

Translated by Richard Howard

Introduction by Bernard Aresu

CARAF BOOKS

University Press of Virginia

CHARLOTTESVILLE AND LONDON

This is a title in the CARAF BOOKS series

© Editions du Seuil, 1956
Originally published in French under the same title
Translation by Richard Howard © 1961 by George Braziller Publishers
THE UNIVERSITY PRESS OF VIRGINIA

Introduction to this volume

Copyright © 1991 by the Rector and Visitors
of the University of Virginia

First published 1991

Library of Congress Cataloging-in-Publication Data

Kateb, Yacine:
[Nedjma. English]
Nedjma / by Kateb Yacine ; translated by Richard Howard ;
introduction by Bernard Aresu.
p. cm. — (CARAF books)
Originally published in French under the same title.
Includes bibliographical references.
ISBN 0-8139-1312-8. — ISBN 0-8139-1313-6 (pbk.)
I. Title. II. Series.
PQ3989.2.Y28N413   1991
843—dc20   90-28436
                                                          CIP

Printed in the United States of America

Contents

Preface to the French Edition

There have been a number of works about Algeria, often by Algerian writers, that deserve respect or even admiration. Yet these same works could have been written, all things being equal, in other latitudes, by men of other races: it would have sufficed for the political and economic conditions comparable to those to which Algeria is subjected to be repeated elsewhere. The stage properties, the setting would be different; but the problem, reduced to its essentials, would be similarly posed. For the books to which we refer bear witness to a situation.

Nedjma bears witness to a people. Kateb Yacine's novel could not be conceived by a Hindu patriot, a Guatemalan revolutionary. Give *Nedjma*'s characters other names, dress them in other clothes: beneath the sari or the poncho, the attentive reader will quickly recognize the Arab in disguise. Rachid or Mokhtar are irreducibly Algerian. The world the novelist builds around them crumbles without them; they die without it. One might say that the relation between this world and these characters is umbilical. This is because Kateb Yacine's narrative is much more than a document. Photography implies objectivity. Here the author is not *objective*, the substance of his novel is not an *object: Nedjma* is the product of a poetic act.

Is Algeria merely an administrative subdivision? In any case the author believes Algerian literature cannot resign itself to being merely a department of French literature, even when it borrows the latter's language and the lessons of its history. Conceived and written in French, *Nedjma* remains a profoundly Arab work, and we cannot arrive at a valid assessment of it if

Preface to the French Edition

we fail to distinguish it from the tradition to which, even in its repudiations, it still belongs.

The narrative techniques Kateb Yacine uses are occasionally disconcerting to the Western reader. The latter, as a last resort, will take refuge in the subtleties of comparative literature to exorcise the mystery: apropos of *Nedjma,* some readers will undoubtedly cite Faulkner. It seems to us that the explanation of this novel's singularities are to be found elsewhere. The narrative's rhythm and construction, if they indisputably owe something to certain Western experiments in fiction, result in chief from a purely Arab notion of *man in time.* Western thought moves in *linear* duration, whereas Arab thought develops in a *circular* duration, each turn a *return,* mingling future and past in the eternity of the moment. This confusion of tenses—which a hasty observer will ascribe to a love of ambiguity and which is actually the symptom of a genius for synthesis—corresponds to so constant a feature of the Arab character, so natural an orientation of Arab thought, that Arab grammar itself is marked by it.

Hence we cannot follow *Nedjma*'s plot development, but rather its involution: the passage from one level of consciousness to another is effected by a kind of intellectual slide down spirals of indefinite length. The reader is furnished landmarks which suffice, we believe, to keep him from getting dizzy. The duodecimal numbering of chapters marks out the trajectory of each "spiral" and indicates the point where it yields to the next. So we can readily follow the rhythm the novelist imposes upon his creation—to the point of being virtually recreated ourselves and penetrating, thanks to this new genesis, to the novel's inmost heart.

To the wary, a summary may appear a necessary guarantee; we present one, with the warning that in truth it summarizes nothing, merely piling up blocks which, as such, will never make a house:

Four friends—Rachid, Lakhdar, Mourad, Mustapha—are living in Bône, obsessed by their common attraction to the same woman, Nedjma, the wife of Kamel. A mystery shrouds

Preface to the French Edition

Nedjma's origin and conception, a mystery they gradually, and through one another, reveal only to discover that it makes Nedjma more inaccessible still: adopted in infancy by Lella Fatma, Nedjma is actually the daughter of a Frenchwoman successively ravished by four lovers, including Rachid's father and a noted seducer, one Si Mokhtar. Nedjma was conceived on a night the two men spent with the Frenchwoman in a cave where the body of Rachid's father was found the next day.

Henceforth Rachid will follow Si Mokhtar everywhere and will spare the life of his father's presumed murderer, haunted as he is by the desire to know the truth about Nedjma (Si Mokhtar had first introduced him to the girl) who might just as well be his sister as the daughter of Si Mokhtar, to whom he is bound by increasingly close ties of family sentiment and friendship. Besides, Si Mokhtar knows himself to be Kamel's father as well, though he could not prevent Nedjma's incestuous marriage without revealing the drama and the mystery of her birth.

After a pilgrimage to Mecca, during which Si Mokhtar finally reveals the secret to Rachid, the two men decide to separate Nedjma from her incestuous husband and take her to the Nadhor, a virtually inaccessible mountain where the remnants of their tribe, the last descendants of the legendary Keblout, still survive. Here Nedjma will be restored to her true destiny, but it is not on the Nadhor that Rachid will fulfill his.

The four friends meet again after various misfortunes and hire themselves out as day laborers. On the first day of work, Lakhdar attacks Monsieur Ernest, the foreman; arrested, he escapes at once. Later, Mourad, touched by the youthful beauty of Suzy, Monsieur Ernest's daughter, kills the obscene old contractor Ricard, whom Suzy has just married. Mourad, in his turn, is arrested. The three friends—the escaped Lakhdar, Rachid, and Mustapha—secretly leave the job and the village. Later Rachid, arrested as a deserter, will meet Mourad in prison. Each man is still obsessed by Nedjma's presence and constantly evokes it: Mourad during his days and nights as a prisoner; Mustapha writing his diary; Rachid talking to a stranger on the banks of the Rummel . . .

Preface to the French Edition

. . . We have told too much—or not enough: this little horological effort leaves the mystery intact. It would be better for the reader to despise such vacillating compasses and entrust himself to the author: the path will not peter out into the sand, and each hesitant step will bring him a little nearer the heart of a world that deserves discovery.

THE EDITORS

Introduction

On 24 May 1947, a young man of eighteen gave an erudite lecture at the Salle des Sociétés Savantes in Paris. The subject was Abd el-Kader, the first organizer of substantial resistance to French colonial expansion in Algeria and the father of Algerian nationalism. At that time, issues of political injustice and freedom from colonial occupation had not yet assumed the prominence and significance that the French defeats in the Indochinese and Algerian wars of independence were to confer upon them only a few years later. In 1948, *Le Mercure de France*, a literary magazine that had been prominent since the turn of the century, published "Nedjma ou le poème ou le couteau" (Nedjma or the poem or the knife). It was an Algerian love poem suffused with spectacular imagery and lyrical density written by the same young man.[1] These two events very early in Kateb Yacine's public life not only launched the precocious and meteoric rise of a brilliantly gifted writer but—in their exemplification of a dialectic of commitment and creativity, political consciousness and poetic effusion—they also embody the creative polarities that presided over the production of a large body of writing to which Kateb was still contributing substantially at the time of his death in 1989.

Now that Kateb Yacine's major novel is being made available

---

1. The poem was reprinted in *L'oeuvre en fragments* (Fragments), (Paris: Sindbad, 1986), pp. 70–72, a collection of poetic, narrative, and theatrical texts (hereafter cited as *OF*). I acknowledge Sindbad's kind permission to quote from the poem, below.

xiv

Introduction

to an American audience once more, some sort of patronymic clarification should be the first order of business: Kateb is the last name and Yacine the first, a mildly confusing peculiarity impishly perpetuated in memory of the administrative practice current in the French schools Kateb briefly attended.[2] He was born in 1929 in Constantine, a Mediterranean city whose rich and tumultuous past had been influenced by several civilizations: Numidian, Phoenician, Roman, Byzantine, Arab, Turk, and French. Constantine plays a role as both a historical and a legendary referent in *Nedjma*. The environment in which Kateb spent his early years is noteworthy. The modest but culturally rich circumstances in which he was born and raised, in the Arab part of the colonial city, shaped both his intense emotionalism and his acute awareness of political and ontological complexities. An array of family dramas played themselves out with almost ritualistic repetition against a backdrop of brutal violence in the nearby military court and the barracks of death where, in those days, Arab political prisoners were frequently guillotined. The vivid remembrance of those years clearly permeates the pages of *Nedjma*: for instance, the passage that describes Rachid's return to Constantine.[3] The close family ties were disrupted often by the family's frequent moves, either because of the father's professional assignments (like Mustapha's father in the fifth section of the novel, Kateb's practiced Koranic law) or because of the ceaseless visits and travels among Kateb's relatives throughout Eastern Algeria.

Another important element of Kateb's experience was his premature severance from the Arab-educated and artistically gifted surroundings of his family, particularly from a mother whose love of poetry and acting made an early and profound impression on him. "As far back as I can remember," he once

2. There exist, for instance, two early pieces signed "Yacine Kateb": the poem "Bonjour" in *Forge* 3 (April–May 1947): n.p., and an untitled prose piece in *Simoun* 8 (1957): 62–67.

3. *Nedjma*, trans. Richard Howard (New York, Braziller, 1961; Charlottesville: CARAF Books, University Press of Virginia, 1991), pp. 203–4, hereafter cited parenthetically as *N*, followed by the page number.

reminisced, "the muses' first harmonious expressions flowed through my mother," adding more recently and not without humor that when his parents argued, it was always in verse.[4] A decision dictated by his father's pragmatism, his transfer from a Koranic to a French school, was thus to become more significant as a linguistic and cultural experience than as a religious one. Kateb experienced both a vivid loss and an excruciatingly self-conscious initiation. The text that closes *Le polygone étoilé* is hardly hyperbolic in this regard. Its signal reference to being cast into the lion's den ("dans la gueule du loup") precisely describes the experience that inaugurated the gestation of Kateb's French works, a severance from both the psychological nurturing of an artistically gifted mother and the rich humus of his native culture: "I thus lost at the same time my mother and her language, the only inalienable treasures from which I nonetheless became alienated."[5] In the novel, Mustapha's comically penetrating perception of the culturally divided universe of Mademoiselle Dubac's classroom represents perhaps the closest fictional approximation of Kateb's own sense of cultural otherness and alienation (*N*, pp. 273–74).

But the episode also prefigures the even more traumatic experience that brought to an abrupt end the course of Kateb's formal education. He was a boarder in the *collège* (secondary school) of Sétif on 8 May 1945, when the first anticolonial uprising in modern Algeria took place. Official reaction was swift and ruthless: estimates of the victims of reprisals by French troops and militia vary from ten thousand to forty-five thousand. Swept into the collective fervor of political conscious-

---

4. The quotation is from Kateb Yacine, *Le polygone étoilé* (The star-shaped, starlit polygon) (Paris: Seuil, 1966), p. 182, hereafter cited as *PE*. Kateb made the comment on his parents' arguments at the Sixth Forum on North African Literature and Culture, Temple University, 21 March 1988, where he visited for an informal talk followed by questions from the audience. Excerpts from the unpublished discussion, in my translation, are cited hereafter as "Kateb at Temple."

5. *PE*, p. 182. Except for citations from *Nedjma*, all translations from the French are mine.

Introduction

ness, Kateb (like Lakhdar and Mustapha in the second section of the novel) joined the demonstrations and was arrested. He was then barely sixteen. Jailed, interrogated, told that he would be executed at dawn, then interned in a military camp, he was ultimately released. Kateb's short-lived passion for a married cousin occurred shortly thereafter in Annaba (Bône in the novel), where he was sent to the lycée after being expelled from the school in Sétif. It is easy to appreciate the symbiotic significance of these two events in Kateb's life. He was to reminisce, more than twenty years later, that "[he] discovered at that time the two realities now most important to [him]: poetry and revolution." [6] Kateb has often mentioned the impact on his adolescence of his profound if ill-fated passion, and it is clear that such a personal defeat in turn exacerbated the importance of the collective defeat looming in his awakening political consciousness. Throughout the novel, the very history of the Algerian nation remains closely interwoven with that of the elusive woman and her many suitors.

The uprising of 8 May 1945 abruptly revealed to this young man educated in a French school the treacherous and repressive nature of French colonial policies. The modern colonization of Algeria amounted basically to the furtherance of the political and economic interests of France and her European settlers. Its social and cultural record was one of racist neglect and cultural arrogance. A turning point in the history of modern Algeria, the May 1945 uprising demonstrated above all the total lack of political education and effective power of the Algerian masses. Kateb's subsequent political activities and his devotion to the cause of Algerian independence demonstrate the impact of such a realization. In a society where political dissent was met with brutal repression, covert political activism became a powerful tool in the hands of revolutionary-minded individuals like Kateb. From the late forties to the mid-fifties, he joined in the militant activities of the short-lived organizations that preceded

6. In "Le maghrébin errant," an interview by Yvette Romi in *Le Nouvel observateur* 114 (18 January 1967): 31.

Introduction

the emergence of the FLN (National Liberation Front). In those days of surveillance by the colonial police, however, he found it both more urgent and more effective to educate fellow Algerians trapped in the prison house of illiteracy and political disfranchisement. Throughout the département of Constantine, he brought together literature and politics in clandestine speeches obviously tailored to the needs of uneducated audiences, an undertaking that foreshadowed his theatrical activities in postcolonial Algeria.

Kateb's first visit to Paris in 1947—it lasted several months—inaugurated the nomadic character of a life marked by periodic exile from Algeria and dominated by his anticolonial militancy and his tireless involvement on behalf of fellow Algerian immigrants. In France, where the political atmosphere remained for a while more tolerant than in colonial Algeria, Kateb was able to organize Algerian workers politically and, later, to mediate their ideological dissensions when the Algerian revolution was still in its infancy. He also joined fellow North African and French intellectuals in several public debates on the abysmal failure of colonialism. His first major works, however, were first published as the military conflict expanded in Algeria, and a climate of increasing official intolerance led to police harassment. In his discussion at Temple, Kateb recalled that not too long after the publication of *Nedjma* in 1956, his Parisian apartment was searched by the police and he had to flee France. Throughout the years of proletarian communion characterized by the uncertainties and deprivations of an immigrant's life in France, he labored as a construction worker and migrant field hand, and even worked briefly in the electronics and metallurgical industries. The personally difficult period of 1954–62, that of the Algerian war of independence, was also a period of intense writing interrupted by frequent traveling, as he fled a situation become untenable both in Algeria and France. His trips took him to Italy, Tunisia, Belgium, West Germany, Sweden, Yugoslavia, and Egypt.

After Algeria won independence from the French in 1962, Kateb's dream of participation in the intellectual and artistic

Introduction

rebirth of his country was constantly thwarted by the harsh realities of political dissensions, and by ideological and cultural intolerance as well. Political parties were not allowed; religious intransigence was settling in. Above all, his creative talent was thwarted by the absence of freedom of expression and by cultural policies that favored the use of classical Arabic—the language of Islam—not only over French but over the more popular colloquial Arabic and Berber dialects as well. The virtual impossibility of staging theatrical productions in French, official censorship, and intellectual alienation effectively dashed Kateb's hopes of playing a meaningful role in the cultural life of his country. He took the road of exile again. From 1963 to the early seventies, he visited a host of nations: not only France, West Germany, Italy, Sweden, Vietnam, China, and Lebanon, but also the USSR. He had first visited the latter country in 1950 with a delegation from the daily *Alger républicain,* went back for medical treatment in 1963, and was to become a frequent cultural guest of that country over the years. Throughout the seventies and eighties, thanks to the popularity of his plays in colloquial Arabic and despite repeated bureaucratic setbacks, Kateb was finally able to secure financial support for his theatrical projects. Subventions from two Algerian ministries thus made it possible for his own theater company to tour Algeria with a very successful repertoire of political plays.[7]

Kateb's manifold activities always reflected the pragmatic commitment and the ideological quest of an exiled writer acutely sensitive to the universal implications of political drama, and unfailingly drawn toward its manifestations worldwide. The main events that shaped a markedly turbulent existence surely enhance our understanding of the psycho-

---

7. "Mohammed, prends ta valise" (Get your suitcase, Mohammed, 1971), which was also performed in France, "La guerre de deux mille ans" (The two thousand years' war, 1974), "Le roi de l'ouest" (The king from the West, 1977), "La Palestine trahie" (Palestine betrayed, 1982) and "La Kahina" (The Kahina, 1985), all unpublished so far.

logical tensions that contributed to Kateb Yacine's creative production, but the ideological tensions are equally important. The complex intensity of a remarkably engaging and modest presence barely masked Kateb's sensitivity to a broad range of problems: the significance of the French Revolution to the Third World; issues of cultural pluralism and of religious freedom and sociopolitical opportunity in his native land; and the Palestinian and South African questions. The pluricultural breadth of Kateb's thematic and poetic registers remains striking throughout his work, and two titles, from the beginning and the end of two decades of theatrical involvement, perhaps best encapsulate the scope of his vision: *L'homme aux sandales de caoutchouc* (The man with tire sandals), a Brechtian play on the Vietnam War, and "Le bourgeois sans-culotte, ou le spectre du parc Monceau" (Robespierre the sansculotte, or the ghost of Monceau Park), a powerful reactualization of the Jacobin's revolutionary experience.[8]

The deprivation, rootlessness, and frequent penury that exile and separation forced upon Kateb also went hand in hand with an experience of creative discontinuity and dispersion. A dramatic succession of poetic outbursts and silences, sallies and withdrawals, Kateb's creative itinerary remains bound up as much with personal tribulations and anguish as with the diversity of his literary interests. His solitude was compounded by economic hardship in 1950, when his father died of tuberculosis. He assumed the support of a family of six that included his mentally ill mother with the meager resources from his job as a fledgling reporter for the daily *Alger républicain*. His mother's long struggle with the demons of insanity had taken a turn for the worse with his arrest and incarceration in 1945, a sequence of events that may have triggered the complex guilt and alienation that surface over and over in Kateb's work. The representation of Mustapha's mother in "Le cadavre encerclé" (In

8. *L'homme aux sandales de caoutchouc* (Paris: Seuil, 1972); "Le bourgeois sans-culotte ou le spectre du parc Monceau," 1988, unpublished.

death surrounded) as a woman "in search of her son gone into exile" who wears "the blue smock of psychiatric patients," and the expressionistic staging of the poignant delirium that follows are apposite.[9] Mustapha's own reference to his combined political and personal ordeal in one of the interior monologues in *Nedjma* (p. 317) is no less significant.

"We spend our lives bidding each other farewell" exclaims Mustapha's mother in "Le cadavre encerclé" (*CE*, p. 62), a comment that echoes Kateb's own allusion to the guilt-provoking scourge that feudal traditions, social conditions, and political brutality alike have visited upon generations of Algerian families: "There is among us [Algerians] a feeling of guilt toward women, because we know how much we oppress them; a strong feeling of guilt can be found deep within every Algerian man, and first of all toward his mother, because no Algerian man can forget how much our mothers suffer, how much they *have* suffered" (Kateb at Temple). As he referred to such suffering, the long and checkered history of Algeria must have been prominent in Kateb's mind. For the war of independence that lasted eight years—and whose violence spared no segment of the Algerian population—was the culmination of centuries of foreign invasions and hegemony. The Berber kingdoms that made up Algeria's original population endured successive invasions by Phoenicians, Carthaginians, Romans, Vandals, and Byzantines. Each wave of invaders attempted to leave its mark on the land, but each in turn had to contend with the stubborn resistance and unconquerable autonomy of the Berber populations. Two historical figures always stood foremost in Kateb's evocations of a period from

9. "Le cadavre encerclé," in *Le cercle des représailles* (The circle of reprisals) (Paris: Seuil, 1959), pp. 62–63, hereafter cited as *CE*. The other two plays in this collection are "La poudre d'intelligence," translated as *Intelligence Powder* by Stephen J. Vogel (New York: Ubu Repertory Theatre Publications, 1985) [*IP*], and "Les ancêtres redoublent de férocité (Ever more fierce are the ancestors), an excerpt of which I have translated in *San José Studies* 4 no. 2 (May 1978): 70–80.

which modern Algeria learned its lesson well: Jugurtha, king of a Numidia "whose cavaliers have never returned from the slaughter house" (*N*, p. 233) and the Kahina.[10]

In the seventh and eighth centuries, the Arab invasion introduced Islam to Algeria, an event that was to alter the course of its history dramatically. By the eleventh century, the invasion had provided the country—indeed the whole of North Africa —with many of the ethnic, religious, and ideological features characteristic of its modern personality. A religious and judicial system, however, Islam was never to absorb the ethnic, cultural, and linguistic complexity of North Africa. Indeed, its rich culture was even further diversified not only by a once important population of Sephardic Jews but by subsequent Turkish and French invasions and by the southern European minorities that would follow in their footsteps until 1962. In response to a series of minor diplomatic incidents, a French monarchy seeking diversion from its domestic problems decided to put an end to Turkish occupation, which dated back from 1514. It sent its navy and troops to Algeria in 1830. Two years later, the emir Abd el-Kader started a series of successful uprisings that inaugurated a hundred and thirty years of opposition to the French colonial apparatus.

A crucial outgrowth of this struggle, Kateb's work and published interviews reflect an intimate and wide-ranging knowledge of Algerian history. It is thus important to realize that although the armed conflict that led to independence did not start until 1 November 1954, and although *Nedjma* deals primarily with contemporary history, Kateb's work remains inextricably bound up with a broad historical perspective that nurtured his political convictions. What we know of Kateb's

10. References to Jugurtha, who unified Numidia before being defeated by the Romans in 105A.D., are frequent in Kateb's work. The Kahina was the legendary nom de guerre of Dihya, a Berber woman from the Djarawa tribe in the Aurès mountains. She organized fierce resistance against Arab conquest before being killed in 702A.D. As noted before, she was the subject of a play by Kateb in 1985.

Introduction

political and literary activities makes one thing evident: ardent humanitarianism and the birth of his nationalistic consciousness were, more than anything else, instrumental in anchoring his vocation as a writer committed to the denunciation of injustice wherever he found it. A brief overview of his literary production is thus in order.

If the genesis of *Nedjma* can be traced from very early pieces (the 1948 poem is the first such text), that novel in turn seminally permeates writings published during its period of gestation or subsequently. As Jacqueline Arnaud has convincingly shown, both the chronology and the content of Kateb's literary production bear the marks of his eventful existence.[11]

Kateb's first known text, *Soliloques,* is a collection of poems originally published in 1946, and the first fragments of both "Le cadavre encerclé" and *Nedjma* were written in the late forties, when Kateb was working in Algiers as a journalist.[12] According to the writer, both were completed simultaneously in a moment of enthusiastic frenzy in the winter of 1954, during a productive period of respite from ruthless material exigencies. Kateb's first novel, and the work for which he is best known, was published in July of 1956. As for "Le cadavre encerclé," it was first published in *Esprit* in 1954 and 1955, before its publication as the lead play of the trilogy *Le cercle des représailles* in 1959. In the meantime, the innovative French theater director Jean-Marie Serreau had already directed several representations: first in Carthage, then in Brussels, and finally in Paris, clandestinely, at the Théâtre de Lutèce. Despite threats of violence from the right-wing extremists of "La main rouge" (The red hand) typical of the kind of reaction Kateb's oppositional discourse has elicited time and again, Serreau went ahead with the representation of the play in the Belgian capital, not with-

11. See in particular Jacqueline Arnaud's *La littérature maghrébine de langue française: Le cas de Kateb Yacine* (Paris: Publisud, 1986), pp. 101–42, the best biographical account so far.

12. Selections from *Soliloques* are reprinted in *OF,* pp. 33–51.

Introduction

out a display of what Edouard Glissant would remember much later as both intense and bemused stoicism.[13] Major texts evolved after Kateb's de facto expulsion from France and during his exile from war-torn Algeria. The imposing trilogy *Le cercle des représailles* was completed in Italy in 1959. As early as 1960, Kateb also read excerpts from *Le polygone étoilé* for the Yugoslavian radio network in Zagreb, and fragments from that prose narrative as well as from forthcoming plays were published in Tunis in 1961. The first open performance of "La femme sauvage" (The woman of the wild), a historical triptych built around "Le cadavre encerclé," compensated for the frustrations of the political setbacks in Algeria. Jean-Marie Serreau masterfully directed "La femme sauvage" at the Récamier theater of Paris in December 1962 and January 1963.[14]

Kateb completed his second novel, *Le polygone étoilé*, in France over the next few years. At times an arcane collage that explodes the notion of genres more radically than any of Kateb's other works, *Le polygone étoilé* was published in 1966. Jacqueline Arnaud reports a comment made by Kateb in late 1962 according to which he intended "to write from now on only in French." [15] His creative career was, in fact, to take an entirely different turn. After the publication of *Le polygone étoilé*, Kateb turned resolutely to the type of political and satirical theater he had first inaugurated with "La poudre d'intelligence," a comic genre whose didactic potential coincided with an old

13. Edouard Glissant was on hand to introduce the play to the audience at the Molière Theatre in Brussels during the International Fair (my discussion with Edouard Glissant, Houston, 26 January 1989). Elisabeth Auclaire-Tamaroff has analyzed the theatrical innovativeness of the play in *Jean-Marie Serreau découvreur de théâtres* (Paris: L'arbre verdoyant, 1986), pp. 113–21, which also contains interviews with both Serreau and Kateb.
14. Jean-Marie Serreau (1915–73) had championed the theater of Brecht, Beckett, Césaire, Adamov, Genet, and Ionesco. The triptych "La femme sauvage" also included a prologue on precolonial Algeria and an epilogue on revolutionary Algeria. Excerpts from "La femme sauvage" are reproduced in *OF*, pp. 303–26.
15. Arnaud, *La littérature maghrébine*, p. 130.

and stubborn dream. Kateb had long sought the efficacy of writing that would fulfill the cultural self-expression that foreign languages (at one time French, but classical Arabic since independence) had kept denying Algerian audiences. This is confirmed in many statements, but in particular by Kateb's response to a recent question concerning the reception of *Nedjma* in France: "French critics have generally emphasized the fact that *Nedjma* was written in French, which is a fact. But a kind of paternalism permeated this way of using and enhancing the notion of *francophonie*. . . . I then felt that mine was a tainted success since *Nedjma* was published when Algeria was at war, when blood was being spilled on a daily basis" (Kateb at Temple). Kateb went on to state that if he had remained in France after independence, he would have found himself in an ideological predicament: "now if I had allowed myself to believe that the book was an actual success, I should have remained in France and would have found myself in an untenable position. For my duty was to carry [the novel's stance] as far as I could, that is to say, to defend the FLN's positions, which I did—that got me a police search of my apartment, and I was forced to leave the country" (Kateb at Temple).

Kateb also felt that independence posed for him the problem of communication with Algerian audiences and the pressing need to adopt and adapt creatively appropriate forms: "When independence was proclaimed, I wondered what I was supposed to do: was I to stay in France and continue writing in inevitably elaborate French forms? For an Algerian writer who would have expressed himself in anything but a very refined form (like the new novel) would not have succeeded there, and I would have had to write something still more complex and difficult than *Le polygone étoilé,* for instance. . . . But it would also have become an impasse, because the Algerian people, who had just won independence, would then not even have suspected my existence. . . . As soon as opportunity knocked, I returned to Algeria in order to attempt writing in languages that the Algerian people could understand, without giving up French entirely" (Kateb at Temple).

Introduction

This last statement clearly points up Kateb's profound dilemma with respect to language and culture in Algeria. He could have expected that independence would bring him the full freedom of Algerian intellectual expression instead of the constraints of classical Arabic imposed by a revolutionary socialist government. In varying degrees, this quandary has become the lot of many African writers for whom French or English were not mother tongues. But it has proved a particularly devastating dilemma for those who, like Kateb Yacine, remained single-mindedly concerned with political commitment and convinced of the progressive and didactic function of art within a plurilingual society.[16] With its caricatural representation of a bloated theocracy, the ferocious satire of *Intelligence Powder* provides the best example in French of the kind of project Kateb had in mind. The character Puff of Smoke remarks with foreboding that: "The enemies of philosophy invented the turban / To protect their arid heads / Against all forms of knowledge" (*IP*, p. 18). Even then, the project was not entirely new, since Kateb had already given free vent to his gift for comic characterization in both of his novels. More systematically satirical, however, the new comedies would also reach significantly broader audiences.

In 1967 Kateb traveled to Vietnam, where he observed at first hand the conflict with the United States. His extensive research into Vietnamese history brought Kateb to a creative turning point. The personal significance of Algerian political problems began to merge, in his creative consciousness, with a broader worldview. By 1970, he had published in Paris the brilliant satire *L'homme aux sandales de caoutchouc,* a play in eight dramatic tableaux that astutely links Ho Chi Minh's organized resistance against Western colonial encroachments to other sce-

16. For important contributions to the debate, see Ngũgĩ wa Thiong'o, *Decolonizing the Mind: The Politics of Language in African Literature* (London/Portsmouth: J. Currey/Heinemann, 1986), and Kirsten Holst Petersen, ed., *Criticism and Ideology: Second African Writers' Conference* (Uppsala: Scandinavian Institute of African Studies, 1988), which contain several texts bearing witness to its widely cross-cultural currency.

Introduction

narios of entrapment on several continents. Although the play was performed both in France (in 1970, in politically sanitized form) and in Algeria (in 1971, in ponderous classical Arabic), it was with theatrical productions such as "Mohammed, prends ta valise," "La guerre de deux mille ans," "La Palestine trahie," "Le roi de l'ouest," and "La Kahina" that Kateb fulfilled his dream of a simultaneously popular and didactic theater. Furthermore, these plays decisively addressed the practical issue of vernacular languages. Dialectal and participatory, occasionally improvisational and resorting to the dramatic adjuncts of recitation and song, they set out to bring relevant contemporary issues, both foreign and domestic, within the cultural grasp of the broadest possible audience. The generous vision of the undertaking (with its implication of enormous personal sacrifice and utter dependence on government support) is easy to gauge. Such projects invariably amounted to a complex, often trilingual enterprise requiring tremendous linguistic and technical resources. They are yet another expression of the indefatigably humanistic spirit that has propelled Kateb's oeuvre from the earliest works to "Le bourgeois sans-culotte ou le spectre du parc Monceau." [17]

Several circumstances lend historical and literary significance to the date of publication of *Nedjma*. The year 1956 is when both Tunisia and Morocco officially acquired their independence from France, as well as the year when a Tunis-bound plane with five revolutionary leaders on board was highjacked on French orders. The plane was diverted to Algiers, where the five men were arrested upon landing by the French police and languished in jail until 1962. This political event found its way, like many others, into the subtext of Kateb's writings.

17. Because of their conception as material primarily for performance, their frequent reworking in relation to changing political issues, and the dissemination of the scripts among several companies, the plays composed after *L'homme aux sandales de caoutchouc* have not yet been published. At Temple, however, Kateb indicated that arrangements were being made for the printing of "Mohammed, prends ta valise," and that other plays were to follow.

Introduction

The ill-fated Franco-British expedition against Nasser's Egypt also took place in 1956. The French joined the attack on the Suez Canal for reasons not altogether unrelated to the Algerian insurgency, thus embarking on an adventure that ultimately proved immensely inspiring to the cause of Algerian nationalism. The year 1956 also marks the date of the Soviet repression of the Hungarian insurrection, an event with considerable repercussions on the French intellectual scene. Four years after the famous break between Jean-Paul Sartre and Albert Camus over the political ideology of *The Rebel,* that event irretrievably broadened the ideological rift between the Algerian French novelist and the progressists who stood firmly on the side of the anticolonial revolution. The hundred and thirty years' war, to use Kateb's mordant paraphrase, was actually undergoing one of its peaks of revolutionary activity on the writer's home front. The Battle of Algiers was to take place the following year, and in the view of historians of the war, 1956 was also the year when the National Liberation Front succeeded in establishing itself as a national movement among heretofore reticent masses. Thus, the years 1956–57 were characterized by convulsive politics, terrorist activities, and counterterrorist reprisals that not only brought the repulsive, graphic reality of the conflict home to France and the world at large but set the Algerian revolution on the irreversible course of its ultimate success. The spasms of nightmarish violence that shook the Algerian landscape at that time provided the specific context in which so poetic and political a narrative as *Nedjma* took root and from which it derived its political relevance. With respect to this background, the novel undoubtedly ranks—alongside *The Battle of Algiers* and Alistair Horne's historical classic on the Algerian revolution—among the most significant documents of the era.[18] In an equally crucial sense, although some of *Nedjma*'s formal characteristics may associate it with the experimental movement

18. *La battaglia di Algeri* (The battle of Algiers), directed by Gillo Pontecorvo (Stella Productions, 1966); Alistair Horne, *A Savage War of Peace: Algeria, 1954–62* (New York: The Viking Press, 1977).

Introduction

of the post-1950 fiction written in French, Kateb's novel also clearly stands out from it in virtue of its substantial ideological content and its primary grounding in a very precise and paradigmatic historical situation.

Some of the major literary events of the year 1956 bear no less relevance to the cultural climate that surrounds the gestation of *Nedjma*. Albert Camus's *La chute* (The fall), whose balanced narrative vividly contrasts with the African vision and the disruptive force of Kateb's novel, was published in 1956. There are other polarities that illustrate the vast differences between the works of these two natives of Algeria. Camus was a member of an ethnic group that, however humble its origins, however harsh its existence, would be spared the institutionalized degradation and violence of the colonial apparatus. An established writer—a year away from the Nobel prize and writing in secure comfort—he was also an influential member of Gallimard's editorial staff. As a struggling immigrant and politically hounded dissenter, Kateb, on the other hand, had long sought a publisher for a manuscript "without a head or a tail," and *Nedjma* languished for an unduly long time at Seuil.[19] Camus in *La chute* and a year later in *L'exil et le royaume* (Exile and the kingdom) could, furthermore, indulge what—to a colonized writer—must have seemed luxurious egotism at a time when the French military were annihilating whole villages in the Algerian countryside. In those years, acts of violence were spreading from the countryside to the larger urban centers, particularly in Algiers. In a conversation about Camus's use of Algerian landscapes, Kateb would later clearly identify the fundamental difference between his intellectual temperament and Camus's: "Literature is not moral discourse and doesn't easily tolerate discussion and theorizing."[20] Despite lucid essays that pointed out the abysmal living conditions of the Arab

19. Arnaud, *Littérature maghrébine*, p. 119.
20. Interview with Hafid Gafaïti, "Kateb Yacine, un homme, une œuvre, un pays" (Algiers: Laphomic, Voix Multiples, ca. 1983,) p. 43.

Introduction

population of Algeria,[21] and despite his desperate stand in 1956 on behalf of some sort of "civil truce,"[22] Camus the humanist could not, in fact, escape the ironic and typically colonial segregation that made it impossible for the majority of French Algerians to foresee the inevitable necessity of radical change. Kateb rightly noted, for instance—albeit with puzzling inaccuracies regarding the fate of the Arab in *L'étranger*—the glaring absence of even one fully characterized Arab from Camus's best-known writings and their singularly narrow sociopolitical frame of reference.[23] Kateb pointed out that the Algerian context was, for Camus, merely a cosmic or symbolic backdrop. He frequently contrasted Camus's avoidance of politics in his works to the existential strength of Faulkner's, and he praised the writer from the American South as a man who courageously came to grips with a political and racial situation very similar to that of preindependence Algeria.[24]

Finally, no survey of the sociocultural context of *Nedjma* can fail to recall the decade of the 1950s as an era of explosive fictional creativity. The humanist novel of ideas, whose discursive form had so brilliantly dominated French letters from the thirties to the fifties, was in decline. Fictional innovation was not an unprecedented adventure, of course. Proust, Gide, and surrealism had left indelible marks on the creative consciousness of the writers whose production would mature from the mid-fifties onward. But with works by Malraux, Sartre, Camus, and others then atop the literary pedestal, with the influence of the Anglo-American novel of the forties in the ascendant

21. Albert Camus, "Chroniques algériennes" (Algerian chronicles), in "Actuelles III," *Essais* (Paris: Gallimard-Pléiade, 1972).

22. Horne, *A Savage War*, pp. 124–26.

23. See "Kateb Yacine délivre la parole," an interview with M. Djaider and K. Nekkouri in *El Moujahid* 156 (4 April 1975): 8–10.

24. Kateb has addressed the issue over and over, particularly in "Kateb Yacine délivre la parole," p. 9, and Gafaïti, *Kateb Yacine*, pp. 38–43. For a perceptive analysis of the Camusian dilemma, see also Herbert L. Lottman's *Albert Camus: A Biography* (New York: Braziller, 1980), particularly pp. 148–60, 189–203, 566–77.

Introduction

in France, a wind of formal change was sweeping the land. In the next two decades, Claude Simon, Michel Butor, Alain Robbe-Grillet, Nathalie Sarraute, and Robert Pinget were to become the foremost innovators in fiction. The lessons of James Joyce, William Faulkner, Virginia Woolf, in the novel, and the example of other art forms such as photography and cinematography had been well assimilated. Between 1955 and 1957, Alain Robbe-Grillet published not only the novels *Le Voyeur* (The voyeur) and *La Jalousie* (Jealousy) but "Le roman de demain" (The novel of tomorrow) and "Sur de vieilles notions" (On a few obsolete notions), two essays that were to constitute the core of *Pour un nouveau roman* (For a new novel), his antitraditional manifesto published in 1963. Another landmark in the theory of fiction was Nathalie Sarraute's 1956 *L'ère du soupçon* (The era of suspicion), whose theoretical questioning of heretofore well-established novelistic models was echoed not only by Claude Simon but perhaps even by Camus, some of whose work from the mid-fifties displays striking departures from previous narrative practice. The artful duality of narrative voice in *La chute* stands out, but the innovativeness of "Le renégat" (The renegade) marks it as the most original and singularly anticolonial text of *L'exil et le royaume*. "Le renégat" is conspicuous for narrative renewal on the part of a writer seldom associated with the theoretical preoccupations of the era.

Because of their North African contexts, then, the dynamics of Camus's and Kateb's very different contributions to literatures written in French assume particular significance. Herbert Lottman indicates that, speaking "of fellow North Africans in Paris, [Camus] said he admired Max-Pol Fouchet's literary columns in *Carrefour*, mentioned Jean Sénac, [and] the Algerian novelist and poet Yacine Kateb."[25] But ideological differences, Kateb's peripatetic destiny, and Camus's early death seem to have cut short a relationship that could have rewritten the cul-

25. Lottman, *Albert Camus*, p. 544. As a forthcoming article by Charles Bonn will show, Camus in fact played a very supportive role in Kateb's early publishing efforts in Paris. I wish to thank Charles Bonn for sharing this information, based on an unpublished letter now in his possession.

Introduction

tural history of modern Algeria. In view of the unique literary status *Nedjma* was soon to acquire, the actual and symbolic shadow the French writer cast on the perception of North African culture should not be underestimated. Concerning the extent to which Camus's success unwittingly contributed to the relegation of autochthonous talent to intellectual marginalization, Kateb's recent reminiscences on Parisian cultural preoccupations of the fifties are suggestive: "When *Nedjma* was published in 1956, the war [of independence] had broken out. I must therefore tell you that *Nedjma* would never have been published that early without the war. Because up to that point, in France, Algerian literature meant Albert Camus. In the mind of French people, Albert Camus *was* Algerian literature and under the best circumstances, Algerian writers were remote provincial cousins" (Kateb at Temple). Kateb also provided a revealing insight into the ugly paternalism with which his creative efforts were first met: "I know that I kept on submitting my manuscript to the publisher for seven years, while he kept on telling me: But since you have such beautiful sheep in Algeria, why don't you write about them? That was it, textually. . . . There was radical ignorance, and such ignorance disappeared as if miraculously with the war" (Kateb at Temple). He went on to point out: "With the first ambushes and France starting to lose her children, Algeria became commercialized, turned into something in which publishers were interested. . . . And the book was a success to the extent that I intended it to be a novel that would show French people, in their language, that Algeria was not French. I wanted to give French people, in book form, an idea of what Algeria was really all about. And the goal was basically achieved, but . . . the book's reception was after all marred by paternalism" (Kateb at Temple).

Against such odds, the extent of Kateb's success as the visionary founder of a modern Algerian cultural identity is considerable. The 1986 award of the French Grand Prix National des Lettres, a distinction that had previously gone to Samuel Beckett, Eugene Ionesco, and Marguerite Yourcenar, belatedly recognized him as the most influential author of the first group of Arab writers who, from the fifties onward, contributed substantially and indelibly to the corpus of literatures written in French.[26] But it is above all as the interpreter of a culture in radical transition and as an intellectual insurgent that he achieved the status of a groundbreaker, distinguishing himself through a paradoxically constructive gesture of obliteration and rewriting. As the struggle with the narrative complexity of his creative vision suggests, Kateb transposed this fundamental act of political and cultural contention into the very boundaries of the French novel. In defining *pensée-autre*, or thought of otherness, as the commitment to both insurrection and mediation, as an experience of both nonreturn and dialogue, Abdelkebir Khatibi uncannily adverts to the very intellectual mechanism of Kateb's own creative adventure.[27] Spontaneously eschewing, on the one hand, the colonizing traditions of French fictional discourse and its generic reductiveness, while paving the way, on the other, for a denunciation of feudal theocracy and patriarchy, Kateb laid the foundations of a truly revolutionary thought from which a successive generation has taken significant cues. As an anticolonial discourse and a discourse of double differentiation, *Nedjma* indeed opened wide the gates for the type of postcolonial literature that has blossomed unabated through a singularly productive generation of writers.[28]

Practical circumstances, financial need, and poetic temperament alike contributed to the simultaneous, overlapping mode of composition that closely interweaves the narrative and thematic fabrics of *Nedjma* with those of other writings from

26. Jean Amrouche, Mouloud Ferraoun (assassinated by a right-wing squad toward the end of the war), Mouloud Mammeri, Mohammed Dib, Albert Memmi, and Driss Chraïbi are among the best known of this group.
27. Abdelkebir Khatibi, "Pensée-autre," in his *Le Maghreb pluriel* (Paris: Denoël, 1983), pp. 11–38.
28. Besides Abdelkebir Khatibi, some of the most talented members of this group are Rachid Boudjedra, Assia Djebar, Tahar Ben Jelloun (who won the 1987 Goncourt prize), Abdelwahab Meddeb, and Rachid Mimouni. On contemporary North African literature, see Françoise Charras and Paul Siblot, eds., *Visions du Maghreb* (Aix-en-Provence: Edisud, 1987).

Introduction

the same period. Since the character called Nedjma stands at the very center of the works from "Nedjma ou le poème ou le couteau" to *Le polygone étoilé,* the relevance of contemporary writings to the novel's poetics and thematics is worth investigating.

The early poem "Nedjma ou le poème ou le couteau" already contains many of the themes and preoccupations of the later works. In its dialectic juxtaposition of eroticism, creativity, and aggression, the poem's title and the latent violence of its imagery obliquely aver revolutionary consciousness. But in "Nedjma ou le poème ou le couteau," Kateb relies upon technical audacity and incantatory mystery rather than on sociological or autobiographical material to evoke the experience of separation and the metaphysical quest. A symbiosis of two cultural discourses, North African and French, the poem relies upon musical and erotic incantation, on the evocation of separation and death but of ancestral memory as well. Thus, many of the practices and preoccupations of Kateb's subsequent works brilliantly come together in the "powerful diwan" (*OF,* 70) that launched his poetic career. The opening of the poem, for instance, sets the tone for the kind of haunting and aggressive quest that will surrealistically unfold over five stanzas rife with hermetic imagery:

> We had prepared two glasses of blood Nedjma opened her
>   eyes amid the trees
> A lute was making much of the plains transforming them
>   into gardens
> As black as sun-soaked blood
> Nedjma lay beneath my soothed heart I breathed shoals of
>   precious flesh
> —Many a star has followed us Nedjma while we have been
>   dreaming
> I had imagined you as timeless as space and the unknown
> And now you are dying and I falter and you cannot ask me
>   to cry.   (*OF,* p. 70)

The surrealist lover of the first poem and the quasi-silent protagonist of *Nedjma* subsequently reappear as a woman mili-

Introduction

tant in "Le cadavre encerclé," the first play of the trilogy *Le cercle des représailles*. Since the play and the novel were written during the same years, the important shift in characterization clearly stresses the dual motivation (poetic and historical, individual and collective) that underlay Kateb's creative enterprise. The play takes place during the Algerian war and, less given to poetic allusiveness than the novel, bluntly stages the conflict between individual passion and political exigency: "Spectators must understand the terrible ambiguity of the past that we have to exorcize on a daily basis" explained Kateb at that time.[29] No longer the autobiographical abstraction of a surrealist poem nor the poetic construct of the novel, Nedjma has further evolved into a warrior figure who actively shares in revolutionary struggle. Mustapha, one of the novel's four male protagonists, recounts the story of reprisals that followed a political demonstration reminiscent of the 1945 events in Sétif. Within the theatrical construct of a violent political tragedy, furthermore, an endlessly repeated drama of emotional failure and alienation unfolds. "Le cadavre encerclé" treats the themes of conflict, violence, orphanhood, jealousy, abandonment, and treachery. In a paradigmatic expression of the motif of generational conflict that is ubiquitous in the novel, Lakhdar—in the play—is stabbed by Tahar, his own stepfather and a collaborator with the French colonialists. The play realistically telescopes and elucidates many of the novel's situations and themes without forsaking stark poetic expressiveness, particularly in monologues that splendidly capture historical adversity and ontological anguish:

> With each year, with each throng
> Of our ghosts stabbed in vain
> Comes the same plunge into the rock
> Renewed perdition
> Ever more difficult to mourn
> But seldom do our souls grieve

29. Auclaire-Tamaroff, *Jean-Marie Serreau*, p. 114.

For like many young dreamers
Burrowed in temples
We hold Time maimed in our claws
For threatening ordeals
Loom from beyond the stelae
Unsettling our death at its very source.   (CE, p. 51)[30]

Jean-Marie Serreau has pointed out that the strength of
Kateb's plays was in their articulation of a new historical
vision.[31] In a personal reaction against Bertolt Brecht's belief
in the demise of tragedy in our time, Kateb resolutely affirmed
his conviction that the tragic genre alone could best accom-
modate the reality of the historical tragedy with which he
was dealing.[32] Let us make no mistake about Kateb's stand:
it reiterated his profound belief in a narrative mechanism in
which poetic and ideational formulations conjoined, a creative
principle that dominates the best of the works published up
to 1966 and of which Nedjma is the fictional exemplification.
"I have repeated a thousand times" Kateb said recently, "that
poetry is the foundation of all my works."[33]

The elaboration of character and plot from one work to
another suggests other important parallels. To the four para-
mours who vie for her attention in the novel, Nedjma is a principle of divisiveness. Symbolically, however—her name means
"star" in Arabic—she is also a unitive principle that stands
for the Algerian nation. She thus assumes in the novel seldom-
acknowledged characterization that strategically foreshadows
her political radicalization in Le cercle des représailles. The
background of colonial domination against which the story of
romantic rivalry unfolds singularly pluralizes one's psychological perception of Nedjma. Images of bellicose independence
and precocious rebellion conjoin, for instance, in a childhood

30. I acknowledge Seuil's kind permission to quote from "Le cadavre
encerclé."
31. Auclaire-Tamaroff, Jean-Marie Serreau, p. 113.
32. Ibid., p. 120.
33. Gafaïti, Kateb Yacine, p. 21.

portrait of tomboyishness that leaves no doubt as to her un-conventional femininity: "Nedjma's eternal game is to reduce her dress to a minimum in the acrobatic poses of an ostrich emboldened by solitude; on such a skin, any dress is a super-fluity of nakedness; Nedjma's femininity is elsewhere; the first month at school, she cried each morning; she hit all the children who came near her; she wouldn't learn her lessons before learning to swim; at twelve she concealed her breasts that were as painful as nails, swollen with the bitter precocity of green lemons; her spirit is still unbroken" (*N*, p. 104). The character-ization of Nedjma also blends images from the animal world with technological allusions that signal the disruptive advent of industrial modernity: "the sea air produced a bloom on her skin combining the dark tint with the brilliance of metallic re-flections, mottled like some animal; her throat has the white gleams of a foundry, where the sun hammers down to her heart, and the blood, under the downy cheeks, speaks loud and fast, betraying the enigmas of her gaze" (*N*, pp. 104–5). De-spite Nedjma's fate in the novel—she is abducted and returned to the tribe's encampment of women, and thus escapes the four men's pointless rivalry—her portrait contains intimations of aggressive strength that foretell the political and mythical characterization in other works.[34]

Seen as a protean incarnation, Nedjma assumes many a real and symbolic projection: the product of an autobiographical phantasm, she becomes an obscure object of desire in the exclu-sive perception of the four male characters in the novel, whereas Kateb's own historical vision inevitably infuses her represen-tation with national symbolism. Within the story's fictional scheme, however, her exclusion and inaccessibility may suggest more than mere silence and submissiveness. In the fact that she embodies the experience of a woman for the first time immune to the successive plundering and abandonment that constitute

34. The poem "Keblout et Nedjma" (Keblout and Nedjma) (*OF*, pp. 81–84) and the characterizations of Keltoum (*OF*, pp. 275–302) and Dihya (*OF*, pp. 427–31), the female protagonists of two later versions of "La femme sauvage," clearly establish continuity of intent.

Introduction

the pathetic background of so many of the novel's mothers, her
fate suggests a historically paradoxical shift. Nedjma's awareness of her domination already went hand in hand with a sense
of impending reversal, whereby her captors would ultimately
fall victim to the very traps they had set (*N*, pp. 89–90). But
that Rachid should solemnize woman's fate in the terms of an
ancient tragedy is significant in view of Kateb's later (and particularly effective) use of the ancient declamatory device of the
chorus of women in his plays (*N*, p. 129). Having benefited
from the kind of ideological elaboration that the progress of the
revolution allowed—and however emphatic their didacticism
may appear three decades later—the plays in turn significantly
reverse the limited portrayal of women so as to usher in a vision
of active participation in an ongoing historical process.[35]
    As the cycle of political upheavals goes on, a further variation
on the novel's setting and an elucidation of its political intent
occur in "Les ancêtres redoublent de férocité" (Ever more fierce
are the ancestors), the third play in the dramatic trilogy. A widowed Nedjma now shares the loneliness and insanity that had
so far been the mother's lot, and the totemic motif first stitched
into the text of *Nedjma* takes on fuller mythical significance.
The romantic rivalry of the novel, which had found its way into
the politically determined and bitterly staged conflict of the first
play, evolves, in "Les ancêtres," into a gripping, if pessimistic,
allegory of Aeschylean proportions.[36] In her incarnation as "the

35. The novel thus carefully reflects (and clearly deplores) a sociopolitical
reality Kateb has frequently denounced. For instance, he eloquently addressed,
during his talk at Temple, the issue of the denial of freedom to women in
contemporary Algeria.
    36. The convergence of Kateb's vision with Aeschylus's constitutes an im-
portant link in the great chain of lyrical composition; witness the following
comment: "When we were working on the first rehearsals [of "Le cadavre
encerclé"], I realized how far theater could go, and I remembered Aeschylus
and the infancy of theater when the latter stood for what today is religion. It
was, however, better than religion because the Greeks could then see the expression of their own lives. They were contemplating their *own* destiny, without mediation, for even the gods were understood and perceived differently in
those days" (Gafaïti, *Kateb Yacine*, p. 28).

Introduction

woman of the wild"—a designation that denotes both dement-
edness and inaccessibility—Nedjma becomes haunted by the
spirit of Lakhdar, who is theatrically present in the avatar of
the ancestral vulture.

The trilogy's farcical intermezzo, "La poudre d'intelligence,"
is not as predominantly poetic a piece as the novel and the two
tragedies. Nor is it situationally related to them. "La poudre
d'intelligence" is nonetheless important as the best reflection
to date of the kind of creative tensions that have so dynami-
cally presided over Kateb's literary enterprise. Above all, its
esthetic conception illustrates Kateb's oppositional production
of a hybrid text free of the linguistic and formal constraints
of established forms. Kateb's will to explode both traditional
genres and linguistic structures is well documented. The following comments, for instance, were made to a journalist in 1958,
at a time when Kateb was still fully occupied with the major
works of the earlier period. Of his work in progress, he stated
that it was: "neither a novel, nor a play, nor a collection of
poems but all of those at the same time. Nowadays, it seems that
art forms thrust themselves upon us with stifling excess. Creative writing is invariably reduced to the production of genres:
are we dealing with theater, poetry, or fiction? For the sake of
marketing or publicity, a writer is today forced to truncate his
work before being able to achieve creative unity. But the latter
is first and paradoxically predicated upon the destruction of all
forms. In the case of my own works, these are not theoretical
concerns but principles that I have actually practiced or am in
the process of practicing. *Nedjma* is not what is normally called
a novel, and 'Le cadavre encerclé' is as antitheatrical as anything one can find. I am presently pursuing this experiment in
order to explode the formal limits that strangle literature." [37]

Within artistic constructs free of the constraints of traditional genres and intent upon the practice of a pluralistic and
open-ended form of writing, Kateb heeded a sirens' song not

37. From "Une heure avec Kateb Yacine," *L'action* 148 (28 April 1958):
16–17.

Introduction

altogether dissimilar from Baudelaire's dream of a simultaneously supernatural and ironic composition. In their spontaneous reliance on creatively compensatory principles, Kateb's texts thus achieve a pluralistic vision of self-modifying opposites. The creative polarities of irony and lyricism, farce and the sublime, satire and symbolic evocation, not only inhabit the comedy's dramatic fabric but articulate *Nedjma*'s vision as well in a dynamics of considerable narrative tension. Toward the end of "La poudre d'intelligence," for instance, the symbolic abduction of the prince and the eerie dream sequence that follows (*IP*, pp. 49–54) completely transform the tonality of Puff of Smoke's mad, farcical outbursts. These outbursts thus serve to allegorize the urgent meaning of a forcibly disguised political actuality from the play's very opening (*IP*, pp. 3–19). Likewise, the novel's picaresque characterization of Si Mokhtar will quickly give way to Rachid's obsessive recollection of his encounter at the clinic and his chimerical evocation of Nedjma's spellbinding beauty (*N*, pp. 140–41, 143–44). Conversely, although the farcical vein remains consistently absent from the two tragedies of *Le cercle des représailles,* realistic dialogues expressing bitter psychological conflict provide a similar sort of tonal opposition, at times deliberately undermining the tragedy's intricate, verselike expressions of mythopoetic consciousness.

The first phase of Kateb's literary production, characterized by poetic effusiveness and lyrical elaboration, thus yielded a complex corpus of poetry, drama, and fiction in which the didactic impulse that dominates Kateb's post-1966 theater remains subservient to solemn incantation and symbolic utterance. Given the thematic interdependency and symphonic reverberation of Kateb's major poetic and theatrical works, *Nedjma*'s greatest originality obviously lies in the high degree of narrative autonomy, thematic cohesiveness, and poetic integrity it expresses. An examination of the artful discontinuities between its narrative content and textual progression is in order.

That a profound dichotomy opposes the novel's narrative

content to the multiple strategies of its polyphonic and achrono-
logical composition is central to one's appreciation of its remarkable unity. As a fictional text, *Nedjma* poetically explodes
a plot whose elements cohere only in synchrony and whose
narrative finality Kateb may indeed never have intended. The
novel's self-conscious reflexiveness in fact provides important
clues as to the open-ended, elaborative intent of its narrative process. An entry in Mustapha's notebook, for instance,
strategically if inconspicuously reflects the very mechanism of
Kateb's art of ceaseless deferral and indirection. Its strategy of
narrative modification and diffusion is both play and source
of interpretive multiplication, the novel's incomparable allusiveness: "lying on my paper mattress, I settle one question
whose solution I finally make impossible . . ." (*N*, pp. 107–
8). Kateb also frequently resorts to a discourse of equivocation
and dubitation that strategically foils or postpones the narrative
clarification about to take place. When, for instance, Mustapha
attempts to reconstruct the history of Mourad's and Nedjma's
relationship, he uses no fewer than four dates to establish the
chronology of events. But recollective speculation soon creeps
into his notebook: "A lot of *hypotheses* here . . . *Naturally*
Mourad left the villa after his cousin's marriage: a matter of
propriety; *but* a neighbor of Mourad's, *basing his testimony
on public gossip*, told *some obscure episode* to a scribe (he too
public and *scarcely affirmative*) . . . *According to* this neighbor,
Mourad left school at his cousin's request, she offered to marry
him if he would take her to Algiers where she hoped to realize
her dream as an 'enlightened' woman, far from the gossip of
Bône" (*N*, p. 111).[38]
    However dilatory its progression, the novel relies on the
narrative hinges of a number of primarily fictional events em-
bedded in the broader framework of a historical consciousness
that reaches as far back as the Numidia of Jugurtha, Abd el-

38. The emphasis is mine. In the French text (*Nedjma* [Paris: Seuil, 1956],
pp. 83–84) *left* and *offered* are in the conditional.

Introduction

Kader's cavalcades, or the dismantling of Keblout's tribe.[39] The personal and political reality with which Nedjma and her four suitors grapple constitutes the chronological foreground of the novel, covering the period from the late twenties and early thirties (the childhood years of the five main characters) to the mid-fifties and the inception of the Algerian revolution.[40] The dating of the novel's most recent events is actually made possible by the passage that concludes "Parmi les herbes qui refleurissent" (Amid the grass blossoming again), a narrative poem originally published in *Le Mercure de France* (1964), then partially reproduced in *Le polygone étoilé* (*PE*, pp. 161–66). Originally part of *Nedjma*, the passage contains an explicit reference to an attack on the bridge near the railroad station in Constantine by Algerian insurgents, and to the haphazard retaliation by the French military. This event situates Rachid's presence in the fondouk within a time span that extends into the revolutionary years. Wounded by a stray bullet, Rachid is brought back to his fondouk, where he lies dying. The events and tonality of the concluding passage of "Parmi les herbes" share many obvious traits with the nine fondouk chapters in the novel's fourth section (*N*, pp. 228–47).[41] In particular, both texts dwell upon the eerie atmosphere of Rachid's refuge, focus on his dialogue with the journalist, and stress the allusive, incoherent nature of the encounter. "A piece of broken pottery, an insignificant fragment from an age-old architecture" (*N*, p. 234), Rachid can "no longer tell what he [is] thinking from what he [is] saying" (*N*, p. 232). While reluctantly sharing his

39. However fictionalized their story in *Nedjma*, the Keblouti are Kateb's true ancestors.

40. *Chronology* obviously refers here to the "real," extratextual occurrence of events, as best the reader can reconstitute them and as opposed to the *textual* progression of the novel.

41. This is the second of two fondouk sequences in the novel. The first occurs after Rachid's return from Bône, when he visits Abdallah's fondouk (*N*, pp. 211–24), located "off a paved alley, a few steps from the medersa" (*N*, p. 212.) In the second sequence, Rachid has become the manager of his own fondouk, perched "at the cliff top" (*N*, p. 224).

Introduction

understanding of Mourad's aggression, he inadvertently unveils the obsessive memory of Si Mokhtar's death to a journalist "more wretched than any public scribe" (*N*, p. 230) and whose point of view is no more reliable than Rachid's is complete or coherent. The second fondouk scene thus plays a key role in determining the chronological span of the novel and its implicit simultaneity with the events of the Algerian revolution. Other facts common to *Nedjma* and "Parmi les herbes" are worth noting. Both texts refer to Nedjma's travels in the company of the old black man from Mount Nadhor (*N*, pp. 244–45, and *PE*, p. 166). In "Parmi les herbes" Rachid's death occurs "in the same clinic where he had met Nedjma" (*PE*, p. 165), which is the clinic mentioned in the third section of *Nedjma* (pp. 143–44). It also becomes clear that Nedjma's unnamed suitor in the novel's last section (*N*, p. 328) is Marc, the French Algerian who, having come to Rachid's rescue, inquires about Mourad and his friends only to realize that it will take more than sympathy for him to remain on the side of the young Algerians (*PE*, pp. 162–63).[42]

Between the two chronological poles of childhood and Rachid's retreat into the second fondouk, several important events are also noticeable: the Sétif demonstration of 1945, in which both Lakhdar and Mustapha took part, is a motif that bridges fiction and historical consciousness; Lakhdar's altercation with Monsieur Ernest and Monsieur Ricard's murder by Mourad constitute a motif of psychopolitical violence that bridges fiction and colonial history; Rachid's second encounter with Nedjma in the Nadhor, Si Mokhtar's subsequent death, and Rachid's ultimate separation from Nedjma mark an episode in which fiction and history, but also legend and myth, conjoin in the complex texture of a story with remarkable poetic dimensions. For "as a palimpsest [that] drinks up old characters" (*N*, p. 94), Kateb's spellbinding text invites ceaseless elaboration of meaning on the part of its readers.

42. *OF*, pp. 207–24, reprints an important section of "Parmi les herbes" that is not a part of *PE*.

Introduction

Strictly from the point of view of textual articulation, the novel is divided into six main sections of slightly variable length, section four being the longest. Each section is in turn subdivided according to a twelve-part arrangement that externally compensates for the totally unsequential nature of the narrative. Sections one, two, and five thus comprise twelve chapters or fragments. Sections three, four, and six, however, are made up of *two* such clusters of twelve chapters, each autonomously numbered from one to twelve for a reason that will become apparent later. One hundred and eight fragments thus replace traditional chapters, in size no more predictable than their elaborate dispersal of events throughout the text. Their relative economy is striking, and they vary in length from a single question ("Will the new men be sacked?" *N*, p. 339) to the twelve pages of section four's eighth chapter (*N*, pp. 200–211). As the preface to the French edition suggests, the hermetic fragmentation and narrative diffusion that ostensibly result from Kateb's six-part and twelve-part scheme have perhaps been overly stressed, especially within the cross-cultural parameters of a genre long accustomed to Joyce's, Faulkner's, or Claude Simon's recondite practices, to name only its best-known practitioners. An effective principle of narrative symbiosis counterbalances the novel's fragmentary appearance and lends it remarkable unity. Political and poetic urgency may appear to have *dictated* the interlacing of as many as three narrative planes: fictional adventure, historical reality, and collective myth. Their associative overlapping—through interior monologues, dreams, or recollective sequences—displaces chronological and narrative univocity in favor of a vision that privileges poetic confluence.

The contrast between the novel's narrative complexity and the arithmetical rigor of its arrangement into sections and chapters is perhaps its most fascinating feature. In answer to a question, Kateb provided an uncannily Faulknerian account of his own struggle with the composition of *Nedjma* that stressed the fundamentally processive nature of his narrative project, its alternately progressive and retrogressive evolution. Stating

Introduction

that, in the absence of any specific narrative plan, he had originally tried to channel a flow of events along a linear trajectory, he pointed out that the will to exhaustive narration took
him back and forth several times along it. He then went on
to explain that, unable to "state everything at once," he ended
up with numberless short fragments that he subsequently attempted to make cohere: "I tried all possible sorts of combinations, and in the end, it appeared to me that it would be best
to have them rotate, as in the motion of time (the division into
twelve is that of time, twelve hours). I thus came up with a rotation. Well . . . theoretically, because when I tried to make it
work, I must admit that I came close to insanity . . . And I remember that at one point, I was left with a pile of rubble! It
comprised all the lines I had drawn in all directions, page one
had become page two hundred, then thirteen, then four, then
twenty-five. The combinations were shuffled in every possible
manner" (Kateb at Temple).

Implying that the structuring of *Nedjma* was both a process that evolved over several years and the chance result of a
last-minute intuition, Kateb attributed the choice of the final
sequence of fragments to the sudden inspiration that followed
a brief and intense period of self-doubt and despair. When
questioned further on the relationship of the clock concept to
the passage of time within the novel, Kateb added: "I felt that
[the narrative fragments] had to rotate, a rotation was necessary, and this is why I quite simply opted for the rotations of
the clock. . . . I tried to make the narration rotate, and this is
roughly what it produced, nine circumvolutions if you wish,
from which I relatively succeeded in giving the novel its own
chronology" [Kateb at Temple].[43] Kateb then denied that he
attached any significance to the final division of the novel into
six sections, pointing out the external pressures that ostensibly
presided over its final structuration: "*Nedjma* and *Le polygone
étoilé* were originally one and the same book. . . . But probably

43. Kateb refers to the nine twelve-part groups that comprise the six sections.

for commercial reasons, the editor limited me to two hundred and fifty pages. With *Le polygone* . . . , there would have been approximately four hundred pages, so that too came into play. Had I kept *Le polygone étoilé* in, the second novel might not have been what it is now, and *Nedjma* might have included a few extra chapters. But this wouldn't have changed things very much!" (Kateb at Temple).

It is obvious that, ill at ease with speculative reductions, Kateb tends to attach much less significance to the twelve-part structure of *Nedjma* than do his readers and critics. Having always preferred to see in the novel a projection of the collective essence of Algeria, he insisted in a not altogether unconvincing fashion, at Temple, that he "could not write the novel of Algeria otherwise," that he had "to try all conceivable combinations to hold together the potential novel of a conceivable Algeria." The point concerning the relationship between national incarnation and historical gestation on the one hand and textual corpus and fictional production on the other is well taken. But the reality of the striking contrast between the novel's internal fragmentation and the external sense of order with which the twelve-part division endows it remains inescapable. Coupled with Kateb's fondness for the kind of numerical references and formulations that abound in the novel,[44] the six-part and twelve-part division of the novel unquestionably enhances the tension between the two complementary creative impulses that provide its sense of equilibrium: narrative polyphony and synthesis within an open-ended internal construct, mathematical periodicity of the external structure. In privileging narration as process over text as product, in favoring textual motion over narrative completion, continuity over closure, *Nedjma* achieves unparalleled

---

44. It would be interesting, for instance, to note the large number of references to the number four and the frequent use of ternary and quaternary patterns in Kateb's speech, not to mention a general predilection for numerical specificity, as in the description of Constantine (*N*, pp. 200 et seq.), and the persistent dating of events, measuring of duration, or age giving that, although narratively dysfunctional, suggest an infrastructure of verisimilitude, order, and stabilization.

balance between scriptural dynamism and visionary stasis. In this sense, Kateb's parallel with the clock becomes crucial: for as the clocklike division simulates textual periodicity, it emphasizes at the same time the contrastive texture of the novel's structure.

Richard Howard became involved in translating *Nedjma* at a time when Third World literatures could barely boast a modicum of recognition, institutional or otherwise. The serendipitous genies of Kateb's Nadhor must have had a lot to do with it, for what he once said about the French view of Algerian literature applied for a long time and probably to an even greater extent to the North American scene. But in 1961, long before Kateb's works had acquired their present status and with scant secondary material available to him, the distinguished American poet completed a translation whose narrative rhythm and descriptive breadth generously serve the untamable genius of Kateb's mythopoetic text. There is no doubt that the American translation successfully captures the narrative vigor and diversity of the novel, and that it preserves its poetic complexity throughout the wide range of tonal idiosyncracies and the variety of idiolects that comprise it. If I have, however, ventured to make comparisons between Kateb Yacine's and Richard Howard's texts, it is not so much to point up cultural or interpretive discrepancies as to stress the fundamentally irreducible character of the Algerian novel. Indeed, one should not underestimate the unique status of a work that did so much creative violence to the language it uses, of a novel written in French but not French, of a text fully exploiting the poetic miscibility of a surprisingly wide range of stylistic and linguistic registers. As it maps out its own cultural space within and against prevalent traditions, Kateb's novel relies not only on theatrical, historical, journalistic, sociographic, and poetic expressiveness but on the linguistic dynamics of a ceaselessly open-ended process of associations, on the kind of figurative intricacy that at times even the broader corpus of his works fails to elucidate.

Introduction

The fate of the text's cultural multiplicity invites reflection. It is not without some justification that one could, for instance, regret the editorial deletion of the eight footnotes that accompany the French text,[45] or the accidental omission of the number for chapter eleven in section six, right after the paragraph ending "She is leaning against the lemon-tree" (*N*, p. 324). The omission risks giving the reader the illusion of a surprising departure from an otherwise unfailingly uniform principle of composition. Somewhat more vexing are some lexicographical or figurative idiosyncracies. Since Kateb has already used *viol* ("rape," *N*, p. 129) in one passage, for instance, doesn't the translation of "rapt" as "rape" rather than as "abduction" in another (*N*, p. 240) tend to overload the semantic field of a word that has become one of the novel's primordial images? Why use the North Americanism "Beaver" (*N*, pp. 45, 344) for *le Barbu* ("the man with a beard") in a text so profoundly rooted in an unmistakenly Algerian ethos? The vision of Nedjma as "irrepressible starlight" (*N*, p. 182) may not carry the poetic significance of *à la façon d'un astre impossible à piller dans sa fulgurante lumière*, and the rendition of *répertoire de pleureuse* as "cry-baby's repertory" (*N*, p. 104) quite simply erases the elegiac and funereal connotation inherent in the Middle Eastern *pleureuse* ("wailer"). It is also somewhat unfortunate that *père défunt tombé à l'orée du bagne* ("defunct

45. Four of the deleted footnotes have been successfully incorporated into the text of the translation. The parenthetical inclusion of the explanation of *Fatiha* on page 103, however, not only breaks the rhythm of the sentence but steals the very comic naturalness of the comment's terseness. "The burial of truth / Is the cause of calamity" (*N*, p. 161) is only the translation of the French footnote. Missing is the actual transcription of the amusing *sabir* (North African pidgin French) version of Si Mokhtar's doubly political declamation: he not only complains about the lack of freedom of speech but also refuses to speak the language of the colonizer. Kateb also pointed out the existence of a factual error in the French text: the second sentence within quotes on page 253 should thus read "He inadvertently killed the *husband* of a woman he didn't love" (emphasis mine). The name of the East Algerian city mentioned on p. 166 should be "Guelma," and not "Cuelma." Other North African terms can be found in the Glossary preceding this Introduction.

father fallen on the threshold of the penal colony") should be
rendered as "defunct father fallen on the brink of bankrupcy,"
déboire ("heartbreak, trial") as "hangover" (*N*, p. 112), or that
outré ("outraged") would be translated as "exhausted" (*N*,
p. 212). The American translation does a fine job, however, of
sustaining the movement of many of the novel's key sequences,
which possess a unity no less lyrical and visionary than their
French counterparts.

The news of Kateb's unexpected death from leukemia, on
28 October 1989 broke as these pages neared completion,
marking the stunning and ironic end of a tragic exile.[46] I had
talked to Kateb in Philadelphia and New York in the spring
of 1988, when he was featured in Eric Sellin's Sixth Forum
on North African Literature and Culture, and the peaceful
surroundings of our next encounter in a small village in the
Drôme did not quite dispel the sense of concern and urgency
that seemed always to prevail over his creative or intellectual
activities. He had called in Décines-Charpieu, which is how I
unexpectedly found out that we were summer neighbors, and
mentioned that he was staying close to Grenoble for the treatment of a recently discovered blood-cell anomaly. He extended
an invitation "just to visit" and to discuss, among other matters, the American reprint of *Nedjma*, which I could tell pleased
him tremendously. When I arrived on Sunday, 6 August, Elisa-

---

46. His death calls to mind the uncannily prophetic conclusion of Kateb's
1962 elegy on the deaths of Fanon, Amrouche, and Ferraoun, words he could
just as well have written about his own:

> War and blood-cell cancer
> Slow or violent, to each his death
> But it makes no difference
> For to those who have learned
> To read in darkness
> And who, eyes closed,
> Will not stop writing
> To die thus is to live.   (*OF*, p. 97)

beth Auclaire-Tamaroff had already joined Kateb. As I now read through the notes I had jotted down in the bus after our conversation, a haunting picture lingers: that of a vital and friendly man, eager, restless too, frail, preoccupied, weary, intense within the Spartan frugality of his flat. A self-effacing man of quiet reserve, he had obviously not lost any of his fierce sense of independence and ideological integrity: as we talked about his just completed revision of *Le bourgeois sans-culotte,* the conversation drifted to the issue of *francophonie,* a concept whose intimation of cultural hegemony he passionately denounced for providing weapons to reactionary religious expansionism. Among the many projects that he was then pursuing, Kateb mentioned a book-length statement on current Algerian problems, in which the language issue was to be prominently addressed. We talked about other projects, too, such as his interest in an earlier English translation of "Le cadavre encerclé" and above all the status of *La Palestine trahie,* a play he wanted to update, before final release, in relation to recent political developments. As the afternoon wore down, the three of us went out for a walk, and I remember his frail appearance in walking attire: the body made seemingly weaker by the slightly oversize khaki shorts, the dark, heavy sweater thrown over the slightly stooped shoulders, the somewhat emaciated but still rugged face with the piercing eyes under the navy-blue Greek sailor's cap, and the knotty cane taken along (he explained in soft Algerian tones) because of the numerous adders in the countryside. But as I recall our last contact, the flow of simple warmth and noble strength remains perhaps the most indelible memory. When we separated with the promise to get in touch soon again, I could not foresee that so momentous a voice in contemporary literature was soon to fall silent.

The permanence of that voice's polyphony, however, remains the greatest gift Kateb bequeathed to us. Not the least because of its dynamic elusion of constraining polarities, and within the rich polyvalence of a pluralistic text, its visionary creation shaped a uniquely humanitarian space. As the scene of an ir-

1

repressibly existential passion, Kateb's work finally embodies an ineffaceable testimony: for his was the most resonant voice of a generation that challenged and conquered the chasm, lived and sang the agony and the ecstasy of a historical cataclysm politically and poetically conquered.

Glossary

bicot: racial slur for "Arab"
Dépêche de Constantine: daily newspaper
gnaouia: an edible plant from Eastern Algeria
hakim: wisdom, knowledge; sage, scholar
kief: variant of *kef,* a mixture of tobacco and hashish
Maître: French title used for attorneys
medersa: a Moslem school
oukil: attorney in Islamic law
periploi: voyages, journeys
sambouk: variant of "sambuk:" an Arab boat of the Indian Ocean

Selected Bibliography

BY KATEB YACINE, IN FRENCH

Le cercle des représailles. Paris: Seuil, 1959.
Le polygone étoilé. Paris: Seuil, 1966.
L'homme aux sandales de caoutchouc. Paris: Seuil, 1970.
L'oeuvre en fragments. Paris: Sindbad, 1986.

BY KATEB YACINE, IN ENGLISH

"Ever more fierce are the ancestors" (a translation by Bernard Aresu of
    a selection from "Les ancêtres redoublent de férocité", *San José
    Studies* 4, no. 2 (May 1978): 70–80.
Intelligence Powder (a translation by Stephen J. Vogel of "La poudre
    d'intelligence". New York: Ubu Repertory Theater Publications,
    1986.
"One step forward, three steps back." In Jacques Derrida and
    Mustapha Tlili, eds., *For Nelson Mandela.* New York: Seaver
    Books / Henry Holt and Company, 1987, pp. 97–111.

ON KATEB YACINE

Aresu, Bernard. *The Poetics of Kateb's Fiction.* Tübingen: Gunter
    Narr (Etudes Littéraires Françaises), 1991.
Arnaud, Jacqueline. *La littérature maghrébine de langue française: Le
    cas de Kateb Yacine.* Paris: Publisud, 1986.
Aurbakken, Christine. *L'étoile d'araignée: Une lecture de "Nedjma"
    de Kateb Yacine.* Paris: Publisud, 1986.
Bonn, Charles. *Nedjma.* Paris: Presses universitaires de France, 1990.
Gafaïti, Hafid. *Kateb Yacine, un homme, une œuvre, un pays.* Algiers:
    Laphomic / Voix Multiples, ca. 1983.

lii

Selected Bibliography

Gaha, Kamel. *Métaphore et métonymie dans "Le polygone étoilé."* Tunis: Publications de l'université, 1979.

Gontard, Marc. *"Nedjma" de Kateb Yacine: Essai sur la structure formelle du roman.* 1975. rpt. Paris: L'Harmattan, 1985.

Sbouaï, Taïeb. *"La femme sauvage" de Kateb Yacine.* Paris: L'Arcantère, 1985.

NEDJMA

I. . .

i. . .

Lakhdar has escaped from his cell.

At dawn, his shadow appears on the landing; everyone looks up, indifferently.

Mourad stares at the fugitive. "So what? They'll get you later."

"They know your name."

"I don't have any papers."

"They'll look for you here."

"Shut up. Don't nag."

No question of sleep now. Lakhdar notices the empty bottle.

"How did you get that?"

"It's Beaver's. He's leaving."

"Don't I get any?"

"Listen," Mourad suggests. "We'll sell my knife."

"Find some kid to buy the wine. Who'll know it's for us?"

They go into the rattiest Arab cafés of all, Lakhdar leading the way. The men inside greet them with gestures of recognition; many offer them

15

coffee. They show the knife to a tattooed man. He offers fifty francs.

"Seventy-five," Mourad says.

"All right."

The knife is easily worth a hundred and fifty. Half price, as usual. The four newcomers order more coffee, paying for themselves this time. Their invitations to the other men are vigorously rejected. They arouse a certain curiosity.

"Which one hit Monsieur Ernest?"

"I did," Lakhdar says, with the simplicity of an old leader.

"Well done, brother. I'll add another twenty francs for the knife."

"Never mind," Lakhdar says. "What goes in your pocket goes in ours."

Leaving the café they bump into a drunk. Rachid exclaims:

"Here's our friend Lakhdar who fixed Monsieur Ernest. Go get three bottles."

They drink until morning in the room they share. At six they leave for the yards, without Lakhdar.

Watching the first swings of the pickaxe, Monsieur Ernest seems to be in a better mood; with his head bandaged, his face has lost its look of sullen outrage; he asks calmly: "Where's Lakhdar?"

"I don't know." Mustapha makes a face.

"He can come back. I haven't reported him."

While the men are working, they talk to each other at long intervals; they are wondering what the foreman's up to.

"Not the first time a foreman's been hit by one of the men."

"Maybe Monsieur Ernest is the kind you have to get tough with."

Ameziane thinks Lakhdar should come back: "If it's a trap, we're still here."

"Watch out for trouble," Mustapha whispers.

At eleven, the girl comes with the basket. God is good! Everytime she moves she astounds them . . .

"Her name's Suzy, like a singer!"

Monsieur Ernest blows on his fork.

The men wonder if eating alone gets him so edgy every day at lunch time. He starts watching them again. This time Mourad seems to bother him most, he doesn't take his eyes off him. The men dig, run around, and loaf as much as they can: trying to throw up a dike against the foreman's ominous silence. Suzy smiles. And by its very innocence her private smile forecasts trouble, even though she makes sure not to look at any workman in particular.

Today the foreman's lunch comes out differently from yesterday's. He goes on chewing, growls something at Suzy. Her smile freezes. She looks down at her feet. The sky is clearing. In the patches of sunlight, bodies awaken, limbs stretch and crack, alert eyes sweep the yards. But

Ameziane still looks tense, muttering in Kabyl. His friends are afraid he might do something bad

"Hey you . . ."

Without looking up, Mourad drops his wheelbarrow.

"Go back to the house with my daughter There's some wood for you to chop."

Mourad walks off, his strides enormous. Suzy seems unwilling to keep up with him; she follows a good ways behind, slowing down whenever he looks as if he's going to turn around.

ii. . .

At seven, Monsieur Ricard climbs behind the wheel of his thirty-three-seat bus. Sixty miserable men are crammed in, along with a cloud of smoke. The conductor gets one foot on the back step. Knowing who Monsieur Ricard is, none of the riders speak to him. Actually they insult him the whole way— under their breath. But they never speak directly to him. After a few moments' silence, Monsieur Ricard asks for a cigarette, his voice expressionless. And since he never speaks directly to an Arab either, no one makes a move. Besides, there is always some stranger or some office worker in the bus who holds out his pack. Which fills the riders with deep resentment. Monsieur Ricard takes the cigarette. He laughs. He begins smoking voluptuously, ear cocked, savoring the insults. What could exasperate the riders more? Matches scrape all over the bus: sick at heart, the wretches smoke their last butts.

When he gets to Bône, Monsieur Ricard lets cars pass him, waves at policemen even when they can't see him. He is not the same man who crossed the village like a cyclone just this morning.

The city is too much for Monsieur Ricard. He is afraid to look at the shopwindows. He has only one thing on his mind now: sitting in the fashionable bar where there is no one he knows. The waitress is nice. Eighteen. She drops a pointed remark: "When are you getting married, Monsieur Ricard?"

Two miles out of the city, he almost turned over. "That bitch thinks I can't find a wife. The Jews and Arabs started that story. They know I got married before they were born, and by correspondence too, it's something they can't even conceive of . . ." He takes off his cap, a fit of anxiety riveting him to the table. He feels as if he wanted someone to punch him hard. The darkness steals down. Seeing her employer in one of his bad moods, the maid sneaks out to the stable. For years now she's had trouble sleeping, like the cows she keeps awake at night with her ghostly presence. Through the rickety door, she watches him get up from the table. Monsieur Ricard goes straight to the Modern Bar where he hasn't set foot since the cigar contest; when he comes in, the owner hides in the pantry. Monsieur Ernest is alone in the bar. Ordinarily the foreman would have made a point not to invite the contractor to his table. But Monsieur Ricard seems to be looking for Monsieur Ernest.

"Have a glass?"

iii. . .

Monsieur Ricard gets out of bed at five in the morning; he pulls on an old moth-eaten pair of pants and begins humming around his house, carrying his shoes, bumping into the walls and the polished furniture, heavy, unstable, noisy as the flies whose nocturnal recess he interrupts, followed by their vague agitation and their buzzing protest against an awakening without the sun's warmth, without the day's cheer which would have gently drawn them from their torpor if the old contractor didn't make a ritual of being up at cockcrow, though it would be another two hours before his bus left. Before his eyes are completely open he pats his pockets, fingers the lighter, the keys of his impregnable apartment; hums over the sink, marveling at how long the soap lasts; plants his leather cap on his head, thereby distinguishing himself from all other citizens who get up as early but cannot imitate the way he wears his cap down over his pepper-and-salt hair by which Monsieur Ricard proclaims his fortune to the still-sleeping village, save perhaps some foreman like Monsieur Ernest, whose shadow stretches toward the quarry where the workers are waiting for him in the dim light, cleaning their tools, while the contractor's bus already reflects the dawning sun from every window . . . Now that Suzy is old enough to marry, the contractor and the foreman watch each other closer than ever, jumping out of bed at the same time and fooling with their caps, on the eve of the inevitable alliance which now depends on nothing more than a gesture: the last-minute proposal Monsieur Ricard will make, according to his position and his reputation, and then the inferior cap will only be tugged at once more, for all Monsieur Ernest's pride and Suzy's arrogance—for all her arrogant experience of the sighs of her father's men, Suzy can provide no argument against her acquisition by the suspicious widower, the old lunatic whose incredible success the foreman constantly curses as he prepares to hand over his daughter. Monsieur Ricard, moreover, would not dream of speculating with his prestige as a wildcat landowner; taciturn, greedy, badly dressed, he will never look like a businessman; his fortune is an effort of will, an act of desperate energy which isolates and sterilizes him, and his Protestant family cannot even sit with the other Europeans when they go to church.

Monsieur Ricard's tools reached the village in a cart where the first *colons* saw him dozing like a caged hawk, drawn by his father's nondescript mule perhaps stolen, perhaps confiscated from its owner and sold for almost nothing by some passing soldier; his mother had died in childbirth between one town and the next, and her unlucky husband soon followed her, crushed by work; still beardless, Monsieur Ricard inherited a kind of prison sentence: the half-century of slavery reserved for him by the defunct father fallen on the brink of bankruptcy, the same future of agonized labor which the scion was forced to accept, having no liquid assets at his disposal; neither the fallow land nor the kitchen garden nor the six horses nor the tiny vineyard could be assessed, any more than the profits from the first vehicle Monsieur Ricard would be driving to Bône each week for the mail, in accordance with his father's plans which turned out to be as profitable as they were troublesome;

it was, in fact, this trajectory which insured the capital. Although thirty years later Monsieur Ricard drives a brand new bus, the only luxury his not too rigorous regime allows—although he owns (outside the village where his house, garage, workshop, stable, milk-shed and other buildings form a kind of outpost on both sides of the road) a thriving but remote farm whose exact location is a mystery to most people—although everything belongs to him outright and no partner has survived, Monsieur Ricard insists on his strange and primitive doctrine of labor; the suits bought after exceptional harvests stand at attention, forsaken except for infrequent pilgrimages to France, Switzerland or Belgium; the wife sent long ago by a matrimonial agency (who didn't know how to separate milk as the marriage contract had stipulated) has faded away like a dream of grandeur, without benefit of divorce or even hearse, and Monsieur Ricard has probably extended self-awareness to the point of engendering only the one son who vanished between the wars—Monsieur Ricard seems to have forgotten all about him. Never the sort of man to be questioned, a hard man and a harder master, he implacably bickered with himself over his own salary, his own rest, as unapproachable and diligent as a chief of state, a convict or a priest.

After gulping down his *café au lait*, Monsieur Ricard examines his provisions while the maid prepares (under his supervision) the lunch he washes down with the wine unsold when it came out of the presses, delivered by the same farmer who was a woodcutter with Monsieur Ricard's father, during the period of the ill-fated cart. It is not even six o'clock when he sits down at the kitchen table, near the liter of rum no one else is permitted to touch, even on Christmas day; on Christmas the master of the house stays in town; he keeps his bus out overnight; after a short nap, he closes his garage; at the end of the day, you can find him, freshly shaved, in clean shirt and overalls, leaning on some bar; he plays cards, warms himself up with triple doses of straight anisette, and intoxication reveals the happy old man he might have been if he hadn't inherited a cart and a Huguenot father; for Monsieur Ricard's loud voice is made for brawling, as his arms are made for thumps on the shoulder and his vigorous body for the mock battles he emerges from lucid and victorious, disappointed that his disabled cronies never ask for the one last round he expected to offer in case of an insult, a challenge, or an encounter with a superior drunkard worth talking to all night . . . But all the other nights end in the kitchen, with the half-awakened flies; on the stroke of six, having revived yesterday's euphoria, Monsieur Ricard puts away the bottle of rum; he hears the servant hobbling along; he starts to leave, then turns around.

"Let me see your dress."

He puts his hands around her throat.

"Have you been stealing the coffee?"

She struggles like a hen, squeezed against the sideboard. "I'm going to bite him. But if I bite him . . ."

The maid leaves, carrying the laundry basket. Near the tubs, she catches sight of Mourad, Ameziane and the other men. Mourad waves at her. The argument goes on. She listens. The men seem to be convinced about something.

She listens.

They are through talking; they wash up, one after the other, solemn and already tired, and start walking back to the yards.

iv. . .

Suzy in her Sunday best. "No need for a bra, thank God. They're so big they even hurt a little"; she dashes to the market and back, leaves her basket in the kitchen, takes the main road, turns into a short cut across an empty lot to a wide pasture; she runs through the thickest grass, and collapses among the daffodils; the sun is hot now; she closes her eyes for a few seconds, shivers, sits up and suddenly turns toward the village, as if a monster had surprised her and bitten her ankle without her being able to escape or feel the bite either. On the road she sees farmers riding mules. Then Mourad appears at the bend.

"Good morning, Mademoiselle."

Suzy imagines the farmers are watching her as they spur their mules; she walks toward Mourad; when the farmers are passing, she's so near him that he steps back.

"Are you going far?"

"I'm out for a walk."

They walk on. Mourad keeps his head down.

"Go away."

"And that's that," Mourad thinks, "the spell is broken, I'm her father's workman again, she'll walk back across the empty lot as if I were following her, as if I were offending her just by walking on the same path, as if we should never be in the same world together, except because of violence or rape . . . And that's that. Already she's told me to go away, as if I had put my arm around her waist. She was offended, and I suppose the farmers offended her too just by looking at her. Because she doesn't belong to their world or to mine, but to a private planet without workmen, without farmers, unless sometimes, maybe even tonight, she dreams . . . What if I felt her breasts?" Then all he can think of is hitting her, seeing her on the ground, maybe picking her up and hitting her again—"until she wakes up, a sleepwalker falling off the roof, with all her superstitions, risking death without having realized that a world exists, not her world, not mine, not even ours, but just the world which has survived its first woman, its first man, and which doesn't keep track of us or our memories long, a second, that's all," Mourad thinks. But Suzy is careful not to laugh now, blushing, her nerves close to her skin, only a young girl can tremble like that; this disarms Mourad. "She's going away." They do not speak to each other. "She's looking at the daffodils, where she was lying just now, moist, lonely, half-open," and Mourad blushes and Suzy's blushing face turns away again; she runs off.

"I almost had her," Mourad says.

"How, how, hmmh? How did you do it?"

Ameziane offers him a drink. He starts walking toward the Modern Bar. It's night. The owner is over fifty. Ameziane hates spending the money, but it's night. Too tired to go to bed. The bar is almost dark, it looks empty. The voices stop, rise, fall like a hen coop at twilight, and the owner is over fifty, not to mention the exhaustion and the boredom that hang over the village after work, even in bars, even in the houses of large families. Ameziane orders a round with a grumble of disappointment, reminding himself that from behind women never look like what they are—old or aging, flirts or prudes—unless they wear veils over their faces. . .

"Hmmm? What?"

"I almost had her," Mourad says.

"Is that all?"

"I know what you mean," Ameziane says, making a face. "What can you say to a girl standing in the road, especially when she's the foreman's daughter! And not even Arab . . . You're better off with your friends. I'll tell you how I used to get my kicks when we worked in the city, before they sent me to another department, when I didn't even know how to hold a shovel . . ."

The owner smiles, a girl's smile: "If you work for Monsieur Ernest, I can give you credit."

Mustapha thanks her and shakes hands. The bar isn't like a hen coop any more; it glows like an airport. Rachid puts on his dark glasses and starts acting big, still grumbling for the form's sake: "I told you we'd find something to drink. Getting credit here's as good as . . ." The owner pours out the pale wine; it's not night yet, only the sun is a deeper color, the sky fades like a heap of ashes revived in each drinker's gleaming eyes and the captive sparks of the bottle pouring, upside down, full of cold and foaming light.

"It was in Oran," Ameziane says. "I was a kid, and I'd do anything. I had a friend my age who came from the desert to make his living. We

28

worked in the same bathhouse, Larbi and I; sometimes, we took the masseur's place, but our regular job was to carry the hot water around and we had another friend, a boy from the Sahara who brought drinking water from the hills and sold it. We were all in the same business: we sold water. We met nights in the main room. One time, the boy who sold drinking water came with this little box here . . ."

"Let's see . . ."

"What did he put in it? Snuff?"

"That's not all . . . Now I only put my nose in it . . . sniff once in a while. But that day, there was something else in the box . . ."

"What was it?"

"Jam."

"So?"

"There were squashed dates . . ."

"In that little box?"

"Yes. The three of us ate them."

"Aiouah?"

"Despite the smell . . ."

"How did it smell?"

"Like snuff. We could even see the flakes in the jam. It was better not to chew . . . 'It's dust,' the boy from the Sahara said, the drinking-water boy, and Larbi ate, and so did I. It was dust all right. But the smell . . ."

"So?"

"We started laughing. Larbi said: 'Funny

jam, funny jam,' but I couldn't stand it any more, I felt as if I'd been eating with my nose. The Sahara boy was pale. He said the smell of snuff came from the room, not from the box. And he was almost right. The room always smelled of sweat and snuff. But we had already started laughing, skating on our clogs to the room where the customers slept on the benches, supposedly drying under the lamps. They chased us out because we laughed too much. And I finally understood . . ."

"What?" Mustapha asked, "what did you understand?"

"I finally understood it was hashish dust. But I kept on eating with Larbi, and I kept on saying 'Funny jam, funny jam, huh?' If one of us had said the word Hashish, I know we wouldn't have eaten it. But by saying jam, we made it jam. First we got hot. We thought it was the steam; and the Sahara boy handed us shirts. 'We'll walk around, it'll stop then.' But outside it was worse. We shivered. But we laughed anyway and sang songs in French, I don't know why we sang in French. But the Sahara boy was bigger than we were and he made us go into a Jewish bar. I don't know how many glasses of anisette we drank. Afterwards, we were dead. The Jew went to get a taxi and paid the driver to take us back to the baths. We sang in the taxi."

"Then what?"

". . . Being drunk that second time wasn't as good as the first."

V. . .

The room Mourad and Rachid share isn't so badly damaged by the rain as the one Mustapha and Lakhdar are in, so they all sleep in the same one; they stretch out one of the hair mattresses and cover themselves with the other, spread crossways; their legs are bare, but their chests and hips covered. The concrete floor is cold; the village is eighteen hundred feet above sea level.

The empty room is no use, but the Italian woman refused to rent one room to four men.

"We'll find a way to use the other hole," Mourad says. "We'll start by putting the dirty clothes and the alcohol lamp in there."

Until morning, it rained into the room where they slept.

They shiver.

They wake coughing. The coffee does them a lot of good. It is Lakhdar who had the courage to borrow half a pound ready-ground from the proprietor of the Arab café; they drink two pots of the scalding stuff, and smoke their first cigarettes. It's six o'clock. Scoured by the night, the village is ominous, commonplace as an actor without make-up; the dawn is cool and gray; there are only heavy footsteps, coughs now and then, brief greetings answering each other, forced cheerfulness of men's voices after sleep; most of the people in the street haven't thought about washing yet; huddling in their burnooses, they pound their broomsticks in unison, with a skill compounded of rage and sluggishness; one after the other they go into the only café open, where they quickly recover their strength at the first swallow; coffee conquers both cold and fatigue; the sky is as threatening as yesterday.

"And it's supposed to be spring," an old, bent sweeper says, spitting.

The farmers shrug and the café empties as quickly as it filled; sweepers, farmers, workmen follow each other along the straight road, and the sound of coughing grows less harsh, the broomsticks more discreet, as if each man had regained his confidence, made up his mind for the day.

vi. . .

A night watchman, rifle pointed toward the sky, watches the loitering group from his sentry box.

Beaver is pleased with himself for not saluting.

"Dirty sneak. Think how many men he's sent up . . ."

"Who hires him?"

"Our commune. Usually they're ex-assistants of the Administrator, retired officials, demobilized soldiers."

"Besides, we haven't done anything," Mourad says.

"But if he knew you were day-workers, if I wasn't with you, he'd whistle."

"We know how to whistle too, we know how to answer . . ."

"He'd say you have to obey the law; in any case, you're better off saluting him as well as the civil and military authorities, especially Monsieur Ricard who runs the bus line. Everyone's his enemy and everyone salutes him. He refuses to stop for passengers if he can't remember their faces. He has plenty of money: he's just bought his fifth bus, and now all he needs is to marry again . . ."

Lakhdar walks faster and Beaver gives up for tonight trying to tip off these "good guys, a little jumpy, a little simple and a little bored too, like anyone who lives in town": that's how Beaver describes the four workmen lately hired by Monsieur Ernest.

vii. . .

Monsieur Ricard's wedding was celebrated in the strictest intimacy. Even though people shinnied up trees and performed all kinds of acrobatic stunts, they couldn't come to the banquet.

Monsieur Ricard was mortified at having to open his house to so many guests: all the Europeans of the village, with their entire families; only the really important notables failed to show up, though their deputies came in great number, despite the fact that they had received neither invitations nor orders. Luckily the local curé, who lived in another village, hadn't got wind of the affair and the Protestant minister wasn't forewarned either; despite the general anticipation, there was no conflict between Monsieur Ricard's faith and his bride's Catholicism, for there were no priests to cross swords with.

The scandal took another form. Monsieur Ricard tolerated the drinking calmly enough at first; but the example must have carried him away; he began to get drunk himself when he

34

realized that this was the only challenge he could accept with a chance of victory; several of his rivals had already fallen under the table and this triumph intoxicated him further. His joy degenerated into hostility; he made everybody laugh, but the lady chairman of the Red Cross received several date pits down the front of her dress and her terrorized infant began to teethe on the corkscrew. Then they put Monsieur Ricard to bed still conscious but incapable of controlling the helpless fury that had assailed him since the start of the dinner. He saw his worst enemies there in his house, laughing at him and spoiling his old bachelor's quarters as they started spoiling his second marriage. But he let them dress him up in an old nightshirt that was too short for him. And Suzy, realizing there would be no wedding night, finished off a bottle of champagne without showing whether she was drowning her sorrow or her joy under her family's eyes. They thrust her into the conjugal bed where she began struggling under the writhing crucifix, while the lady chairman of the Red Cross took her revenge by mounting guard over the vanquished couple and brandishing the screaming baby, drowning out Monsieur Ricard's yells of rage, so that no one could hear the end of the hymn intoned by Monsieur Ernest in a fanatic outburst provoked by his wife, either to save face, or to stir up some protestant reaction from Monsieur Ricard that would pillory him for good. But

35

the lady chairman of the Red Cross remained at the heart of the scandal, and Suzy stopped struggling; finally she turned toward her bridegroom and pummelled him to her heart's content, meeting no resistance, for Monsieur Ricard was apparently in a coma; actually his mind was on other things; he had not heard the hymn, but his eyes had closed on a group of guests rummaging through his wardrobe.

At the start of the orgy, the maid was in the sun-drenched kitchen; she came out at twilight to put a stop to the pillaging. They seized her at once and dragged her into the nuptial chamber. The postman's wife took a half-empty bottle of rum and applied it to the girl's lips. "That's it!" the bailiff exulted. "That'll spoil things for her with Saint Peter!" The maid resisted, stiffening until the postman's wife knocked the bottle against her gums and all the rum flowed down her throat at once. Eight men held the girl fast, not to mention the children. Finally the postman's wife threw away the empty bottle. The maid fell down, then stood up, her eyes bulging out of their sockets. This was her first and her last imprecation: "You're all unbelievers!"

Monsieur Ricard leaped out of bed.

"Get out of here. Now. Get out."

She staggered to the middle of the room, retching, repeating under her breath, without seeing her employer or distinguishing his voice:

"You're all unbelievers!" The postman collapsed in a chair; if his wife hadn't ben running things he would have dragged himself to the girl's knees: not to console her, to make her shut up. He saw Suzy jump out of bed to arm herself with the riding crop hanging on the wall.

Monsieur Ricard forestalled his bride's gesture. He grabbed the crop. The first stroke landed across the maid's eyes. She gave a single groan of pain, as if she were afraid that screaming would make her throw up on the sacrosanct floor. The second stroke hit her across the eyes again. She remained standing, hands stretched out, without unclenching her teeth. Blows rained down. Monsieur Ricard lashed at her with a look of outraged stupidity on his face; he no longer understood that the girl was making no attempt to shield her face, and he began to miss his cap; he knew now, as the liquor's effects faded, that he could neither stop hitting nor finish off his staggering prey without turning against the guests who formed a circle around him. Then Mourad walked in, his steps noiseless. He did not shoulder aside the guests. A thrust of his knee doubled up Monsieur Ricard, just when Suzy was dragging him back, and now it was Mourad's turn to wield the crop—he was unable to restrain his blows. When he came to, he was bound fast near the two bodies which seemed offended for eternity; the maid began groaning and the corporal cut the ropes around Mourad's wrist. The guests were still there, standing in the same circle, as if there had been no crime, as if everyone had been told beforehand that Suzy wouldn't keep her pretty dress, that the wedding would end in a wake; and the policeman who locked Mourad up felt like embracing him: it was the same policeman Suzy had called to arrest Lakhdar at the yards, the same policeman who was in love with Suzy and with whom she was in love, the same policeman who locked Mourad up when he really wanted to bear him through the streets in triumph, the same policeman who carried Monsieur Ricard's coffin, for he was a protestant too.

viii. . .

Lakhdar refuses to go back to work at the yards, much to everyone's surprise.

"I won't go," Lakhdar says. "Monsieur Ernest's losing his touch. I won't go."

"He'll let bygones be bygones. His daughter's getting married today."

"Yes," Rachid says. "If you come tomorrow, he'll still be thinking about the wedding. He won't dare have you arrested."

"I'm going to have a look at the party," Mourad says. "If I run into Monsieur Ernest, I'll mention Lakhdar to him."

Lakhdar keeps shaking his head stubbornly as he cuts into a cold fritter. Mourad has gone. "The sun's gone already and we haven't set foot outside."

Mustapha finishes peeling the potatoes. "If Beaver doesn't bring the pot and the oil, what'll we eat?"

"Instead of worrying about this wedding just to get me back to work," Lakhdar says, "Mourad should ask Monsieur Ernest to advance us some cash. I want to get out of here."

Rachid has fallen asleep on a corner of the mattress.

"Should we light a candle?" Mustapha asks. "Here's our man . . ."

Beaver comes in, with two others they don't know: Si Salah and Si Abdelkader, employees from the mixed Commune. Beaver's winded. He's forgotten all about the pot and all the other things he had promised . . .

"Haven't you heard? . . ."

Rachid jumps without opening his eyes. Mustapha watches Lakhdar light the candle, while Beaver tells about the crime, and the darkness roused by the flame seems to have swallowed up the ominous news. And Beaver finishes, seconded by the sighs of the two new arrivals: "This time,

39

he won't get out of it . . . You should turn yourselves in. They'll probably call you in for questioning."

Rachid has stood up. He steps across the
mattress to take a look at Beaver. Lakhdar and
Mustapha stand up too. All six look at each other.

"Impossible. What time is it? Mourad left at
sundown. What time can it be?"

"It all happened in a flash. The police are
still there."

"Allah!"

"Alas!" Si Abdelkader says.

"By now the whole village is cursing you . . ."

"Talk about trouble! First the fight, the arrest, Lakhdar's escape. And now Mourad . . . The
village was quiet, too quiet before you got here;
and of course the outsiders get blamed for everything. People are tired of it. Some are even locking
up their wives. The Europeans went to the administrator, with their city councillors. They're demanding your expulsion, insisting that French
sovereignty be respected. And you're no better off
with us Moslems. Even when they enjoy whispering
about your misadventures, they condemn you all
the same; they say you sold stolen goods to buy
wine; even the drunkards can't conceal their dis-
gust. Really, everyone's against you."

"Allah! Allah!" Si Salah echoes, but Beaver
recovers:

"It's no good getting cold feet. Let's spend

40

our last night together . . . I have my own suspi-
cions; my friends here can bear witness: so long as
they didn't know each other, my rivals didn't give
me any trouble. Now they've showed their hands
and joined forces. If that was only all! Their wives,
whom they have so generously forgiven, love them
all the more! They surround me, follow me all
night long. If one of them recovers his honor I'm
lost!"

"Poor friend!" Mustapha says, already preoccupied by his own misfortunes . . .

"Ordinarily my mistresses would save me.
Today they arm their pimps against me. And
cuckolds never heard of pity . . ."

"Courage . . ."

"That's life," the employees sniff, while
Beaver makes despairing gestures.

"That's not all. They saw me come here . . ."

All six look at each other, and the candle
lugubriously collapses.

"We have to get out now," Mustapha says,
and Lakhdar, furious, adds:

"I've wanted to for a long time, we should
have left already. But it's my fault. I ought to
have taken care of that dungheap."

Beaver makes terrible faces. "It's a sure thing
they followed me tonight too. The woman in the
bar told them I knew you, she even told them we
were drinking in her place the night you came.
It's a sure thing."

Si Abdelkader picks his teeth.

Si Salah and Si Abdelkader look at each other.

If Mustapha were talking (but he's stopped), he might make bitter remarks to Si Salah and Si Abdelkader, the two strangers: "All right, get out, our problems aren't any of your business, we're leaving and all we're taking from your village is another memory of more trouble . . . So what if your masters kick us out: there's never enough slavery to go around, they'll end up by kicking themselves out. And if someone got hurt, so . . ."

Beaver takes a mandolin out of his burnoose, then a bottle. Si Salah takes something out of his pocket. Ah? Lakhdar has just leaped up.

"Give that knife here. It's mine. Don't bother opening the bottle. The candle's going out."

"Ah!" Si Salah gasps.

And Si Abdelkader: "Don't get excited!"

"Get out!" Beaver orders, dismayed.

The strangers run like rats.

Lakhdar slams the door on their heels.

"He had the nerve to buy back the knife Mourad sold . . ."

"And to hold it under our noses on a day like today! That's the kind of visitors you bring us . . ."

Beaver feels sorry for himself. "What do you expect, the traitors are always on my tail—it's my fate."

Mustapha, holding back his tears: "So nothing's sacred? The memory of a friend we may never see again . . . The knife sold to celebrate another friend's return . . ."

Lakhdar: "And knowing the whole story, this so-called man buys back the knife without even thinking of giving it back, and comes to rub our noses in it."

Rachid yields to the general anger: "And to celebrate with a bottle, as if we were going to drink to Mourad's arrest!"

"I've brought other bottles," Beaver says, his hand on his hood. "I'm sorry. I didn't mean to make it worse."

The bottles are put on the floor.

The mandolin too, near them.

Beaver will not sing.

He realizes it's a night of farewells.

"If I didn't have kids, I'd go with you . . . I'll die a violent death. Better that my rivals kill me. If I leave with you, they'll turn on my wife . . ."

But none of the men has the heart to laugh.

Rachid walks Beaver home.

Lakhdar waits until they've gone to close the door.

"Hand me the knife," Rachid says. "You never know . . ."

"You never know," Beaver says.

ix. . .

Toward the end of the night, the three men leave
the room, a good distance from one another; they
meet on the road, turning their backs to the
quarry; they stamp on the ground strewn with
bare branches; the north wind pushes them over
the brush and they plunge into the fog; the absence
of any itinerary abolishes the notion of time; still
fresh, by the end of the morning they have reached
a *douar* of some dozen huts. The village is invisible
now. The three men head for the *douar* with a
single impulse. The farmers watch them coming.
They ask them into the elder's hut once they find
out that the strangers are from the city; they
leave them alone with the cakes, the dates, the
curds, so they won't be ashamed of their appetite.
The elder comes later to take coffee with them, asks
them questions about salaries in the city and in the
village, about the wheat harvest, the grape and
olive crops. But the elder doesn't seem pleased that
the three young men are thinking about staying
in the forest; he talks about police interrogations,
elections and reprisals. Rachid assures him. Finally

44

the elder tells them to gather firewood and take it
to the old women of the *douar*, who will sell it in
the village so long as the forest-ranger keeps out
of the district. For the rest . . .

"There's an abandoned house, not far from
here."

"I don't know how we can live," Mustapha
snarls. "Will the people of the *douar* drive us out
like the villagers?"

Nothing is left of the abandoned house but
the bare walls, the stripped rafters. All afternoon
the newcomers carry thatch.

"Don't light a fire," the elder suggested.

Lakhdar groans, his head buried in the straw.

The stars swarm.

It is bitter cold.

Mustapha hums, both to fight off the cold and
to fall asleep; the stars swarm.

At sunrise they follow the bad forest paths.

They don't talk to each other.

It is the moment to separate.

They don't look at each other.

If Mourad were here, they could each take
one of the cardinal points; they could each stick
to a specific direction.

But Mourad is not here. They think about
Mourad.

"Beaver gave me some money," Lakhdar
says suddenly. "We'll share it."

"I'm going to Constantine," Rachid says.

"Let's get started," Lakhdar says. "I'll go with you as far as Bône. What about you, Mustapha?"

"I'm going a different way."

The two shadows fade on the road.

X. . .

"I left the yards a long time ago, I haven't worked in a long time, for three years I haven't had a thing ahead of me"; he keeps ogling the women passing, dressed up and perfumed at this hour, in the Place de la Brèche; he compares them to Marcelle, the famous madam who must have been young once, who must have had her time of grace, of disdain . . . *Marcelle: the ugliest men in the department got into her; she's a rich woman now. She's big and never had a child, the fat comes up to her ears; Marcelle is hairy; she smells of kerosene; her arms are covered with bracelets and they make Chinese shadows on the walls; her heels stick out over the edges of her slippers, as if her gummy feet were about to come through the velvet. Everyone wants her to break her neck on the stairs, she doesn't like noise and doesn't give credit. But her middle-aged visitors, the ones she sends, one by*

46

one, to her creatures, politely and authoritatively,
her visitors tell their friends the next day that that
Marcelle is a Madonna; they imagine they spent
the night with magnificent mistresses; sometimes
they stop boasting, imitating the jealous silence
of men who, having tasted unheard-of delights,
prefer not to divulge their good fortune; they re-
turn faithfully to the maternal madam's and per-
fect their lies that are unutterable anyway, for
such passion is not discussed, Rachid tells himself,
turning back toward the *fondouk* on the Boulevard de l'Abîme. He staggers slightly, walking
down the middle of the street . . . Like a whirlwind
. . . Rachid throws himself onto the parapet, gropes
for a stone . . . The shock of the projectile. The
driver gets out.

"Where do you think you are, you tramp?"

Rachid keeps his head down.

"You think the road's made for cats and
beggars? What if I had run you down? I still can,
if that's what you want. What's wrong, you lose
your nerve?"

Rachid puts his hand under his coat, fingering
the lining; the man is thickset, wearing golfing
knickerbockers, bald.

"A no-good like you . . ."

With his index finger, the driver lifts
Rachid's chin, brings his shiny round head even
closer; Rachid steps back; the stab is made;
Rachid runs to the end of the street; the driver,
his face reflected in a puddle of blood, wipes him-

self off without knowing what's happened, and the policeman, ominous and distant, blows mournfully on his silver whistle, racing along the trees that soothe Rachid's still undetermined flight with a murmur of complicity; he isn't running any more; he hammers at the door, a long silence; a woman's hand opens the little window, draws back the bolt, and the shadow vanishes; Rachid steps over the porter sleeping at the end of the corridor; in the moonlit courtyard he finds the woman crouching bare-legged over a terra-cotta brazier, a bellows in her hand, boiling coffee; it is an intractable Rachid, born of the Place de la Brèche and the assault on the street, who is talking now, his foot next to the coffeepot, his knee on a level with the sleepy face; Rachid has never spent more than one night here, not with this woman; "luckily the porter's asleep."

"You don't happen to have your veil?"

The woman jumps.

"What's the difference? Who do you want to see?"

Rachid is feverish; he grabs the woman by the sleeve.

"I'm telling you to give me your veil. They're after me."

"I've never heard of a man asking a woman for that. If anyone's after you, it must be the devil. Leave me alo . . ."

"All right," Rachid says.

He has slapped her; he walks away, shakes

the stupefied porter, then comes back toward the woman. She screams; "a baby, that's what, a crazy fool"; Rachid seems riveted to the ground, on his short legs, his eyes half-closed; and she quiets down, staring at him, panting, with a last scream toward the porter who has no trouble hearing *her*, as if he could only recognize women's voices because of his work:

". . . as if a prostitute had to have a veil! . . . Go find him a sheet, maybe he can get buried in it, and he's lucky to be crazy or else . . ."

Rachid wraps himself in the dirty cloth; he takes the bellows from the woman and crouches down over the stove; she laughs aloud; "now I hope he'll buy me something, he could even take my place when I'm sick if he likes playing house so much, the son of a bitch"; she keeps her ears cocked, talking to the porter, while Rachid pumps the bellows, his head completely hidden under the sheet; "another lunatic knocking, closing time is closing time, we have a right to sleep too, what does that policeman want?"

"Here, Monsieur, here he is, take him away in his sheet, like a son of a bitch, and watch out, he's crazy."

The policeman's sleepy; he leads Rachid away by the arm, walking nonchalantly.

"You'll talk later; the relief's on now."

And he hands Rachid over to another policeman, standing in front of the commissariat, as tired as the first apparently, although he's just gotten out of bed, his face swollen, his voice hoarse.

Before sitting down, Rachid notices an elegant prisoner sleeping at the rear of the cell. He sings softly so as not to wake up the other man, who doesn't seem to have seen or heard him. Rachid is sitting on the concrete floor; "I'll be here all day at least"; a spider creeps toward him; "as if she were flirting with me"; a big spider, gray, terribly old, dusty and tottering; he wakes the other man who begins fuming through his gray moustache, his raincoat carefully folded under his head; Rachid's companion talks lying down; it is like a dream.

"That's bad, another one afraid of bugs! Why didn't it bite me, that spider of yours? I've been here three days. There are more than spiders, there are worms and rats. I'll even bet there's a snake in a hole like this."

"All right," Rachid says, "I won't be able to sleep. What are you doing in here?"

"What do you think, enjoying myself? I know my way around. They call me Little Joe, if that means anything to you."

At noon the policeman calls Little Joe and hands him a big package full of fried potatoes, grapes, stuffed peppers between slices of hot bread, a bottle of milk, three packs of cigarettes, different brands.

"It's a woman's present all right. Eat with me, kid."

"I'm no kid," Rachid says.

They swallow the potatoes first, then scorch their mouths with the peppers and finally torture themselves nibbling at the grape seeds without admitting that they're thirsty.

"We'll keep the milk for later."

"I'm full now," Rachid says.

"That's nothing, not all my wives have heard about it yet. Otherwise we wouldn't know where to put all the stuff."

They smoke, picking their teeth. Then they take a nap, but Rachid keeps waking up, remembering the spider staring at him, another prisoner; "as if it was lonely, looking for company, maybe caresses"; Rachid takes off his belt; he holds the buckle so as not to wake Little Joe; Rachid whacks at the spider; it jumps on his neck, graceful, grateful, forgiving.

"Help, it's still alive!"

Little Joe opens his eyes again.

"All that fuss over a bug! If your skin's so tender, stay home with your mother."

Rachid tears off his clothes, but the spider keeps ahead of him with a kind of frenzied joy; it dances, contracts on his heaving chest as if it were patiently waiting to be petted, as if it had helped Rachid take off his clothes with all the modest diligence of a lovesick woman.

"Take it off, Little Joe, please!"

"Leave it there, kid. Why bother the beast? Didn't the Lord say something about that? Let it alone. It'll understand what you want all by itself.

Don't look at it like that, you're scaring it instead of making it sorry for you. Let it have its little fun. God says so. You have to tolerate God's creatures."

"It's on me, on my chest, don't you see?"

"Don't move, I'm going to sing you a little song. You see . . . It's happy there. It's dancing. I don't have anything against that spider; I was getting bored, that's how dull I am, and I liked having that insect put in this cell with me by a merciful God who does nothing by accident."

Enter the police commissioner.

"All right, out, upstairs you!"

"I can't, monsieur commissioner," Rachid moans. "Give me your riding crop or kill it yourself, otherwise I'll go crazy here, and you're responsible."

"Don't move, clown!" the commissioner says, "I'll try, but I'm not wearing my glasses. You may get it right across the face. *Tac*."

"Help!" Rachid screams, "you missed. Try doing your job right or give me the crop."

"I'm doing my best," the commissioner says. "*Tac*, and *tac*."

"Missed!"

"What?"

"Missed!"

"Now it's sure to get mad," Little Joe says, "especially if it's a female; they don't like clumsiness. Now, monsieur commissioner, supposing she gets mad? If she jumped into your mouth, you without any teeth left, or in your eye when you're not wearing your glasses? She might sting you, that filthy spider that's spent her whole life with the Arabs and the tramps, and then what would you tell your pretty little grandchildren who throw away the Lord's own bread if a fly, a simple fly comes to share it with them; you can be sure your grandchildren won't forgive you for punishing everyone else if you let yourself be victimized by an insect, a paltry spider born in your own cell; you should let us leave with it and not wear yourself out with all these responsibilities . . ."

The commissioner's not listening; he's sitting on the floor wiping the sweat off his brow, watching the spider run away, next to Rachid who's scratching his thin, bare chest.

"You can take your stuff with you," the commissioner says at last, without looking at Rachid. "You're a deserter, aren't you?"

xi. . .

Night, Mourad gasps, night coming back, the cell overflowing, the moon landing, coming in the win-

dow, Mourad gasps. He gasps. The guard keeps
the door half open. He hasn't seen the blood on the
floor.

"You crying?"

The guard gallops down the corridors, across
the courtyard, into the guard room.

"One's killed himself!"

The orderly lifts Mourad who hadn't seen the
thickened pool himself. He sees it. He stops gasping. He lets himself be carried, drained of his last
agony.

"I tell you he was fighting."

"No, he stuck the knife in his belly."

"No, that's just it. They found the knife on
the other one."

"What other one?"

"The one from Constantine. The young one.
The little one. The one who just came."

The convicts sing in the courtyard. *Mother
the wall is high.* They sing in the courtyard.
Mother the wall is high. They sing. Now and then
they stop singing, whisper, can't sleep, whisper in
the courtyards, the cells:

"I tell you they were fighting."

"I tell you he killed himself."

"Is he dead?"

"No."

"It was nothing."

"A couple of stabs in the belly."

"In three weeks it'll all be over."

"They'll fight again . . ."

"Did you see them fighting? Maybe they don't know each other."

"They know each other."

"Mourad and the other one?"

"Yes."

"But who saw them fighting?"

"No one."

"They found the knife in the room."

"What knife?"

"This is the story: Mourad, the man who was hurt, says it's his knife, even though they found it under the other one's pants. When they were looking for it. It's the only weapon they found in the room . . ."

"That's just it. So they showed Mourad the knife, and he said it was his. That's not all. The other one too—they questioned him. He said it was his knife. That's the story."

xii. . .

Mother the wall is high!

Here I am in a ruined city, this spring.

Here I am inside the walls of Lambèse, but it's Corsicans instead of Romans now; all Corsicans, all prison guards, and we play the slaves' roles, in the same prison, near the lion pit, and the sons of the Romans do guard duty with rifles on their shoulders; bad luck was waiting for us at the edge of the ruins, the penitentiary that was the pride of Napoleon III, and the Corsicans do guard duty, with rifles on their shoulders, perfectly balanced on top of the wall, and the sun shines for us only off the guards' visors, off the barrels of their rifles, until twenty years' labor are over . . . I'll be free when I'm forty, I'll have lived my sentence and my age twice, and maybe when I'm forty I can have my twenty years free, *Mother the wall is high!*

You have to be a prisoner to get a good long look at your rival. I know who Rachid is now. The friend who comes back to me in prison, to wound me with my own knife, Rachid who was my friend, the friend of my brother, who then became our enemy though he was still living in my room, he who followed us, Lakhdar and me, to the yards . . .

II. . .

i. . .

Monsieur Ernest is waiting on a pile of loose stones at the edge of the quarry rising above the village to the east.

"Just do what I say. You work ten hours. Including Saturdays."

Mustapha shows his disappointment right away.

Lakhdar forces him to be quiet and Rachid preaches calm: "It's already something to be working . . . A lot."

"Besides, you're not going to haggle over twenty francs, like the French."

"You get your money when they know you're staying, not before . . ."

"Yes," Mourad concludes, "Patience . . ."

The other workers say Monsieur Ernest tries to be decent, but that you have to watch out for him.

Ameziane unties the rope he uses for a belt and shows an infected scar at the small of his back: "That's what Monsieur Ernest is like . . ."

The friends are divided between anxiety and delight.

"From a kick or a shovel?"

"Let's not waste time waiting around . . . I'm here to get my father out of jail."

"His father killed a Frenchman who stole his cattle," another workman explains.

Monsieur Ernest clumsily hoists himself off the slope he had been sitting on, smoking a cigarette. He watches the men in silence for a few minutes; his red, ill-shaven face reveals nothing through the thick puff of smoke he has just breathed out, still sucking his butt between his thumb and index finger. The men don't look up, aware they are being watched, and their words grow heavy; their eyes lowered, they seem to lean on each word, letting the foreman understand they are discussing him. And they look as if they want to stop talking, not too suddenly, so that they can watch too, watch Monsieur Ernest, and be on the lookout for his signal, maybe forestall it . . . The men and the foreman seem to abide by an obscure treaty consisting of many precise details by which they maintain constant communication, still keeping their distance, like two armed camps long familiar with each other, occasionally warranting an unjustified truce, until one side catches the other out.

"What are you waiting for?" Monsieur Ernest shouts.

His voice is unreal in the cloud of smoke; you can't tell the butt from his bent thumb, still close to his unshaven face. The men start walking toward a freshly dug trench, visible three hundred yards away from the quarry.

"I went to see two big lawyers in Constantine," Ameziane continues, "and I sold our last property to pay them. My savings and my mother's were used up too. But at least we got speeches! Three whole hours, especially when Maître Gauby began, the judges looked down. They talked in whispers. I thought they were telling each other papa was innocent. At each proof I put a hundred-franc note on the defense-attorney's desk. The police wanted to get me out of the courtroom. The interpreter made a good translation of my father's noble words. The audience didn't conceal its emotion. After the defense plea, the judges left the court, walking heavily. I thought they looked like angels, with their robes and their silly caps. Maître Gauby was smiling at my father so I knew he was saved. Then the judges came back. Condemned to death."

Monsieur Ernest sneaks over. "All right. What's all the talking about?"

ii. . .

Ameziane knows a lot; he knows the story of
Ernest the soldier, promoted to a non-com, store-
keeper in Tunisia, cook in Italy: "He bought the
villa with money he made in the army"; and the
other men know a lot too: ". . . Never one day in
prison, and he almost had his gold braid, but he
said he gave up his rights and didn't ask to be put
on half pay. Because of rheumatism." Monsieur
Ernest has been foreman of the same yards, for
the same owner, for ten years; the war hasn't
changed him much. Scarcely anyone noticed that
he had come back the day he got his old team together at the quarry, without mentioning salaries,
without discussing the absentees, as if nothing had
happened for ten years.

"They're building a market."

"The commune's paying three-quarters of
the expenses. The rest is covered by the administration. Monsieur Ernest's boss is only supplying the
materials. The foreman gives the orders; the workers count for nothing. Some died without ever be-

ing sure they really worked on something; supposing the project is a real one, who knows if the market won't be turned into a police station? Work is often interrupted without the municipal council's being able to explain why. Monsieur Ernest probably doesn't know why either . . . Deep down he's convinced they're going into debt. He saves everything, including the sand from the quarry; he often refers to the bad days, says the Americans made a fortune out of the war . . . Still, he has a daughter like . . ."

Monsieur Ernest sneaks over. His heavily bearded face is warm with kindness. "All right, what's all the talking about?"

Ameziane starts off, his mattock over his head; he seems not to have understood, showing his respect for the foreman merely by lifting the mattock; all the men immediately start to work, without fumbling or arguing over the tools; Rachid lifts a barrowful of sand he has found and walks off with it; Lakhdar is leaning over a piece of freestone he examines with the gravity, the eagerness and the arrogance of an archeologist, and Mustapha, jumping into the trench, begins picking up stones that have slid down the embankment while Mourad vigorously shovels them away; the others apply themselves to more specific labors, already indicated on the preceding days. Monsieur Ernest pretends to ignore the entire scene. He continues staring at Ameziane, a gleam of interrogation in his cunning eyes, blurred by sleep and the smoke from the butt stuck on his thumb now, burning still in the imperceptible bit of paper yellowed by saliva, gradually devoured by the fire without the foreman moving his stained finger, as if he were waiting to be burnt to have an excuse for an outburst.

"Nothing," Ameziane says, in the breath that accompanies the mattock's fall.

The tool is buried about a foot and a half from the trench ; the earth is torn away at the right level, in a single flat thick block. Ameziane smiles ; the splendid mattock stroke he has just made appears as a ceremony worthy of everyone's respect (most of the men stop to look) except Monsieur Ernest's :

"Why do you stop talking when I come around? Do you think I'm a complete fool?"

"Far from it," Lakhdar murmurs.

Monsieur Ernest hits Lakhdar on the head with the yardstick he is holding.

The blood.

Lakhdar goes back to staring at the stone, reddened drop by drop.

Here comes Suzy, up through the quarry ; she stops in front of Monsieur Ernest.

"What's the matter with him, papa?"

Lakhdar drips the blood on the stone, his back turned to the rest of the men ; the foreman prowls around the yards, staring at the men, who have gone back to work; he makes the soles of his boots squeak; he stops in front of the yardstick on the ground, near the entirely charred butt. A last thread of smoke floats under Mourad's nose where he is sifting gravel, his mouth open as if he were singing under his breath, his face brushed by the girl's dress as she hesitantly walks toward her father.

"Was there an accident?"

Without a word, Monsieur Ernest snatches the basket out of his daughter's hands; he steps into the trench, sits down and takes out his lunch: meat and cauliflower in a pot, a bottle of wine, oranges. He eats and he stares.

Despite the cold, the girl is wearing a thin knee-length dress that swells with the breeze; she has long moist lashes; she widens her round eyes that are green, yellow, gray—birds' eyes. She bridles as she walks, the way birds do, and you can see her little pink claws through the openwork sandals. Lakhdar does everything he can to wipe off the blood. He presses one finger against his temple and looks for something in his pockets, maybe a mirror; his friends do what they can to show they're on his side, in the silence; he is paralyzed with hatred, standing over the stone, but slowly he turns away, speaking to no one, staring at the girl's sandals while her eyes burn and fill with spite, probably on account of the general silence, the stares not bold enough or eager enough to touch her, and the exasperating, ridiculous, humiliating noise her father's new shoes make, moving toward the water trough to wash out the pot.

"That one hasn't had enough!" she screams suddenly, blushing and holding her head high as if to control her voice, as if she were about to weaken after screaming, like a child uncertain whether to burst into tears or hysterical giggles.

And she adds in a jerky tone of voice:

"He hasn't had all he deserves."

The shadow of a smile passes across her soft lips, and she walks toward her father again, disdainful and proud of realizing that the man was beaten, that there was no accident.

The foreman has finished his meal.

Far from calming down, he is in a towering rage.

He pushes his daughter away, not looking at the slender body that seems, standing there in the yards at such a moment, to encourage his men to lustful, bloody thoughts.

His lips flecked with the cauliflower sauce, Monsieur Ernest walks toward Lakhdar; this time, his daughter's apostrophe having raised him to the peak of heroism, he throws the yardstick into the trench; Lakhdar turns around, seizes the foreman by the throat, and with one blow opens his head along the eyebrow; *a draw!* say the witnesses' involuntary smiles.

Monsieur Ernest collapses across the basket.

The empty bottle rolls into the trench, as though out of loyalty to the foreman.

Blood streams over the yellow tie, and Rachid's barrow has taken a nose-dive, arms in the air; the sun now illuminates the yards like a stage set suddenly appearing in the most depressing banality.

A handkerchief over his face, Monsieur Ernest holds his head between his knees, surrounded by the powerless crew, while Lakhdar stands motionless behind a grove of trees, facing the trench, and everyone stares after the girl running away, a parachute blown by the wind along the road that is straighter, wider and shorter than ever.

The police.

Lakhdar has seen them.

He remains motionless.

He lets them put on the handcuffs. "It's not the first time," Lakhdar thinks, as if he were looking for old scars on his skinny wrist.

Meanwhile the corporal takes Monsieur Ernest home, walking slowly, and the girl meets them on the road; the policeman who has handcuffed Lakhdar suddenly moves away; he leaves his prisoner and scatters the crew with swats of his crop which hit no one, then he returns to Lakhdar, still motionless where he had been left.

On the road, Monsieur Ernest lets himself be led, walking slowly; when he notices his daughter in tears, he turns around; he quickly ties the handkerchief around his forehead and tries to return to the yards, restrained by the corporal who makes impatient gestures at Suzy; she stands beside her father; now the girl and the corporal are walking on either side of Monsieur Ernest with their arms around him, encouraging him, keeping him from going back; Lakhdar stares after them; the policeman takes Lakhdar away.

iii. . .

The crew, put to flight, has stopped in front of the trench, Mustapha, Mourad and Rachid in the first row; they do not speak and make no gesture toward Lakhdar, who will soon no longer be able to see them, for the policeman pushes him from behind and keeps him from turning around. "It's not the first time," Lakhdar thinks, lowering the handcuffs toward his knee to scratch himself. "It's a little over a year" . . . Lakhdar sees himself in prison even before getting there; he is in a cell with a sense of having been there before; the last ray of light from the setting sun makes his absence felt on the road that is gray now and narrow; here Lakhdar recovers the vanished atmosphere of his first arrest. "It was late spring, a little over a year ago, but it was the same light; the same day, May eighth it was, I left on foot. Why bother leaving? First I had come back to school, after the demonstration; the three courtyards were empty. I couldn't believe it; my ears were like sieves, choked with explosions; I couldn't believe it. I couldn't believe that so many things had happened.

I saw S . . . at the first dormitory window. He looked like an orator; he was making a speech to the Europeans.

There weren't any more Arabs in the dormitory; S . . . was talking loud and gesticulating, standing on Mustapha's bed; my bed wasn't made; others had been moved around. I still didn't understand. I glanced through the window without going in; I didn't want to prowl around the courtyards but I couldn't jump through the study window either. I'd have to break open Mustapha's box, take the pamphlets out, and I stood there without saying a word, not trying to hide behind the post, squinting toward the dormitory where S . . . was talking, standing on Mustapha's bed, and I couldn't even hear what they were saying;

I was standing there like a stork on one leg in the open field, cold and stubborn as a stalled engine, as if I knew I was on the prison threshold, condemned to inaction, temporarily self-paroled. But I wasn't arrested until the next day. A year ago.

There were not enough handcuffs; the cook was fastened to me; we were locked up in the heart of the police station, in the hayloft: the cook, the baker boy and me. Each of us had one hand and one foot free. A sheep, a real sheep bounding around the loft. It had stopped bleating. The corporal had pushed it in there without hurting it, and he brought its food in separately, kicking vaguely at the bundle of men in passing. But this time I'm alone . . .

iv. . .

I shouldn't have left. If I had stayed at school, they wouldn't have arrested me. I'd still be a student, not a laborer, and I wouldn't be locked up again, for a knock on the head. I should have stayed at school, that's what the district chief told me.

I should have stayed at school, at my job.

I should have listened to the district chief.

But the Europeans had ganged up.

They had moved the beds around.

They were showing each other their fathers' weapons.

There was no head-master or under-master left.

There was no smell from the kitchens now.

The cook and the steward had run away.

They were afraid of us, of us, of us!

The demonstrators had evaporated.

I went into the study. I took the pamphlets.

I hid the Life of Abd-el-Kader.

I felt the force of the ideas.

I found Algeria irascible. Its breathing . . .

The breathing of Algeria was enough.

Enough to keep off the pigeons.

Then Algeria herself turned . . .

Turned stool-pigeon.

But the ants, the red ants.

The red ants came to the rescue.

I left with the pamphlets.

I buried them near the river.

I made a map of a future demonstration.

If some one would give me that river, I would fight.

I'd fight with the sand and the water.

With the cold water, the hot sand. I would fight.

I had decided. So I could see far. Very far.
I saw a farmer bent over like a catapult.
I called to him but he didn't come. He made
me a sign.
He made me a sign that he was at war.
At war with his stomach. Everyone knows . . .
Everyone knows a farmer has no brains.
A farmer is only a stomach. A catapult.
But I'm a student. I was a flea.
A sentimental flea . . . The poplar blossoms . . .
The poplar blossoms burst into silky fluff.
But I was at war. I amused the farmer.
I wanted him to forget his hunger. I clowned.
I clowned for my father the farmer. I bombarded
the moon in the river.

V. . .

"Whew," the baker boy said, "I left my mother
this morning . . . She had insulted me. I went to
the café. A Frenchman was following me. A
civilian. Your papers, he said. Nothing to say. He
was a civilian."

The sheep rested its muzzle on the baker boy's

shaved head. The boy was singing, his eyes closed,
full of the ancient aroma of the people.

"I kept to the pastures. I practiced laying an
ambush for the streetcar. Each time I crossed the
French road, I glanced around for the high grass;
I looked for patriots; I met only kids or tramps. I
wondered if I would find my grandfather in the
village, and if he had any other weapons besides
his double-barreled rifle. I slept again half way
there, mouth against the earth, and I didn't shake
off the ants. I was still comparing them to the
demonstrators. They dug their feet in hard and
sometimes stood up on their hind legs; I envied
their readiness. I didn't stop again until the European graveyard. The clouds clubbed the pale night
with slow concussions; I followed the orderly uprising of the firs—*it is not for nothing that there
are no birds in their necropolis*—I inhaled the
alien dead and I made a speech in which I reminded
each of the deceased of all the filth he thought had
been forgotten. A future as a revolutionary general
or a cross upon my life! It wouldn't be fair to go
ask grandfather for weapons, *I would see him after
the victory,* and I was annoyed with him for buying
me pajamas a few months away from the rebellion.
From the graveyard I could reconstruct the village and assume command. The main street was
empty; hunger led me quickly from one sidewalk
to the other; I greeted people and I felt them
on my heels, but I was ashamed to announce the

great day to villagers with neither heart nor honor . . ."

"Whew," the baker boy said, "I left my mother this morning, she had insulted me, and I didn't know . . ."

"I didn't last long in the village," Lakhdar thinks. "Neither father nor grandfather was there any more. The sun gripped me by the ankles, I had to do something. The one I fished up first was the lawyer, Mustapha's father, the other one, the rich one. He was wearing a *gandoura* over his clothes. His dark glasses were turning in his hand. The people were all around, so that you couldn't see them, mixed in with the trees, the dust, and I could hear them bellowing even where I was; for the first time, like in Sétif, I realized that the people can be terrifying, but the lawyer was bravely playing the peacemaker. His apprehension for his money and his land was stronger than his fear of the people, and the lawyer begged the people to go away, or to wait . . . And the crowd began roaring:

Wait for what? The village is ours,
You rich bastards sleep in French beds
And you help yourselves to whatever you want
While we get a bushel of barley and our cattle eat us out of house and home
Our brothers in Sétif have risen

The lawyer beat a retreat, followed by the

74

mufti whose beard jumped up and down: "My children, be careful, in times like these we cannot fight against tanks, have confidence in your leaders, we promise you . . ."

Let the leaders show the way, we're tired of lying around, attack!

I told my wife: I'm going out to find grain.

Let's get our hands red, we're tired of lying around: the people listened to no one but its own sudden orators. An old man from the mountains, standing on his mule, fired at the police station: "I swore to empty my rifle, if there's a mother's son here, let him give me cartridges."

"I was nothing but a leg of the unyielding crowd," Lakhdar remembers, "there were no more words now, the lawyer and the mufti brought up the rear. *No more talk, no more leaders,* old rifles were spitting, *far away the donkeys and mules were loyally leading our young army,* there were women at our heels and dogs and children. *The whole village came to meet us,* people had changed, *they didn't close the doors behind them any more,* it happened to be the day for diplomas, those who had failed cheered the fellahs, I noticed the administrator's assistant disguised as an Arab creeping along the walls, *grandfather was among the demonstrators,* no use talking to him.

"*The machine-gun tanks,* the machine guns, *the machine guns,* some fall and others go running through the trees, *there is no mountain, no strat-*

75

egy, we could have cut the telephone wires, *but they have radios* and brand new American guns. *The police are using their sidecars,* I don't see anyone around me any more.

"All right you bastard, you too!"

"And now here I am in prison."

vi. . .

There were nineteen in the room now.

The barber Si Khelifa was still shouting.

The heavy door had opened four times.

Tayeb had not come back. They were shooting close by.

Close to the prison. Close to the prison.

In a green field. Close to the police station.

Mustapha was splashing around in a pool of black water.

A farmer with blue eyes was sobbing.

Lakhdar had got up on the empty bucket.

Lakhdar stuck his nose through the bars.

Like a calf.

Lakhdar was happy. Nose happy. Happy.

Happy to lean against the bars.

Those who had their bones broken by gun

butts, like the farmer, couldn't pull their arms and legs in to make room.

It was the fourth time.

The fourth time that the guard opened the door.

Boudjène Lakhdar!

Here.

"This way," the guard said.

They had gone upstairs to the police station. The hay loft . . . The watering trough . . .

"Wait here," the guard said.

Music.

News. The corporal's wife was changing stations.

General de Gaulle has convened the government.

"What are you doing here?"

The policeman takes a strong grip on Lakhdar's collar.

"You listening to the radio?"

"I'm waiting for the guard."

Another policeman. Finally the guard.

"You leaving him here?"

"No, it's his turn."

The barber Si Khelifa wasn't shouting any more. He was gasping. Where could he be?

The guard went into the room Lakhdar hadn't noticed. A large, low room with whitewashed windows. Again the guard left Lakhdar alone and closed the door behind him.

Lakhdar knelt down. The barber Si Khelifa

didn't recognize him . . . His long, streaming body appeared, bent, criss-crossed with swollen blue tattooed areas. His teeth chattered, then he sighed, as if he were coming out of a sweat-room. He had his coat and his shirt under his arms. Lakhdar stared at him hard.

The guard came back out of the room, pushed the old barber down on the floor, near the trough, and let him take a breath. Then he came back to Lakhdar and pushed him through the door. It was a laundry room.

The guard wanted to leave. His gray eyes seemed to suffer from the room's dim atmosphere.

"Aren't you going to help me?" the lieutenant asked, lighting another cigarette.

The guard turned and went back deferentially.

There was a chair and a table covered with papers in the middle of the laundry room.

The officer turned on the water.

He went over to the table.

The officer didn't look up when three inspectors came in the door.

The guard went out without a word.

"Your name," the officer said, holding the pen.

Lakhdar hurried closer to the table, under the blows of the inspectors. He gave his identity, his family and other details of his civil status.

The inspectors went on hitting him.

The officer was rereading his sheet.

"So the gentleman is a student?"

"Student," Lakhdar gasped.

The inspector hung his crop back on his belt. He picked up a wet rope that was lying on the edge of the sink. The other two inspectors stopped kicking him. Lakhdar kept his head buried in his arms, on the floor.

While he was waiting to be tortured, he had prepared himself . . . He wouldn't deny his presence at the demonstration. He wouldn't mention the old revolver he had buried near the river. If the torture became unendurable, he had decided to give the names of his pro-French schoolmates; besides the investigation would prove they were innocent.

Lakhdar had only the vaguest general idea of all this. He couldn't feel his head any more. The rest of his body was apparently unhurt; second by second, a remote, flashing pain localized itself in the small of his back, his knees, ankles, sternum and jaw.

Lakhdar let them tie his hands and feet. Then the inspectors ran a long rod through the two bindings, which immobilized the prisoner whom they grabbed around the waist and threw into the tub.

Lakhdar skinned his left shoulder and, in his inertia, found a way to remain half immersed, his body upright. The rod was wedged against his chin.

Struggling to free his head, Lakhdar often hit the inspectors.

Lakhdar kept his eyes closed.

He felt something cold pressed against his lips. From the taste, he realized that they were sticking a big stone down his gullet to keep him from closing his mouth. Then another object was pressed to Lakhdar's lips, and he could tell what this was too: it was the metal tip of a drain pipe.

The water was turned on.

Lakhdar couldn't.

He couldn't not drink.

At first it felt as if all his nerves were twisting, and that an icy current was filling his guts.

The water flowed.

The officer increased the flow little by little.

Lakhdar struggled harder.

"Animal! He's trying to kill himself."

"All right, talk. You're young. You'll be released."

"Who are your leaders?"

"Come on, fairy, you want to croak?"

Lakhdar made up his mind. He made a sign to turn off the water.

"Our leaders . . . We don't have any leaders. All right, I'll talk. First take away the pipe. Our leaders? . . ."

"He's faking, the cocksucker."

The blows rained down.

The officer's crop wasn't enough now.

The policemen picked up other wet cords.

They aimed for the soles of his feet, panting as they worked.

Lakhdar heard the policemen panting.

He realized why the inspectors were aiming for his feet.

He bent his knees, and dived.

vii. . .

The first person Lakhdar met was one of the non-commissioned officers who had been his guard in La Sûreté, a stocky fellow from the north of France, with red mustaches.

He noticed the canteen at the soldier's belt and remembered that the man used to drink often, taking long pulls, during guard duty.

They went into a little bar. The non-com tried to protest. Lakhdar insisted on paying.

"You acted decent. You never hit a prisoner."

"Don't talk about that! . . ."

Through the half-open door, they could recognize people in the street. The sun hadn't set, but the city was already turning on its lights for the night.

"What day is it?"

"Friday, my friend. For me, a glass or two doesn't need to wait for a holiday."

Lakhdar mentioned the Ramadhan of captivity. "Do you know this is only the second time in my life I've ever taken a drink?"

"I know none of you guys drink. And you have a funny way of praying. Like a slow-motion film of calisthenics!"

"Why does everyone in France treat Algeria like a zoo?"

"I don't have anything against your prayers! You can fly around like angels in your burnooses if you like doing exercises for Allah! I come from the North. For me, a church is no different from a mosque. I'm not going to break my head open for either one. Where I come from, there are Proletarians."

Lakhdar thought it was a slang word.

"Pro . . . What?"

"Proletarians, workers, you know! I don't give a damn about the army. Go take a look at what the Schleuhs did back where I come from . . ."

The what?

"The Schleuhs, the *Boches*, you know!"

Dissatisfied, Lakhdar shouted in the soldier's ear: "Schleuhs! Another word like *Bicot!* But when we fight the Boches together the French can't tell which is the enemy."

Already he regretted using the word *Boche*: "He's given me his race sickness."

"No reason to look like that!"

Lakhdar burst out laughing.

The sergeant showed honest regret as he poured out a full glass for Lakhdar.

"I'm not drinking any more."

Lakhdar went out, after embracing the astonished non-com.

viii. . .

Surrounded by stubbed-out butts, Lakhdar stares through the doorway at the fields of tobacco, the plain . . .

To labor with nature, like grandfather, wouldn't that be the best way to live, now that he couldn't study any more?

In this third-class railway car, a farmer family is about to get off. A young French sailor helps the husband get together a half dozen crates where hens and vegetables are jumbled in with the baby's rags. Lakhdar nibbles his mustache: a sign of emotion or confusion?

". . . The eighth of May has proved that this sailor's kindness can turn into cruelty; it always begins by condescension . . . What's he doing in an Algerian train anyway, that sailor with his Marseillais accent? Of course the train is furnished by France . . . If we had our own trains . . . First of all, the farmers would be comfortable. They wouldn't be fidgeting at each station, afraid of missing their stop. They could read. And in Arabic too! I'd have to reeducate myself in our own language. I'd be grandfather's classmate . . ."

The sailor takes out a pack of cigarettes. He offers one to the farmer, then to Lakhdar.

"Why so nice? They want us to forget their crimes . . ."

Lakhdar quickly dismisses this notion.

"A decent one! Maybe his father's poor too . . . Maybe he used to be hungry in Marseilles . . . He hasn't had time to be contaminated by the ones around here. Besides, he'll change like them. They'll tell him: they're thieves, ingrates, all they respect is a bludgeon. He won't offer cigarettes to a fellah any more . . ." Between the sailor and Lakhdar is a young woman in sunglasses, yawning over a magazine. It's good to feel her relaxed body next to his. Bitter odor of her painted nails . . . Lakhdar has pasted himself in his corner. His revenge is to blow puffs of smoke into the face of this third-class empress.

The farmer family gets off. The sailor sweats a lot as he hands them their crates.

"Two more stations to Bône. God, what a

sun!" the sailor sighs, probably trying to entice the empress away from her magazine.

Lakhdar stares sourly at his own drill trousers.

"Not much of an outfit for a first visit to rich relatives. What can you do in a town like Bône with five hundred francs? I could write grandfather. That would be shameful. I was right to leave without saying anything . . . They must have heard I was released. I'll write grandfather from Bône. Except for him, they'll all be glad to hear I was expelled. They think I'll make more money for them by working. They're wrong. Poor mother!"

He digs in his pocket for an old piece of paper.

Beauséjour.

ix. . .

The apparition stretches, trembling, and the porter presses his seat as if to slow down the streetcar; deceived by the intensity that makes his chest shudder like an engine, is the porter afraid of flying off his seat and landing beside her?

And if his customer, once home and rid of her veil, had turned into this apparition . . . Neither he nor she knows who they are; this remote encounter has the futility of a challenge.

Mustapha will not go back again, back to the station, but will see the villa again, and the terrace, and the woman with auburn hair standing on the lawn: this scene will burst upon him in the streetcar, at the last station, where he is the only passenger . . . The Maltese driver and the Kabyl ticket-taker have headed for two different bars . . . Finally Mustapha gets off the air-cooled car; he will walk back, without seeing the terrace, hypocritically convinced that the apparition will not occur again; Mustapha the porter makes straight for the center of town, gradually straightening to his full height, frank and bantering; his eyes will reflect the boldness, the carelessness of the great apartment buildings he will certainly live in some day; he will spend his second night under the station clock, swearing not to follow the veiled women of Beauséjour any more—a quiet, disappointing neighborhood . . . *"All those villas, all those second-rate palaces named after women . . ."*

Rising above a haunted patio (before the war, a whole family committed suicide here), the Villa Nedjma is surrounded by residences which cut across the streetcar tracks, at the bottom of a gentle slope covered with nettles; the ground floor has four rooms off a corridor which turns so that it too opens onto an overgrown garden and a terrace with a worm-eaten staircase no better than a ladder; the peeling walls are the color of mould, with a thick outcrop of moss; at the top of the slope, there are steps of native stone, emerging from the brush which the tramps' shanties have sheared away, burned to ashes, reduced to a cinder bank, without quite extinguishing the jujube trees and the twisted cedars, dazed runners out of space and light in their vertical sprint, trunks bare, branches stretched toward the ground that in spring is dotted with Barbary figs, hawthorn and whortleberry; though far away, the oranges fall of their own accord into this natural refrigerator; an old cat limps by, meditative and calamitous, satanically staring at a spiderweb hung in his whiskers; does this feline pride produce the illusion of being caged in the brush by the demons of the dog days? The whole noon bombardment, concentrating its fire, does not exhaust the thick shade of its irresistible suctions nor the conflagration's desperate thirst for air; on the road, barefoot children go on kicking their collapsed ball . . . Paradox of children, solemn savagery! A bicyclist skids to a stop and straightens up, enjoying the distraction of the children; playing, they no longer think of ridiculing the flayed cyclist; but the ball wheezes as it bounces down the slope, and this object consumes all the comedy of its fall . . . The road joins the top of the slope by an alley; a new rush of foliage vanishes into a background of red earth, where there is a spring; it rarely rains on the eastern Algerian plain, but when it does, in torrents; the miraculously impregnated Seybouse here delivers its unseasonable showers of a river in agony, vomited up by the ungrateful shores it has fed; ecstatic, in a single huge swell, the darkened sea imperceptibly eats into the river, a near-corpse jealous of its springs, liquefied in its bed, forever capable of that desperate undulation which stands for the passion of a country sparing with its water, where the meeting of the Seybouse and the Mediterranean has something of a mirage about it; the shower rises in a whirlwind, degenerates into an abortive sneeze; the constellations are drowned from one night to the next in the damp, refined like flotillas in the vaporous camouflage; draining some planetary fuel from the troubled waves, despite the warlike cracklings of the surf, the great ship of the storm gathers its forces with the unforeseeable fracas of a tank falling from one abyss to the next; a crimson ghost fraying its shroud on the west wind, the painted sun lingers, a nerveless calumet drowning in the slaver of a lamentably wallowing sea, that low, cold-blooded mother who spreads through the city an odor of sorcery and torpor, all of nature's hatred for the least action, the slightest thought . . . "*A nation of beggars and parasites, fatherland of invaders,*" Mustapha thinks, "*a country of hooded women, of femmes fatales . . .*"

88

Garment and flesh new-washed, Nedjma is naked in her dress; she shakes her stifling auburn hair, opens and closes the window; as if she were endlessly trying to drive the air away, or at least make it circulate by her movements; against the cool and transparent space of the glass, the clinging flies let themselves be felled, or feign death at each shift of air; then Nedjma attacks a mosquito with a handkerchief she fans herself with at the same time; exhausted, she sits on the tile floor, her eyes staring into the darkness; she hears the bushes rustling; "*that's not the wind . . .*" Her breasts rise. She stretches. Unendurable consumption of the zenith; she turns, turns back, her legs stretched along the wall, looking strangely as if she were sleeping on her breasts . . . "*Climb back up to the terrace? Too many peepers . . . Too many people I know in the streetcars . . . How clumsy he was! The fruit almost fell out . . . He had white hands, dirty nails . . . Nice, without that Chimpanzee build . . . Not from around here, obviously. Kicked out by his family? That way of cutting his beard. If Kamel knew I gave a hundred francs to a porter! . . . Why did I do it, actually? To send him away . . . I imagined him spending it in some bad place . . . I shouldn't go out . . . A whim would be enough . . . A trip . . . Starting all over again . . . Not giving myself to a man, but not alone the way I am . . . They've shut me up to defeat me, isolated me by marrying me . . . Since they love me, I keep*

them in my prison . . . In the long run, it's the
prisoner who makes the decisions . . ." Nedjma lies
full length on the floor while her mother, Lella
Fatma, with the help of visiting ladies the girl
doesn't bother to speak to, prepares the meal;
Nedjma answers Kamel's questions with grunts;
ordinarily she treats her husband with a kindness
heavy with sarcasms he takes for reproaches.

Kamel married because his mother wanted
him to.

Nedjma married because her mother insisted
on it.

Kamel, the happy bridegroom, had an incontestably noble father who died without making an
appearance in town; an orphan, Kamel sells his
share of the land, moves to Bône, lets his mustache
grow; his mother finds him a newspaper-and-to-
bacco store; Kamel reads the papers, but remains
faithful to the traditions of the deceased, who
never smoked, never entered a bar or a movie theater . . . The two mothers meet at the baths, then
at the shrines of various saints; they confide to one
another that they are both of aristocratic birth, one
with an eagle's profile, the other with a condor's;
they both live in Beauséjour, talk constantly about
Constantine and Algiers back when men were men,
gradually show each other their jewelry, climb up
their family trees as far back as the Prophet, jump
over centuries, and finally remove their false teeth
to embrace one another, with no further reserve;

the daughter of the one can only marry the other's son; Lella Fatma explains that she doesn't want a dowry, but loves her daughter; Lella N'fissa proclaims that her son is a man to make three women happy. The two mothers-in-law coexist until the seventh day of the marriage; on this occasion, Lella Fatma hires the greatest pianist in Algeria; Lella N'fissa, who has not been consulted, refuses to appear at the party, and collapses, blue in the face, in the hall.

"It's her heart," Kamel says.

"Her stomach," Nedjma says.

That's how the cold war begins.

Kamel transfers his mother to allies in Constantine.

Victorious, Lella Fatma has the villa painted green.

Unendurable consumption of the zenith. This morning, Nedjma woke up sore all over; she has not done well by Lella Fatma's simmering eggplants; Kamel has come home without making a sound, his heart heavy with unsold papers and tobacco sold on credit! Satisfying his hunger, the husband takes down the lute; he tries to associate himself with the conjugal spleen. Nedjma flees to the living room, frowning. The musician feels his talent collapsing in the solitude; he hangs the lute up again; Kamel's passivity merely thickens the mask of cruelty Nedjma assumes against anyone who doesn't fall into her trap; she weeps, ignoring

Lella Fatma's protests: "... *such a good man, so sweet, you wouldn't believe he's his mother's son! What do you want then? A no-good who'll sell your jewelry, a drunkard?*"

Unendurable consumption of the zenith! First fruits of coolness ...

X. . .

First fruits of coolness, sightlessness streaked with rippling ochre and ultramarine that soothes the traveler standing opposite the metallic, flickering strait of the outer harbor; the tracks turn toward the sea, follow the Seybouse at its mouth, cut across the road, a burst of pavement shimmering grain by grain in the somber future of the city decomposing in architectural islands, in oubliettes of crystal, minarets of steel screwed into the heart of ships, in trucks loaded with phosphates and fertilizer, in regal shopwindows reflecting the unrealizable costumes of some century to come, in severe squares where human beings, makers of roads and trains, seem to be missing, glimpsed in the distance from the train's calm speed, glimpsed too behind the

wheels of cars, masters of the road, adding to their
speed the human weight ominously abdicated, at
the mercy of a mechanical encounter with death,
humming arrows following each other alongside
the train, suggesting in series a schedule ever more
crowded, bringing closer to the passenger the moment of the naked, demanding city which lets every
movement break up within it as the sea fawns at its
feet, tightens its knots of rails as far as the plat-
form where every track, whether from south or
west, converges and already the Constantine-Bône
express gives a centaur's start, a siren's sob, it has
the broken-winded grace of the choked machine,
creeping and twisting around the knee of the city
evasive still in its lustfulness, postponing its swoon,
seized by the hair and mingled with the sun's ascen-
sion, stooping to receive these locomotive effusions;
the cars release the passengers: so many indecisive
beasts, quickly restored to their somnolent watch-
fulness; no one dares look upon the God of the
pagans now at his daily summit: noon, image of
Africa seeking its shadow, unapproachable nakedness of the empire-eating continent, the plain swollen with wine and tobacco; noon subdues like any
temple, immerses the traveler; noon! the clock adds
in its sacerdotal roundness, and the hour seems re-
tarded along with the machinery under the ventila-
tion of the palms, and the empty train loses its
charms, an abandoned tyrant; on September 15,
1945, the Bône station is besieged as it is every

93

day; the great glass doors attract a number of idlers, taxi drivers, shabby coachmen whose impatient horsebells give every sign of unemployment; stampings of idle horses and men; once off the train, the traveler is surrounded by porters he neither hears nor pushes away; the traveler is overexcited; the sun raises a column of motes above his steaming mop of hair; long uncombed, such a fleece is irritating enough; under thick curls the circumflex eyebrows have something of the third-rate actor about them; deep parallel lines, like inner rails, absorbed in a seism, appear on the wide, high forehead whose whiteness drinks up the wrinkles as a palimpsest drinks up old characters; the rest of the face is hard to see, for the traveler lowers his head, swept on by the crowd, then lets himself be outstripped, though all he has for baggage is a schoolboy's notebook rolled around a clasp-knife; observers have already noticed that the young man, jumping down from the train, dropped this knife—its size intolerable to the Law —rapidly picked up the prohibited weapon and then, in his confusion, wrapped his notebook around it instead of putting it back in his pocket.

That same evening in Bône, they describe the traveler "dressed like a madman": this is the expression of a young man called Mourad, speaking to his friends Rachid and Mustapha.

"Imagine a real 'Paleface,' but his blood and nerves right under the skin! He probably had a

fever. His cheeks were hollow, and not one hair!
He stared at the ground, as if to keep from getting
dizzy. Was he drunk? Had he been smoking the
weed? I don't think so; he didn't look up to it. He
was like a spoiled child lost during the moving!..."

Mourad, when his friends neither interrupt
nor encourage him, assumes a pseudo-sarcastic
tone:

"Well, after all! He was wearing a black
tuxedo jacket; his shirt was hidden under a white
silk scarf. He was dragging gray drill pants that
were round as stovepipes, a real sack! The traveler
was rather tall but he must have bought the pants
from a peddler, they probably belonged to some
American giant, luckily for him, the crazy fool . . .
He could hide the fact that he didn't have any
socks, and he traipsed around in shoes he had to
put back on at almost every step . . ."

"All right," said Rachid, who for a long time
will be characterized by his silence . . .

"If you want to know what I think, I say he's
a student expelled from somewhere, like our friend
Mustapha . . ."

Mustapha breaks in: "There you go jabber-
ing again, worse than a woman. What does the guy
matter to me?"

During Mourad's story, Mustapha has done
nothing but show signs of impatience; the way he
raises his voice now interests his friends; they guess
Mustapha doesn't like hearing the same jokes

about someone else that his own arrival must have provoked, when he got off the Constantine-Bône express, two months before . . . Mustapha turns his back to Mourad and sits down on a pontoon . . . *"She was wearing a wide hood of pale blue silk, the kind emancipated Moroccan women wear now; funny hoods; they cover the breast, the waist, the hips, fall straight to the ankles; a little more and they'd cover the gold anklets (the customer was wearing a very fine and heavy one) . . . The new hoods are only an excuse to show the face by covering the body with a uniform rampart, so as not to give any excuse for prudish criticism . . . She spoke to me in French. Trying to cut off all communication by treating me not only as a porter, but as a criminal she could have nothing in common with, avoiding conversation in the mother tongue. Didn't want me to come with her on the streetcar, I saw her climb up a slope, vanish; then I looked up at the top. She had taken off her hood; I would have known her from any other woman, just by her hair . . ."* Mustapha breaks off his daydream, without leaving the pontoon, his eyes fixed on the water. Night is falling; Mourad hasn't stopped talking; he says he was the only one of the three to be at the station a while ago . . . Seeing Rachid walk over to the pontoon now too, Mourad blunders again, with a kind of insistence:

"I just can't explain what was so ridiculous and sad about that traveler; maybe it's because he was expelled, like Mustapha . . ."

The traveler happens to be a student. In his little jacket pocket he has a five hundred franc note folded into eighths and a piece of paper with a relative's address.

But it's only an aunt on his father's side whom he's never seen . . . He has asked directions; the aunt lives in Beauséjour. The traveler wonders how he's going to manage with only five hundred francs; he leaves the station as fast as he can and collapses in front of a table. He happens to be in Bône's one ultra-chic brasserie whose terrace overlooks the station, the harbor and the Cours Bertagna, the promenade of elegant citizens; the manager is away; at the end of this stifling summer, the inhabitants of Bône are all taking naps; the traveler orders a bottle of beer; his notebook fell on the ground when he let himself drop into the chair. He doesn't pick it up until after he has emptied the bottle. He decides to call over a little newspaper vendor, then changes his mind . . . After paying, he stammers in front of the waiter in the white shirt with white hair, and abruptly moves away, so as not to have to look at the ten-franc tip he has left; more than one pedestrian turns back in a fury after colliding with the fixity of those calflike pupils, elbowing the unreacting wanderer who evidently doesn't realize he's walking in circles; again the station clock is on his left, but you can tell he is attracted by the slope of the Place d'Armes from the way his gait swerves and retards, while the smell of the roasting food makes him catch his breath; he stops in front of the slope; his direction is decided by this pensive halt, and he starts walking again, his face the mask of a patient seeking by scalpel to escape some past of witchcraft and cruelty, a prairie of chloroform growing upon a young body imperceptibly attacked, even as the dew corrupts metal; hard pupils watering under the luminous hail in a fog of insomnia, cornea bloodshot, iris dimmed and overrun; a wrecked stare, a splendor straying beyond the slope, the same old stare, pure and secret, that the traveler had three months ago, walking to the torture; with his sidelong gait, he advances with the ubiquity of animals for whom the road is no longer ahead, having made so many forced marches without seeing anything; perhaps the traveler owes the oxlike closeness of eye to ear to his peasant origins; unless the strangeness of his face is the result of accident, a fight; like boxers when their eyebrows are opened or their eyes swollen; the traces of the fight are done away with but something has vanished along with the ecchymoses, and the boxer, delivered of the swellings, shows only an anachronistic mark that has the flatness of a battlefield once the corpses are buried; the traveler makes a point of not asking his way; night surprises him at the Sidi Boumerouene Mosque. Some ten men are praying on the terrace; he watches them bending, intoning; they seem to be pleading with God: "*Spare us the sight of such a madman*"; three hundred years old, a prow mounting the horizon, the minaret intimidates the concrete armada buttressed between heaven and earth as it conquered nomads and pirates in the city fallen before the boldness of the new sites it delays and invests; the traveler, resting in the twilight, takes out a cigarette and turns away; he knows that a moment will come when the iman will interrupt his sermon and order the smoker to be driven out; the iman is facing east, according to the ritual, and sees nothing from his throne; the traveler takes out his lighter; the lips of the believers move faster and faster, and the traveler savors this prayer releasing a flood of imprecations which only the iman's distraction dams; the cigarette is still not lighted; the traveler's gaze unsettles many turbans, lingers on the half-closed eyelids of the faithful: "*Meditation and wisdom are good for the brave who have already joined battle. Rise! Return to your posts, pray on the job. Stop the world's machines if you fear an explosion; stop eating and sleeping a while, take your children by the hand, and make a good strike-prayer, until your prayers, even the humblest, are answered. If you are afraid of the police, do as the bears do: a seasonal nap, with roots and tobacco to hibernate on; I understand you, my brothers, understand me in your turn; act as if God were among us, as if he were a man out of work or a newspaper vendor; manifest your opposition seriously and without remorse; and when the lords of*

99

*this world see their subjects dying together, with
God in their ranks, perhaps then you will obtain
justice; yes, yes, I understand you, I approve of
your presence in the mosque; you cannot dream at
home with the shrews and the children, you cannot
be sublime on the conjugal hearth, you need to
prostrate yourselves with unknown men, to refine
yourselves in the temple's collective solitude; but
you are starting at the wrong end; you scarcely
know how to walk and here you are kneeling again;
neither childhood nor adolescence: right away it
has to be marriage, home, the sermon in the mosque,
the garage of slow death"*; at the exit, he passes
beggars holding out empty tin cans, asking for
their pittance from the mufti's servants; around
ten, the men in the Place d'Armes notice the wanderer sitting on the steps of a store that has been
shut up; finally he notices the sign of a Turkish
bath. He sacrifices fifty francs and falls asleep on
the edge of the matting, near an old farmer who
slips him a piece of honey-cake early in the
morning.

"You have to get out at seven to let the bath-
ers in: the boss's rule."

The traveler dozes; the streetcar makes a
shrill turn, crosses Beauséjour and all the platitude
of the suburb surrounded by the sea; the porter
argues with a sailor at the market bar; Mourad
and Rachid reach the meeting-place at noon;
Mustapha has left with the Canadian sailor who

100

has fifty cartons of cigarettes to sell; the business comes just at the right time; the trio has debts in half the cafés and cookshops of the harbor; *"if it keeps on, I'll go back to carrying packages for women in the market,"* Mustapha grumbled yesterday; then the three friends happened to find the Canadian staggering along the docks; they delegated Mustapha, who is the biggest of the three; walking away beside the sailor, he said they should meet him at the usual place.

The "Café de l'Avenir" is run by a horse-dealer who has made good; the clientele consists chiefly of young Egyptian music-lovers who like mint tea and hashish; the room is narrow, dark; Rachid spends a good part of his nights here; the habitués meet here, but stay only long enough to settle business; they prefer to sit outside; some lean their chairs against the rotten wall of the alley; they mingle with the crowd without impeding traffic.

The morning passes; Mustapha does not come back. Mourad and Rachid cannot leave together; they don't have enough money to pay for what they have drunk; they go on talking.

Mourad describes the traveler.

"He's still in Bône. Just this morning my aunt says Kamel found a filthy fanatic sitting on the bedroom windowsill, the one window where the shutters are always open, no one knows why. A real case for an asylum. And what was the crazy fool doing? He was writing in a notebook, and almost never looked up; Kamel wanted to tell him it was wrong to sit on the windowsill of a respectable family; Nedjma wouldn't let him; she said there was nothing about 'that poor boy' to be afraid of and all he wanted was a place to sit and write." (Mourad's face reflects a timid jealousy.)

Rachid smiles.

"Still, he's got his nerve . . ."

"Mustapha can't get over it," Rachid breaks in, knowing Mourad's eloquence when he starts talking about his cousin . . .

Toward the end of 1945, Mourad was going on eighteen; an orphan at six, he was adopted by his paternal aunt, Lella Fatma, who had only one daughter, Nedjma, after losing four boys, one after the other. Mourad's father died in an auto accident with a retired prostitute from Tunis; in this bold flight, the deceased had sacrificed the vestiges of the ancestral inheritance which supposedly amounted, before the French invasion, to three thousand gold pieces, not to mention the land. This fortune, when Sidi Ahmed met with disaster, was swallowed up in a series of mishaps, some fatal, others merely stupid; the land, for instance, was lost in the struggle against the French: Mourad's great-grandfather had fought under Abdelkader, exposing himself to Bugeaud's reprisals, the latter distributing the finest estates to the European colonists; on the other hand, the liquid cash was squandered by Sidi Ahmed, who practiced polygamy and the Charleston; Mourad's mother, a poor countrywoman named Zohra whom Sidi Ahmed had met during a trip in the Aurès, was carried off at fourteen, in return for a sum which dazzled her family; since Moslem law forbids any girl under fifteen to marry, Sidi Ahmed took possession of his wife with no ceremony beyond a Fatiha (the first sourate of the Koran) read by a chance priest; Mourad was born a year later; to celebrate his birth, Sidi Ahmed took the bit in his teeth, got drunk, almost beat the woman in childbed because she cried too much, and disappeared; it came out that he was living in Tunis with a magnificent woman for whom he fought a duel with a notary from Marseilles; a year later, Lakhdar was brought into the world. Lella Fatma, the fugitive's elder sister, was obliged to send mother and child back to the Aurès, but kept Mourad, who was never to see Zohra again; Lella Fatma received many letters from the repudiated wife's father, most of them requests for money and threats of legal action; but the rake had influence; the day of the accident, Mourad was playing with Nedjma in front of the villa. Three men carrying a blanket stopped in front of the children. The men had a strange expression on their faces. They could not make up their minds to go in. Nedjma pointed to the blanket.

"That's blood!"

The remains of Sidi Ahmed were watched over by relays of priests carrying pastry in their burnooses. Mourad had fever.

As a little girl, Nedjma was very dark, almost black; her flesh was firm, her nerves delicate; her waist slender, her legs long, and when she ran she looked like the high carriages that swerve left and right without leaving their route; the width of the little girl's face! The skin, for all the delicacy of its texture, has not kept its native pallor; Nedjma's eternal game is to reduce her dress to a minimum in the acrobatic poses of an ostrich emboldened by solitude; on such a skin, any dress is a superfluity of nakedness; Nedjma's femininity is elsewhere; the first month at school, she cried each morning; she hit all the children who came near her; she wouldn't learn her lessons before learning to swim; at twelve she concealed her breasts that were as painful as nails, swollen with the bitter precocity of green lemons; her spirit is still unbroken; her eyes, however, are losing their wild fire; sudden, rare and tantalizing Nedjma! She swims alone, dreams and reads in dark corners, an amazon of the attic, a virgin in retreat, Cinderella with an embroidered slipper; her gaze assumes secret nuances; childsplay the shape and movement of her lashes, a cry-baby's repertory—a dancing girl, a tomboy? Spared by the fevers, Nedjma matured quickly, like any Mediterranean girl; the sea air produced a bloom on her skin combining the dark tint with the brilliance of metallic reflections, mottled like some animal; her throat has the white gleams of a foundry, where the sun hammers down to her heart, and the blood, under the downy cheeks, speaks loud and fast, betraying the enigmas of her gaze.

xi. . .

MUSTAPHA'S NOTEBOOK

There is a great number of drunkards, judging by the plates of snails that strew the counters; he who drinks dines; the people of Bône are quarrelsome; they all know how to fight, but their soccer has fallen off; they are full of contradictions! They cheat at cards and cry in the movies. The refined influence of Tunisia is the cause of it all . . . I've seen Mourad at the café. I was listening to a record by Osmahan, the Lebanese woman killed in a car accident . . . Mourad nodded his head, on the verge of tears. Mourad loves me like a brother; he offered me his room in Beauséjour . . . I would never dare live so near Nedjma. That would be a good one on her: show her that her morning's porter is a friend

of her respectable cousin Mourad. He's in love
with her, the glutton! Couldn't I sleep instead of
making up phrases on a bench? Midnight soon!
No more trains . . . And not even a butt. Every
door shut, nothing in sight. To be a street porter,
you have to have a permit from the mayor's office.

. . . .

My father won't recover from the cyst in his
lung. He's dying in the Constantine hospital. My
mother's lost her mind. She's gone to stay with my
two little sisters on my uncle's farm; I'm the
smalah's only hope; my only protector in Bône is
a fritter vendor, a friend of my father's. A short
man in overalls, laced into an incredible shirt that
once was white, God knows how he got it. I've never
seen him take off his wool cap, he must be scabby
or bald at least; knock-kneed, broken-winded, mild-
mannered, he spends all day over his huge platter
of boiling oil, tirelessly throwing in fritters, pulling them out on a long wire without a word or a
glance at the street running the length of the European quarter, the Canebière of Bône; at night, the
vendor leaves his platter and becomes the sociable
citizen *par excellence;* he picks up a lot of talkers,
young and old, stuffed with peanuts and newspapers; they crowd into the shop that he trans-
forms into a night-school; like all illiterates, the
vendor is willing to make any sacrifice for a grammar lesson, natural science or simple demagogy;
since I've been living with him, he's put up a black-

board and sent out invitations to all his acquaint-
ances, so that the presence of the young scholar
(me) won't be wasted. The vendor knows I left
school because of politics; what could dazzle his
visitors more? I'm tacitly supposed to feed the conversation, dropping whatever phrases come to
mind, let it be said in passing, from previous read-
ings financed by the vendor: "*The French vocabu-
lary includes 251 words of Arabic origin . . . Thus
we influence their civilization as well . . . Two thousand European retailers share the benefits, and we
drink water* (neither the vendor nor the listeners
know I drink wine). *We go barefoot and our
Ouenza ores produce the best light steel for pursuit planes! Not to mention our cork . . .*" My role
as a lapsed student makes it a duty for me to
answer questions of this importance: "*How many
sons has Ibn Saud? Do the Turks have the atom
bomb?*" The reverses of the French army, the
eighth of May, the entry of UN troops into Arab
countries; such is the folklore of the fritter vendor.

The vendor has a brother who has just been
demobilized. B . . . hates me and makes no secret
of it. He is sumptuously dressed; this is not the
least reason for the vendor's resentment, confining
himself as he does to one filthy shirt; B . . . sleeps
in the shop too, and tells me in the most elaborate
way what I should do; I should clear out . . . The
two brothers are asleep; there are rats under the
bed. I give up mewing to scare them away; lying

107

on my paper mattress, I settle one question whose solution I finally make impossible . . .

I was in a dive, watching a young prostitute, when the vendor came in. Seeing me, he started to leave—too late, I went over to him, asked him to sit down at my table. He knows I never chase after women, having no money for it; yet he smiles as if to ask my pardon in advance for some unworthy action he is about to commit.

"Let's drink some wine."

"I'm not used to it, but I'd like to. Yes, let's drink."

I thought I would stun the vendor just by mentioning the word wine, and he hasn't turned me down. He's counting on my imminent drunkenness to take the woman behind that staircase where there's a corner specially reserved for modest types like himself, but he's not allowing for the irritation that overcomes me once I see his hypocritical face.

"To your health!" he has the gall to say . . .

He's won the first lap: I'm tight; without being taken in, out of bravado even, I've drunk much more than he, who brings up some sickness or other as an excuse. His only sickness is his desire to get into that girl, a delicate creature of sixteen . . . The bastard's never had a little sister, I suppose! Far from weakening me, the alcohol's effects increase my resentment. Now he's gesturing to the wretched girl to sit down with us. She seems to be infected by the demon too. So they're two against one now, lusting after each other horribly. All right. Each one has already left the table, innocent as you please . . . I grab the vendor and hold him back. I drag him to other dives where we drink until eleven. He's beaten. He knows it's not alcohol that makes me behave like this, and he's long since guessed I hate him. Is it my hatred that forces him to take me in? Does he do it in memory of my father? . . . We go back home. The vendor follows me, timid as a child; didn't I surprise him in the vilest debauchery, he the paragon of virtue, according to his friends? Damn vendor! He stumbles outside a movie theater; his eyes gleam at the vision of some new lechery but I'll keep him out of it. From now on, while I serve them tea, he and his visitors will be tortured by fear, will bow effusively, afraid to mention virtue, waiting politely until I leave the room to complain about the peculiar servant who deals so severely with their existence . . .

The sea is rough; nothing to eat. Walking along the Saint-Cloud beach, I passed a Restaurant-Grill-Bar-Dancing-Baths-Sandwiches — let out your rage, jackal! I sat down on the beach, face to face with the gluttons; an impatient virgin at the bar drinking, next to her an infantry captain caressing her; I stare at the virgin and I see Nedjma, as if she were really there: hair of glowing steel, delicate, hot where the sun strikes it, disordered like a hive of hornets! Huge breasts raised toward God, huge and tiny. Icy mouth melting under the captain's kisses! What are these two

pigs doing in my fantasy? It's always Nedjma I
see, still it's the virgin too; Nedjma laughing at
the breaking wave, tending an orchard, the present
vanishes, and I fall asleep, giddy . . .

I think of my sisters, between the madwoman
and the tuberculous man. He may be dying at this
very minute. Somewhere in the shop is a razor; it
wouldn't take much to set the vendor's head rolling
at my feet . . . Can crime alone assassinate injustice? Mother, I'm dehumanizing myself, turning
into a leper-house, an abattoir! What's to be done
with your blood, madwoman, whom can I take vengeance on for you? It's the idea of blood that leads
me to wine . . .

That would-be suicide who comes to his senses
no longer knows the illusion of dying.

Summer dresses . . .

In the movie-houses the policemen's wives
gesture furiously at the kids who whistle at the
lovers . . .

Since the eighth of May, 1945, fourteen members of my family have died, not counting those
shot . . .

Summer dresses: Nedjma . . .

There's no reason to suppose that Mourad
and Nedjma are lovers, and no reason to suppose
the contrary; Kamel married Nedjma in 1942;
Kamel sells tobacco, his firm character and lack-
luster past conceal his imminent ruin. He's thirty,
not bad looking, believes without practicing, is

moderately nationalistic and the only thing he's against is his status as a small businessman; he's elegant; he plays the lute and admires the Egyptian avant-garde whose leader has brought off the prodigy of imitating on his violin the tremulous calls of the muezzins . . . Kamel lives with his wife and his mother-in-law in the Beauséjour villa; now in July 1945, when I knew Mourad, he hadn't lived with his aunt for years; Mourad still visits Lella Fatma; she gives him money—discreetly, although he abandoned his studies not long after Nedjma, in 1941, despite Lella Fatma's advice. A lot of hypotheses here . . . Naturally Mourad left the villa after his cousin's marriage: a matter of propriety; but a neighbor of Mourad's, basing his testimony on public gossip, told some obscure episode to a scribe (he too public and scarcely affirmative) . . . According to this neighbor, Mourad left school at his cousin's request, she offered to marry him if he would take her to Algiers where she hoped to realize her dreams as an "enlightened" woman, far from the gossip of Bône; they planned an elopement in the worst romantic tradition: Mourad was caught pillaging Lella Fatma's savings, the latter called the police and then withdrew her complaint . . . Is Kamel aware of these events? The neighbor has no answer to this question; he emphasizes the fact that Mourad is no longer in Beauséjour where he used to live; his aunt was supposedly on the verge of retracting her affection for him, after renting him a furnished room not far from the villa; this room became the refuge of unemployed men like Rachid (the public scribe does not know I am unemployed) who have completed Mourad's debauchery, etc. The tone in which these confidences are made is only too convincing; perhaps the neighbor is jealous . . . There would be nothing astonishing about that: the scribe himself says that the day he saw Nedjma close up, for the first time, his heart leaped in his breast. There exist such women, capable of electrifying public opinion; they can be asses and even owls in their phony midnight solitude; Nedjma is only the sapling of the orchard, the foretaste of the hangover, the odor of lemon . . .

The odor of lemon and the first jasmine rises with the delirium of the convalescent sea, still white, wintry; yet the whole city clings to the brightness of the leaves, as though swept away by the wind at the approach of spring.

xii. . .

The traveler is nothing but a dolt, in rags; he waits for summer to throw his jacket in the sea;

one last coquetry: he has made himself sandals out of string and a tire left by the roadside.

Mourad has not seen the wanderer again, never hears him mentioned. The traveler disappears from each neighborhood, backtracking as if he could neither leave nor stay; when the siren blows, does he walk along the docks? No one notices him. He stares at the sea: that's all. He's waiting for the birth of the abyss, the future of the harbor; "if the sea were free, Algeria would be rich," the traveler thinks; the year of May eighth is over now . . .

It's May again.

One heavy twilight, Mourad heads for the villa.

The traveler arrives from the opposite direction, along the corniche road; the gaze of a vanished woman hurries the traveler on. She dare not have Nedjma's face; he swallows the aquatic obsession in a sigh; walking has made him feverish. He walks quickly, turning toward the villa, a new pitfall in his heart into which he must descend again—with Nedjma faceless for the moment, with his cold visionary brides.

Mourad skirts the stadium wall.

He sees the villa's closed shutters.

He sees a man crouching on the windowsill.

A beggar?

A beggar would have leaned against the wall, wouldn't have climbed up.

Mourad comes closer.

He recognizes the traveler and makes a vague gesture of greeting; the other man does the same, after putting his notebook down; Mourad remembers his aunt's words; he remembers that Kamel has already found out about the wanderer at the window.

Mourad's stare hardens.

He stands still.

The tramp doesn't get down from the window.

He has opened his knife and adjusted the catch.

Mourad and the traveler are face to face.

"What are you doing here?"

"What about you?"

"I'm visiting my relatives!" Mourad exclaims.

"Me too."

Mourad decides to show him up; he reaches for the bell without paying any more attention to the wanderer; the latter, while no one answers, stands behind Mourad and rings a second time, with an expression of profound boredom.

Nedjma appears in the doorway. Her bewildered expression reflects a childish joy, inquisitive, unworried.

Mourad hesitates to go in.

The traveler pushes him aside.

"I'm your cousin; my mother Zohra married your uncle Sidi Ahmed, Mourad's father."

Mourad starts toward the traveler.

The traveler pushes him away.

"I want to tell about Sidi Ahmed. He died with a prostitute."

Nedjma recoils.

The traveler regrets having spoken; Mourad embraces him despite their mutual repulsion and leads him down the hallway; Kamel is sitting at the table, skinning a fish; he watches the wanderer advancing down the hallway; the three young people pass without noticing him; he folds his napkin to wipe his mustache.

Lella Fatma:

"I knew Sidi Ahmed's tricks would come to no good," she says to Mourad. "Nedjma, fix your hair!"

The aunt hands the traveler a cushion.

She forces him to sit down near her, on the divan.

". . . Lakhdar! A farmer's name! No, Sidi Ahmed was no man . . . How is your mother? Say something! Are you hungry?"

"Rest in peace, my aunt . . . I've forgotten my notebook . . ."

"What notebook? He's out of his mind! . . ."

Lella Fatma feverishly unties the scarf around his head, a tramp's scarf; she drops a number of velvet bags, furiously picks up her amulets, sending Mourad and Nedjma away.

"Go on now, out! I've a right to be alone with my nephew!"

The aunt has a long conference with Lakhdar,

who as he leaves passes the married couple's room;
Nedjma introduces him to Kamel; Lakhdar makes
a gesture of greeting and goes away, followed by
Mourad.

"Why didn't you marry Nedjma?"

III. . .

i. . .

Too many things I don't know, too many things
Rachid hasn't told me; he came here with an old
man named Si Mokhtar, treated him like an old
friend; Si Mokhtar would have talked to anyone,
if Rachid (all we knew was that his name was
Rachid), with his brutal manners, his loud voice,
hadn't imposed his despotic presence on him all
day. The two men, Rachid wearing dark glasses,
Si Mokhtar sporting an Egyptian fez too tall for
his height and too bright for his age, were a perpetual subject of curiosity; people liked them for
their abstract friendliness, their gaiety, really for
the mystery the younger man seemed to cultivate
with his dark glasses, his half-civilian, half-military
outfit, and the dominance he seemed to exercise
over this friend who was at least twice his age, perhaps more . . . This went on a whole year before
people found out they came from Constantine;
people in Bône were beginning to get used to them
—you rarely saw one without the other; no one
had been able to learn anything specific about the

two friends, the one at least twice the other's age, perhaps more, and yet they were always together. Then someone noticed they were gone, without paying much attention to the fact, for they had often gone away during the year, but had reappeared each time, as if something in Bône alternately attracted and repelled them. When Rachid and Si Mokhtar came to Bône, I was still in school; I couldn't leave often enough to find out about their comings and goings. However, it was impossible not to meet them or hear about them; they were at every wedding; you found them wherever there was a crowd; in the stadium, on the docks and the boulevards, on the beach and in the cafés; actually, they wouldn't have attracted much notice if it hadn't been for the flagrant disproportion of their ages. Si Mokhtar—white hair, scarlet fez and silk tunic—could hardly be less than sixty, although he was astonishingly lively, a good walker and a great talker, in contrast to Rachid's impudent silences; Rachid was in his twenties, and the second-hand jacket he usually carried over his arm, his American shirt with its starched front, his khaki trousers that might just as well have come from army stores as from the open-air tailor you find in every Algerian city—these details escaped no one: Rachid's dark glasses, his occasional brays of laughter and martial bearing, Si Mokhtar's tall Egyptian fez, the ridiculously long English shorts he sometimes wore, showing

his graying calves without a thought for the curious pack following a few yards behind, never embarrassed, simply furtive, with a kind of ostentatious humility about him.

ii. . .

There were plenty of displaced persons in the city
of Bône; the two wars, the growth of the port, had
surrounded those of us who were citizens by birth
with people of every circumstance, especially
farmers without land, men from the mountains,
nomads; and of course the tides of the unemployed
were swelled by the discharged soldiers; it all ebbed
and flowed through the same harbor, where anyone
can find work by the hour, unexpectedly pull some
miraculous deal, the kind transacted only on a
dock or the deck of a foreign ship, just as anyone
can also spend his whole life without work, or die
of poverty in broad daylight, never having had
one lucky break; the city turned breathless, stifling, like a gambling den, for best and worst alike;
the permanent residents no longer could be distinguished from the adventurers except by lan-

121

guage, accent, and a certain tolerance for the foreigners who enrich, populate, vivify any maritime city washed by the human tides it involuntarily canalizes; but the two friends, Si Mokhtar and Rachid, had shown themselves in too many different circles, spending the wildest nights without forgetting themselves for a moment, without dropping a word to indicate their origins or their intentions . . . They constituted only a meager subject of intrigue; if their costume and bearing was extravagant, you could only laugh at it, and in other respects they compelled respect, merely by keeping their distance; not only did they go to cafés; you found them at certain meetings, sometimes even in the mosque. As for their inactivity, it was far from being exceptional at a period when the demobilized men themselves remained unemployed; what remained was the enormous disparity in their ages.

iii. . .

I met the two men for the first time shortly after they landed, in a harbor bar. Si Mokhtar was talking to a British officer. Rachid was listening to them, a cigarette in his mouth. There was something about war and about freedom. The fried sardines brought us together. I found myself standing near Rachid.

iv. . .

A month later I learned that Rachid and Si Mokhtar had met at Nedjma's wedding. She was my paternal aunt's only daughter. My Aunt was Lella Fatma and I hadn't lived with her since leaving school . . . One strange thing, Rachid had never mentioned the wedding, although he was already my friend, more or less; since at first he didn't talk at all, he showed his feelings by his imperious way of waving to me, then of keeping me near him when I happened to be going his way. Of course Si Mokhtar was generally with him, but sometimes now they would appear separately—solitary, calm, occasionally crossing each other's path with sidelong looks; then they would be together again as before, with their false mystery, their pseudo-quarrels, their deaf-men's dialogues, their meditations in common and the respectful crowds that followed a few yards behind . . . They never mentioned Nedjma's marriage to me; I hadn't been invited.

v. . .

Then they disappeared; no one was surprised, for the two friends went away from time to time; but this time, whole months went by. Meanwhile I visited my aunt a few times. About the same time I made the acquaintance of a young student expelled from school named Mustapha; that was how I heard Rachid was back. This time he was alone. Si Mokhtar had not returned.

vi. . .

I also heard from Mustapha that Rachid had fallen on bad days; Mustapha, who had his own story, hadn't been in town long enough to be interested in Rachid. He had noticed him one night, walking along the docks, had tried to talk to him, then had left when the man in dark glasses barely returned his greeting. From this description, I recognized Rachid and immediately started to look for him; finally they (Mustapha and Rachid) came to stay in the room Lella Fatma had just rented for me, near where she lives, after the scandal that forced me to leave school . . .

vii. . .

In a few days, I more or less reconstituted the story Rachid never told me to the end; he referred only vaguely to the thing, but more and more frequently, shutting up or starting in again when he felt I was particularly attentive, as if he wished both to confide in me and to make sure I would never take his outpourings to heart.

viii. . .

It was a woman Rachid was after in Bône. He
claimed not to know her name, but he couldn't
keep from describing her, making her completely
unrecognizable, speaking with a suddenness, a
perplexity that reminded me of my own torments
. . . Several times, judging from his contradictions
and from other signs, I knew he was trying to
divert my attention, to put me on a false trail.

ix. . .

There could be no doubt that Rachid was very
disturbed; he smoked, slept hardly one night out
of two, lying awake or roaming the city alone or
with me, for I attached myself to him as much as

to Mustapha, though unable to link them in the same friendship. As for Rachid, if he talked to me at all (feverish words, outbursts followed by sullen silences), it always seemed to be against his will. I felt our relations had become strained at the same time that they were growing stronger; he was pretending to be calm now; but he grew thinner from day to day, grew completely taciturn; then an attack of malaria kept him in my room over a week; after violent fits of fever that made his teeth rattle, sitting on the bed with a handkerchief tied around his head, he collapsed into a strange light sleep, interrupted by seizures of violent delirium, sudden awakenings that kept me up all night, impatient and feverish in my turn, anxious as I was not to disturb Mustapha who lay against the wall, imperturbably unconscious, leaving early every morning as though fearful of contagion, or foreseeing that Rachid would confide something to me when he awakened . . .

"Do you understand? Men like your father and mine . . . Men whose blood overflows and threatens to wash us back into their old lives like disabled boats floating over the place where they capsized, unable to sink with their occupants: we have ancestors' spirits in us, they substitute their eternal dramas for our childish expectations, our orphan patience bound to their paling shadow, that shadow impossible to dissolve or uproot—the shadow of the fathers, the judges, the guides whose

127

tracks we follow, forgetting our own way, never
knowing where they are, whether they're suddenly
going to shift the light, ambush us, resuscitate
without even coming out of the ground or assuming
their forgotten outlines, resuscitate just by blowing on the warm ashes, the desert winds that im-
pose the journey and the thirst upon us, until the
hecatomb where their old, glory-laden failure lies,
the one we'll have to bear after them, even though
we were made for unconsciousness, for frivolity—
in other words, for life . . . Yes, those are our
fathers; every wadi ransacked, even the smallest
brook sacrificed to the confluence, the sea where
no springs recognize their own sound: agony, aggression, the void—the ocean—haven't we all seen
our origins blurred like a stream in the sand, closed
our ears to the underground gallop of our ancestors, played on our fathers' graves . . . That old
pirate Si Mokhtar, the fake father who brought
me to this city, lost and abandoned . . . Do you
know how many sons, how many widows he's left
behind, without even forswearing himself? . . . He
was my father's rival. Who knows which of them
is Nedjma's father . . . The old bandit! He told
me about it a long time ago, before the last time
we were in town, he followed me here without seeming to, knowing I was looking for his presumed
daughter, Nedjma, he had introduced me to her
himself; but he had talked to me before, in
snatches, always in snatches, no one else could talk

like that: '. . . I wonder what came of all the old nights,' he used to say; 'nights of drinking and fornication; nights of rape and burglary, fights in every city we went to; fights in hallways and on terraces; fights in procuresses' houses . . .' The chorus of women, women seduced and abandoned—he didn't think he'd forgotten a single one, the only ones he kept quiet about were the ones in our own family, for Si Mokhtar was descended like me from Keblout; he told me that later, when we were sailing on the Red Sea, after dropping off some pilgrims for Mecca . . . That was before our last stay in Bône, long before . . . And the old pirate told me a little more every day, but I still didn't understand his clown's confession, although he had already hinted at most of it: a congenital liar's story—caught in his own tricks, reduced to spitting out the truth by the sudden materialization of his own lies: '. . . What escapes me,' he said, 'is the spawn, the vengeful spawn of all the mistresses seduced, the married women whose second husband I became just long enough to confuse the chronology of blood, to abandon one more piece of property to the suspect rivalry of two progenitures—one, tradition, honor, certainty, and the other, the offspring of a dry root that may never sprout, yet everywhere green and growing despite its obscure origin . . .' And the bandit, the second husband, neither polygamist nor Don Juan, but only the victim of his monumental polyandry, cared nc more about eliminating his legitimate rivals than he wanted their prolific wives. But he almost wanted to seduce their children, like a tree too high to attract the moss that would save it from the icy embrace of the deadly altitude; it was late to recognize his children, to see the childhood velvet climbing toward him—a childhood that was really his own, one he created by himself, and finally it was Si Mokhtar who capitulated, bending his trunk, ripping out his dead roots, seeking a hitherto alien lichen . . . He was on the brink of the grave, stripped of the ancient luxuries of blood, a despot rejecting everything, not foreseeing that he was emptying his heart and only bringing the banal moment of his fall that much closer; it was no use appealing to paternity courts, to orphanages, not to mention to the mistresses who wouldn't look at his shadow any more. Not even a man in the street to proclaim at the hour of his death: 'I am the child of this corpse, I am a bud of this rotten branch'; but Si Mokhtar would end his days in ridicule; the clandestine wives had left him in doubt, as if, after accepting the sowing, they had annihilated or concealed the harvest; all the old pirate had left was the horrible conviction that the product of his crimes would always be secret, until they flowered around him, a grove where the plunderer finds only insomnia, the illusion of waking renewed while the sudden and studied matriarchal vengeance that all women must satisfy

130

sooner or later takes its course, sacrificing to the primitive polyandry from which men have reaped only survival—women enjoying the fruits, men picking up the pits, each taking root despite the other—and now it was Si Mokhtar's turn to endure the matriarchal flight: the abandoned women who were poisoning his death drop by drop, weighing down his depraved body with the burden of the long sticky tears he had blindly made them shed, from which rose now the ghost of a son like Kamel, husband of another problematic daughter . . . I will not speak her name again. And Si Mokhtar even had a semblance of certitude about Kamel, who had quite innocently invited him to his wedding, and he had brought me with him, probably so my presence would keep him—at the time I knew nothing, or almost nothing—from perpetrating some scandal or other . . . Kamel's mother had been one of Si Mokhtar's few Constantine mistresses whom he had kept for several years, partly because he was sure of being her only lover, and partly because he hated the class of puritanical nobility to which her husband belonged; finally, a curious rivalry had just developed among the deceived husband, who had his mistress too, Si Mokhtar, who wanted to get this mistress away from him after having already supplanted him in his wife's favors, and my father, who was then Si Mokhtar's closest friend: my father and Si Mokhtar had heard that the puritan, Kamel's legitimate

a foreign mistress, contrary to the
:iples, the wife of a Marseillais notary
a off with a Bône landowner . . ."

:hid suddenly broke off, his teeth chattering, and I pulled the covers up over him . . . He
looked worried; his eyes were red with a new fit
of fever:

"Tell me, Mourad, tell me the truth. Do you
think it's the fever that's making me talk?"

I answered, trying to laugh: "No, no, go on,
who was the man from Bône?"

"It was your father, Sidi Ahmed, your own
father who had run off with the notary's wife who
abandoned him in his turn: yes, the Frenchwoman
ran away from your father to follow the puritan
whose wife was then Si Mokhtar's mistress, and
Si Mokhtar was keeping *her* as a hostage, because
he was in love with the Frenchwoman too, and in
the same town where your father, his best friend,
was showing off his conquest, before it was the
puritan's turn to seduce the Frenchwoman, spending all his money to put her in the biggest hotel in
Constantine, to the North, near the ruins of Cirta,
and Si Mokhtar announced in front of Sidi Ahmed,
the flouted lover, your own father, that this couple
didn't deserve the moonlight under the arches,
swearing to humiliate the puritan again, and to
avenge Sidi Ahmed, but the old pirate had made
too many friends to be faithful to any of them, for
he was as close to my father as he was to yours . . .

Si Mokhtar couldn't admit, maybe didn't even know himself that he simply wanted to take the Frenchwoman away from the puritan, when he had already taken his wife, who was pregnant with Kamel at the time, but Si Mokhtar didn't admit paternity, which of course was attributed to the legal father, that puritan who had supplanted your father Sidi Ahmed, yes, your father, and whom Si Mokhtar was waiting for at the cross-roads . . ."

"What crossroads?" I interrupted Rachid in a tone of irritation; he finished his story anyway, sweating great drops under the blanket.

"At the crossroads my father was standing, the fourth suitor . . . Si Mokhtar and he had been friends for a long time, not because they were re-lated but because of their folly, their love of vio-lence and rapine and defiance, my father was on the Rocher de Constantine then, a kind of centaur, always on the make, galloping around on eternal shooting parties, as if by bringing him into the world after 1830 Fate had condemned him to this futile carnage, he whose intrepid existence would have been covered with glory if he had been able to turn his rifle against the invader instead of quenching his hatred in pursuit of boars and jackals . . . I'm telling about this without ever having known my father, for he died by his own rifle, murdered in a cave by an unknown man who must have run away or hid himself during the in-

quest, and no one was ever able to identify him . . .
It doesn't matter . . . The Frenchwoman didn't
stay at the hotel a week: in league with my father,
Si Mokhtar had carried her off in broad daylight,
offering to take her for a ride in his gig; the old
pirate was holding the reins; my father followed
on horseback, carrying his rifle; but there was no
struggle. The ravished Frenchwoman was taken
into the woods, to a cave where the reprobates of
Constantine still hang out today; it was in that
cave that my father's body was found; his neck
was spattered with bullets; the empty rifle was
under his feet. When I was born, when my first
cries joined my already widowed mother's curses,
the inquest was being held."

X. . .

"Don't think that all those crimes had anything
excessive about them at the time; the splendor of
the Turks, the concentration of wealth in the hands
of a few tribes, the size of the country, the incon-
sistency of the urban population couldn't resist
the upheavals imposed by the conquest. The chiefs

of tribal Algeria, the ones who had access to the treasures, the guardians of tradition, were mostly killed or dispossessed during those sixteen years of bloody battles, but their sons found themselves facing an unhoped-for disaster: ruined by the defeat, expropriated and humiliated, but retaining their opportunities, protected by their new masters, rich with the money their fathers had never turned into liquid assets and which the colonists who had just acquired their lands offered them in compensation, they had no idea of its value, just as they no longer knew, facing the changes brought by the conquest, how to evaluate the treasures saved from the pillage; they found they were richer than they could ever have expected if things had remained as they were under the old order. The fathers slaughtered on Abd-el-Kader's raids (the only shadow that could have darkened the whole country, a man of the pen and the sword, the only chief capable of uniting the tribes into a nation, if the French hadn't come and cut short his efforts that were initially directed against the Turks; but the conquest was a necessary evil, a painful graft promising growth for the nation's tree slashed by the foreign axe; like the Turks, the Romans and the Arabs, the French could only take root here, hostages of the fatherland-in-gestation whose favors they quarreled over) had never taken inventories: and the sons of the vanquished chiefs discovered they were rich in money and jewels, but frustrated; certainly they felt the offense, yet in their retreats they had not kept the taste for the battle that was denied them; they had to drink the cup, spend the money, and take their places as supernumeraries at the feast; then the torches of the orgy were lit. The heirs of the valiant took revenge in the arms of *demi-mondaines*; there were *agapes*, banquets of the defeated, gaming tables and first-class passages to France; the enslaved Orient became the cynosure of cabarets; notaries' wives crossed the sea in the other direction and surrendered themselves in gardens up for sale . . . Ravished three times, the notary's wife, the seductress of Sidi Ahmed, of the puritan, and of Si Mokhtar, was to disappear a fourth time into the cave where my father was discovered, cold and stiff near his own hunting rifle, which had betrayed him as the Frenchwoman was to do, fleeing with Si Mokhtar . . . Ravished three times, the easy prey of Si Mokhtar, the virtually admitted father of Kamel and perhaps of Nedjma as well— Nedjma, the retort of the insatiable Frenchwoman three times ravished, dead now or mad or repentant, three times ravished, the fugitive had no other castigation than her daughter, for Nedjma is not Lella Fatma's daughter . . ."

"That much I knew," I said. "It's true that Nedjma's mother was a Frenchwoman, and more precisely a Jewess, according to what Lella N'fissa, Kamel's mother told me, out of mother-in-law's spite, probably, before the wedding . . ."

xi. . .

The malaria attack over, Rachid never mentioned
the subject again; he seemed to consider everything he had told me a delirium; and I—I didn't
want to bring it up again either, for I thought I
knew everything that had been revealed to me . . .
But Kamel's mother hadn't told me everything:
she hadn't told me that Si Mokhtar was also her
late husband's rival, and on two counts, having
taken first his wife and then his mistress, and that
wasn't the worst for Rachid, for who could have
killed the other rival, the dead man in the cave,
if not the old bandit and seducer, old Si Mokhtar
who is both Kamel's father and Nedjma's and
probably also the murderer whom his victim's son
pursues without knowing it, for Rachid cannot
know what I know, for he was never acquainted
with Kamel's mother, who told me other things
too . . . Yes, Kamel's mother knew the whole story
of the little girl adopted by Lella Fatma's late
husband: that was Nedjma, three years old then,
abandoned by her mother, the Frenchwoman, and
entrusted by Si Mokhtar to Lella Fatma's hus-

137

band, for Lella Fatma was known to be sterile. Si
Mokhtar didn't explain that it was his daughter
when he gave her to the childless couple she was
never to leave again, at whose home I was to find
her after my mother was repudiated and my father
Sidi Ahmed died, a few months later . . . Kamel's
mother didn't tell me how she had learned this. I
didn't believe it at the time. I didn't know Si Mokhtar then, nor Rachid, nor Lakhdar . . .

xii. . .

She came to Constantine without Rachid's knowing
how. He was never to know, neither from her nor
from Si Mokhtar.

The meeting between Rachid and the unknown woman had taken place in a clinic where Si
Mokhtar had *entrée* . . . Rachid was dead with
sleep. He was going back to his mother's early in
the morning when Si Mokhtar gave him a lecture
(the old man and Rachid had already spent a lot
of time together) and dragged him to the clinic
where there was a blank, somber, vacant woman, a
young woman whose hands Si Mokhtar began

kissing, chanting something between a lovesong and a paternal blessing; then Rachid was alone with the woman in the darkness (the shutters were closed); in the doctor's absence Si Mokhtar had gone off to visit with the nurses, most of whom had left off the veil, thanks to the old bandit's influence with their families . . .

i. . .

"She came to Constantine without my knowing how, I was never to know. She was standing there, blank and somber, in the examination room of a clinic where Si Mokhtar had *entrée* (having been the childhood friend of the doctor who was now councillor-general), a clinic he dragged me to one morning, among the nurses—he knew them all; 'not one is European,' he had told me once, 'and they would all be veiled if the doctor and I hadn't picked them out of school or got them away from their parents . . .' He spent the morning surrounded by them, girls not over twenty, timid and eager, whom he openly called 'my daughters,' chattering behind the doctor's back without pay-

139

tention to him, as if the clinic were one
htar's residences, the doctor merely a
the staff and coming far below in the
hierarchy, far below the smiling girls—Si Mokhtar knew them all, knew their fathers and their
grandfathers, had traveled around the world,
visited Europe by way of Turkey, had almost
been stoned in Saudi Arabia, played the prince in
Bombay, squandered his inheritance in Marseille
and Vichy, returned to Constantine, still vigorous
and not yet ruined, had invested other fortunes in
women, bad company and politicians, contracting
and annulling marriages, intrigues, stirring up
the city from top to bottom to get back the lost
money, always ready for bankruptcy and brawling, quickly replacing his false teeth and his
ruined clothes, but not leaving his home town
again, having no one left but a centenarian mother
as sharp as himself, without a wife or a business,
forcing doors, vomiting in elevators, forgetful
and impartial as a patriarch, inventor of sciences
without a future, more erudite than the Ulémas,
learning English from a soldier but never pro-
nouncing a word of French without mutilating it
on principle, colossal, broken-winded, stoop-shouldered, muscular, nervous, bald, eloquent, pugna-
cious, secretive, sentimental, depraved, cunning,
naïve, famous, mysterious, poor, aristocratic, doc-
toral, paternal, brutal, whimsical, wearing sandals,

140

boots, slippers, espadrilles, dress shoes, wearing cashmere, mattress ticking, silk, tunics too short for him, baggy pants, English rep ties, collarless shirts, pajamas over suits, burnooses and extorted gabardines, wool caps, incomplete turbans, glistening, wrinkled, heavily perfumed; Si Mokhtar had known the city, so to speak, in its cradle, and he had given the clinic girls their first candy, their first bracelets, their first lovers (the old devil had even thrown me into the arms of I don't know how many women during his mad career as a pander, a Mentor), but the woman he showed me that morning seemed not to know what kind of subtle and turbulent old man she was dealing with. I had never seen such a woman in Constantine, so elegant, so untamed, with her incredible gazelle's bearing; it was as if the clinic were a trap, and the wonderful creature about to collapse, her delicate legs made for running, or suddenly leap away, escaping at the first gesture toward her; Si Mokhtar had left us face to face, struck dumb by a fit of emotional terror there in that shuttered clinic where sickness seemed unreal and the nurses paraded their delicacy, their charming dexterity ("you see, we're not French but *their* medicine, *their* manners have no secrets for us, daughters of old Arab, Turkish or Kabyl families")—all dark, some almost black—I don't know how many unveiled girls passing back and forth, smiling over the instruments, the magazines, the huge ashtrays,

141

while I stood there stunned in front of the woman who wasn't dressed like a nurse and who didn't seem sick (anything but!) . . . I followed Si Mokhtar when I was falling asleep on my feet after a night of roaming around the city; he gave me a lecture (the old scoundrel had appointed himself my censor) . . . And what fate, what ironic providence had made me Si Mokhtar's inseparable companion? I couldn't say just when we really met. He had always belonged to the ideal city that's been lying like a deposit in my memory since the blurred age of circumcision, of escapes from the house, of the first weeks when Madame Clément had given me a slate—for me he was one of the tutelary spirits of Constantine, and I never saw him age, any more than there is an age or one particular countenance for the historical Barbarossa, the legendary Jupiter; I had always lived in Constantine with ogres and sultanas, with the locomotives of the inaccessible station, and the specter of Si Mokhtar. Sometimes he walked in front of our house; like all children, I rushed after him, begging for money, following him and throwing stones at him; he terrified us but we loved him with all the fierce dissimulation of childhood, and we couldn't do without him; all the proverbs, all the jokes, all the tragedies were Si Mokhtar's; everyone knew what he said about war, about religion, about death, about women, about alcohol, about politics, about everyone and everyone, what Si

142

Mokhtar had done or not done, the people he fought with, those he heaped with bounty. How could a man like that attach himself to anyone? With his disciples, he could have made up a small army . . . Yet there came a time when he interested himself in me particularly, day by day, paid my debts, but refused the room I offered him in my house; it was just when I entered the Medersa. Partly to comfort my mother, and partly to make up for squandering what I had inherited from my father, I asked to be accepted as a boarding student in the only institution in Constantine where you could complete your studies in Arabic . . ."

ii. . .

And Rachid recalled that gray morning, without being able to fend off the specter that immediately rose between the tremulous gazelle and the stupefied orphan: "The old bandit! He introduced her to me there, 'the daughter of a family that is yours as well,' he said, leaving me alone with her, struck dumb with terror there in that clinic where sickness seemed unreal, as if the old rake had made it up on a whim, to astound the poor boy that I was, dazzled by illusions; and the chimera smiled at me, in her unheard-of sumptuosity, with her chimerical forms and dimensions, personifying the child's city: the old world that bewitched me like a *fondouk* or a beautiful pharmacy, the utopian universe of sultanas without sultans, of women without a country, homeless save for the dark tents of pirates and princes (Si Mokhtar's disappearance had alarmed me, already suggesting sacrilege as I faced the strange woman still smiling at me, neither a local girl nor an invalid nor a nurse— simply a sultana—and the enchantment grew with the timid complicity her smile showed me, without my having to speak; we stood motionless in the gray dawn, unnoticed despite the clinic's bustle; Si Mokhtar avoided us diabolically). The nurses vanished one after another; so that my twitches, my cigarettes and my swaggering smiles seemed to be addressing her, without a word, merely by the grace of the haunted atmosphere that kept us together as though in a train or a bus; her face, her expensive clothes, her hair tied with purple silk made a halo of darkness around her eyes that were full of sudden, unfathomable looks now; I wasn't surprised to be there, I stopped hearing the clock which I glanced at now and again for assurance and out of superstition: the two hands soon met. It was going to be noon."

iii. . .

I left with her. But towards midnight, as I had
expected, she left me on a street corner, walking
fast and firmly, without a word of goodbye—and
afterwards, not a sign of her, nor of Si Mokhtar,
who claimed not to know her by her new name (she
had just been married, the old rake told me
laconically)—and concluded in an imperious tone:
"You were dreaming . . . Be calm. If you found
her again, you'd be flouted, deceived, betrayed. Be
satisfied."

iv. . .

Si Mokhtar left for Mecca at seventy-five, laden
with so many sins that forty-eight hours before

setting out for the Holy Land, he took a tube of ether "to purify myself" he told Rachid.

Rachid was a deserter at the time; returning from Tripolitania, he had been living in the Rimmis woods, not far from a cave of sinister memory . . . Si Mokhtar visited the pariahs of Rimmis, and preferred spending his time there with Rachid; it was all feasting by torchlight, monstrous banquets (one day they butchered a colt), during which the extravagant friendship between the septuagenarian and the adolescent sporting his runaway soldier suit was reinforced, until the Friday when Si Mokhtar suddenly stopped drinking, put himself on a daily ration of snuff, made his ablutions and his prayers, bought *eau de Cologne*, energetically washed his tunic, stamping on it in the stream's icy water, talking about the Holy Land that he had already visited half a century ago and wanted to see again "one last time." Rachid watched him pensively, still drinking and smoking, without washing his military jerkin; then he quietly left the bivouac and returned the following week, shoving under the old man's nose navigator's papers daubed with a cork; the photograph of Rachid (in peculiar sailor's outfit) was in the phony passport, but with another name, another birthday, all thanks to the good offices of an unemployed navigator who had agreed to sell him the certificate, and after a few days Si Mokhtar managed to find the two thousand francs Rachid had promised.

V. . .

Rachid was even better informed than Si Mokhtar:
he found out the sailing date, the ports of call,
learned about the ship, the crew, the food, all the
probable incidents, and even the religious rites Si
Mokhtar no longer remembered very well, fifty
years after his first pilgrimage . . . According to
Rachid, the question of cash came up only for the
impotent, the timid or the rich . . . As he put it, the
only difficulty would be in being taken on as a member of the crew, for the owner of his papers hadn't
managed to be included on any long voyages,
hadn't even found a berth on the worst freighter,
not even one from Bône to Oran. There was a maritime crisis, unemployment for many sailors, even
veterans, even Europeans, but Rachid had made
up his mind: he took Si Mokhtar aside:

"All right, we'll go together? Get ready. I'm
ready now."

"I knew you'd want to come."

"It's your move, boss. If you say no, I'll go
without you."

"Oh no," the old man said. "It's all settled for me: the ones who've given me their sins have paid my expenses, delighted to see a scoundrel leaving in their place, they tell themselves that only people whose case has to be argued on the spot need to go . . . Everything's settled. All I have to do is buy my ticket."

vi. . .

Si Mokhtar's father had been buried in Mecca; therefore he was selected to sit among the dignitaries, his seventy-five years merely made matters easier; as the sacred month approached, it was inevitable that the old fool became the supreme delegate not only of the few pilgrims who already surrounded him, but of the whole city, the whole department which because of its relation to Tunisia and the Middle East had always passed for the cradle of Moslem faith in Algeria—an Algeria that Si Mokhtar was perhaps to represent as a whole, at the side of Moroccan pashas, of Tunisian Ulémas, of Indian fakirs and Chinese mandarins, who were the only ones, actually, who might touch the Black Stone ahead of him. Three months before leaving, Si Mokhtar was invited everywhere, and, no longer able to drink ether, he secretly swallowed a tumbler of *eau de Cologne* when he felt he was losing his fervor; he now believed he had recovered his faith; he confided in Rachid, who dared not mock him, living largely on the money and the various favors the citizens lavished on the departing Sheik in order to be named in his prayers; at last Si Mokhtar was escorted to the pier in a superb sedan, and along with his pious congeners was officially received by the sub-prefect of Bône in a vast official chamber; Si Mokhtar almost overturned the tray of liqueurs in his eagerness to turn his back to it, while Madame, her bare feet sticking out of her green mules touched up with satin, cool and flaccid from her bath, ruffled her silk trousers, sucking on a long cigarette holder, referring to Islam with a catch in her throat, as she might have spoken of a dressmaker or a grocery she was annoyed with, in order to commiserate with, to distract, to soften this delegation of rickety screech-owls about to fall from the last branch: the youngest pilgrim wasn't under sixty; Si Mokhtar was the most vigorous, the only one without a cane or a crutch, clutching the vial of perfume under his sweaty chaplet . . .

vii. . .

Rachid was still in Constantine; he galloped from street to street, purposeless, tireless, looking for the old man; then he managed to find enough money to take the train to Bône, no more; he expected to triumph over everything, provided he found Si Mokhtar. They came face to face under the dock floodlights, the night of the sailing, in the crowd. They waited until the whistle stopped blowing, shouting in the uproar as the last groups came up the gangplank.

"Don't worry," Rachid said. "It's my problem."

"You think you're at the bus station, with your mamma?"

"I'm waiting for the man from the union. No good without him. He's busy now. He keeps getting on and off with other sailors. They want to strike . . ."

"You hear that?"

It was the second whistle.

Visible on the gangway, the officer kept on

150

blowing; the moorings were cast off at each end of the hull; the whistle stopped; the officer was shouting now, no longer directing operations but accompanying them in a persuasive, serious tone, like a farmer ploughing, encouraging his ox's somnolent effort at the end of a furrow; the docks, the ships, the city observed the same attentive silence no longer violated by the belated screams of relatives or the rumbles of the nearby yards that also seemed to have vanished or to be on the point of yielding to the challenge of the open sea and the starless night that melted into the sheet of heavy, gleaming water.

"Go in peace," whispered Rachid. "I've been waiting ten hours. My hard luck. You have just time to climb up. If they take off the gangway . . ."

"Follow me," Si Mokhtar said. "What are you waiting for?"

viii. . .

Rachid had traded his semi-military clothes for a striped jersey, stoker's blues, a brown wool hat, a runner's flat-soled shoes that were twisted and

tough, their blunted toes obliging him to change
feet like storks, an absurd position that perhaps
made him scuttle on board more than Si Mokhtar's
exhortation, which he hadn't understood, following timorously, without answering—not as if they
didn't know each other, but as if they had always
been mortal enemies—for they had suddenly and
simultaneously decided to play for high stakes:
they reached the gangway. The two spotlights
seemed to focus on their lowered heads, rigid in
the vibration of the rigging, the peaceful hum of
machinery: the sense of being two guilty shadows
that the crew would certainly unmask, surprise,
then lock up or lead off at the last minute, last
spectacle of the departure that the whole city
would talk about, pitying Rachid's clumsiness, Si
Mokhtar's frivolity, while insisting that such a
trick had often succeeded in other cases. Rachid
stumbled on the second step; he patiently pulled
himself up, avoiding the rope railing, in order not
to feel the space, the wind, the lure of the open
sea, and not to lean on the loose rope, lest he fall
into the hands of the police he heard walking up
the gangway behind him—actually it was a ladder,
a long wet trembling ladder. Si Mokhtar was already on deck.

Rachid started walking again.

He was stopped when he let go of the rope
and was getting his breath, not having noticed the

officer on the gangway, although Si Mokhtar had signaled his presence by a ringing salutation.

Rachid took out his papers; the officer handed them back to him without a glance and he passed on board, not even surprised by this mark of confidence, as if fate had vexed him by smiling at him at the height of fear, or as if he really belonged to the crew, irritated by a pointless and poorly performed formality, so that he did not immediately join his companion, savoring this introduction into the wolf's mouth, he who had just deserted on land to find himself fictitiously enrolled on board a big ship, so big that the officer on duty claimed to recognize him . . . Si Mokhtar was biting his nails; more than a hundred stowaways had been discovered; not only discovered but locked up in the hold by the time Bizerte was sighted.

Si Mokhtar went ashore to buy two virtually complete pilgrim outfits for himself and for Rachid: seamless sheets to be tied around the waist, unstitched sandals, and various baubles; meanwhile Rachid had laid out a mattress on a plank just wide enough, in the infirmary bathroom; he had found the key on the door and had installed himself there at nightfall. Si Mokhtar congratulated him; he brought him food and news of the voyage, urging discretion: "now that you're there, stay there." There was no question of passing as a navigator now; all the men of the crew were known, each at his post.

ix. . .

Every night Rachid mingled with the passengers;
he couldn't resist the simple pleasure of strolling
when the air was cool.

At Port Saïd, the ship docked for a whole day;
this was the moment to change money into Egyptian pounds that were more easily convertible into
rials; Si Mokhtar calculated he had scarcely
enough to pay the guide assigned to accompany
each *hadj* from Jidda to Medina, as far as the
Prophet's tomb. He confided in Rachid, who hadn't
a centime.

Port Saïd was no longer in sight. There were
only ten days left before they reached Arabia; that
night, Si Mokhtar made an unexpected speech:

"We'll go together or we won't go. It doesn't
matter . . ."

Rachid didn't say a word.

The engines slowed; the anchor chains began
to rattle. Rachid had locked himself in the bathroom, had removed the key; Si Mokhtar called him
several times, but without getting any answer.
When he looked through the porthole and saw the

last *sambouk* leaving, overloaded with men and baggage, Rachid hastily pulled on his stoker's blues again, wrapped the sacramental outfit in a newspaper, opened the door, pocketed the key and strolled across the deck; he felt his shaved head was a poor way to finish off his sailor's disguise, but neither the wool cap nor the soft fez Si Mokhtar had brought him from Bizerte had seemed much good; he hugged his package, his future *hadj* outfit, gradually walking faster, testing his belt buckle, trying not to hear the sound his stiff trouser material was making, as at the time of his still recent desertion, from which he had inherited this anti-militaristic nonchalance he considered necessary, leaving the army, in order to inspire if not the respect at least the sympathy of the passengers at whom he smiled mechanically, standing aside and careful not to salute . . . But he was no longer a deserter. On this ship he was nothing; he had simply followed the old pirate out of habit, and perhaps too because of the chimera, the unknown woman in the clinic, the night of last summer, and no other reason, not even to see the country, since he had just crossed the Suez Canal without opening the porthole, just as he was quite unmoved at now meeting on deck several of the men he had avoided since the start of the voyage, various groups of crewmen moving in all directions, making a great racket. He stopped one of them passing near him and without a hitch:

"They're all off?"

"And good riddance," the Tunisian said (Rachid recognized the accent, which had been his own, when he had recently crossed the Tripolitanian desert, passed the frontier and taken the road to Carthage in shorts and a soldier's shirt . . .). "The whole boat's filthy. And slobs like that think they're going to paradise . . ."

"You're not going off?"

"I don't know yet."

"You don't like Jidda?"

"Just for business . . . No café, no hotel, and you have to have a license to buy a radio, on condition you don't listen to singing, just psalms; it's not like in Egypt, their chiefs are wild men and they're all poor devils living off foreigners' faith. I may go off though . . . Some things . . ."

"What things?"

"Some gold," the Tunisian said (Negroid, grease-stained, with tears of sweat on his nose), "yes, gold, but I don't have enough on me . . . The other men won't want to get off . . . Most of them have gone through too often; they don't like this kind of stopover, and if no one else wants to get off you can't take the boat for just the two of us, the Second won't let us."

"Which one?"

"Over there."

Rachid went straight over to the officer, who took him for one of the crew (there were almost three hundred) ; a little later, a group of stokers, galley boys, sailors—among whom Rachid and the Tunisian—took seats in the boat, with the chief officer and the ship's doctor. A light breeze cooled the September afternoon, but the sun still weighed heavily on the apparently deserted harbor, and the distant city shrank to some patches of low walls above the glowing ochre earth in high relief, a cruel nakedness that it hurt to look at; the red sun was closer than the land, the boat after crossing the breakers, the coral reefs surrounded by wrecks, landed at the custom house, and Rachid, turning his head, discovered rows of sails swaying in the breeze, as though another harbor, rising out of another age, had faded in the spaceless sun, and Jidda was no more than a desert betrayed. Rachid could only guess at the weight of the turbans swollen with duty; he saw the officials in their English gaiters, the suspect uniforms evidently taken from the rejects of too many foreign armies; he thought how the fathers of these men, these clowns glistening with vanity, had banished the Prophet as they were banishing progress now, along with faith and all the rest, merely in order to choke the desert with their arrogant ignorance, probably the last flock to wallow in the dust, knowing no better than to renew their cast-off clothes and doze, murmuring the very verses that should have roused them, "but that's just it," Rachid thought, "they're doing what their fathers did: they've banished for good the only one of their number who woke up one morning to tell them of his dark and legendary dream, and they wouldn't stand for it; it took other peoples, other men to face the immensity, to believe that the desert was simply the old paradise, and that only a revolution could reconquer it . . . Others would believe him, would follow the Prophet, but the dreams couldn't be naturalized . . . It was here, in Arabia, that they should have believed the Prophet, passed from nightmare to reality . . . but here they banished him, forced him to transplant his dream, to disseminate it wherever there was a favorable wind; and the ones the Koran was created for aren't even at the stage of paganism or in the stone age; who can say what monstrous expectation they've settled for from their thirsty land?" The customs officers had come over to the boat, while the sailors jumped ashore; then there was some squabbling; the chief officer's camera was seized, and Rachid was beginning to find Ibn Saud's officials sympathetic while doing a good deal of elbowing himself, but the incident almost kept him from accomplishing his plan, for now insults filled the air; sailors suggested returning on board at once rather than let the camera be seized; then the doctor declared it would be better to lodge a complaint with the French consulate, and Rachid was finally free in the crowd, though he left his papers at the customhouse according to regulations. Si Mokhtar ran into Rachid wandering alone in the *souks*. He burst into a fit of rage.

"Forget it," Rachid said. "You can see I got out all right. Go rent your guide and don't bother about me."

"What are you going to do?"

"We'll see."

"No use. Without money you won't get far here. They all live on pilgrims, their famous sultan's nothing but an oil salesman . . . Have to have a guide; even then, there's a whole series of privileges (I left thirty pounds at the customhouse), almost wherever you go, not to mention the Aïd's sheep . . ."

"I'll get there on my own . . ."

"I tell you I know the country; it hasn't changed much in forty years. You can get to Mecca by paved road, but there will still be over four-hundred kilometers to reach the city of the Prophet; if you don't get to Medina, you might just as well give up your pilgrimage."

"I'll walk; I'll find someone . . ."

"It's a path in the desert. People from all over the world will get there before you. You'll die of thirst, I've made the trip already . . . At the time, I had a fortune. I've come back without anything. Stay with me."

"Why, though? You're old enough to be selfish. I'll find a way."

They were joined by the Tunisian who was glancing searchingly around them as they walked.

"You don't know the man with the tooth?"

"No," Rachid said.

"The one who sells gold . . ."

Si Mokhtar said he didn't know such business was even conceivable.

"Ah, my father, how innocent you are. Half of those who come here have nothing but business in mind; it's a kind of annual fair under God's protection . . . But I don't have enough on me . . ."

"Yes," Rachid said, "the ones who come by plane, and others less powerful; besides, it's only the businessmen who are passed when they ask for their passport; that's how it is at home, probably here too."

"Right. If all the believers were sailors, they'd be as down on the pilgrimage as I am. I'm as good a Moslem as the next man. I've made the trip five times. That's enough."

Si Mokhtar nodded approval, delighted to have the Tunisian support his own views. But Rachid persisted.

"Then members of the crew can join the official caravan?"

"It all depends on the chief officer. This time, you can't. We're not going to stay in port the whole month the market lasts. Tomorrow all the men have to be back on board. We're going after coal and supplies . . . In Port-Sudan."

The Tunisian left.

Si Mokhtar took Rachid by the arm.

"I didn't come for Paradise. Your father was my friend . . ."

And the old devil, leading Rachid, made a scandal at the custom house. He insisted on returning to the ship, claimed he had lost a purse. The chief officer refused. Then Si Mokhtar made a speech; planted before the chief officer, who was preparing to get back into the boat at twilight, he took off his turban, tore his ivory teeth out of his lower jaw, and holding his hands over his enormous, shiny skull, exclaimed:

"Oh my God! Three times! Why this injustice?"

Si Mokhtar had declaimed in French, here a foreign language; the customs officers weren't listening; as for the crew, they burst out laughing; Si Mokhtar hadn't screamed; his laughable person contradicted the notion of madness, aside from the disappearance of the dental plate, the fall of the turban and the old man's fierce appearance, still declaiming, restoring silence:

> *The burial of truth*
> *Is the cause of calamity.*

And again, in a strident voice:

> *My father Charlemagne*
> *My mother Joan of Arc.*

The chief officer beamed. Was he surprised to hear a *hadj* refer to French history? Did he choose to extricate himself politely from a situation which might cover him with ridicule? He questioned Si Mokhtar; and Rachid, the unofficial navigator with the false papers, served as his interpreter.

The ship wouldn't be loading until the next night, and the official caravan had forty-eight hours of formalities before leaving Jidda. Hence Si Mokhtar's re-embarcation seemed quite normal; he would take his purse and rejoin the caravan in a *sambouk*, "At your expense, of course," the chief officer told him. On the gangway, Rachid gradually separated himself from the group of sailors clustering around the old pirate and made straight for his bathroom, where Si Mokhtar lost no time joining him.

"Now we're going to Port-Sudan."

Rachid was dragged to the infirmary attendant.

"I am dying," Si Mokhtar said.

The doctor was called.

"I'm dying. My purse has been stolen."

"Stolen?"

"Unless someone's thrown it into the sea. Dying is all that's left to me."

"But what was in it?"

"My money and my mother's and the alms of my friends. Now I'm no longer worthy of Mecca. Give me a bed and let me die. Be charitable, give me a bed . . ."

The doctor had a hard time getting in a few words.

The old clown grew more and more upset, simulating despair; he tugged the attendant's sleeves, calling him to witness, laying all four hands on his heart, sobbing, crumpling his clothes. Finally, coldly:

"I no longer wish to go to Mecca. You cannot force me. I have paid my passage both ways."

This time, no objection could be made. He obtained a bed in the infirmary, near Rachid's hiding-place. Rachid hadn't understood a word.

"What purse?" Rachid asked, when they were alone.

"Never mind. I know what I'm doing . . . Without the pilgrimage, would they have given me a passport? Imposture for imposture, better to see the world . . ."

Until that day, Rachid had never asked himself what reasons Si Mokhtar might have for returning to Mecca. Or did the old fool simply want to leave his city one last time, afraid to die abject, abandoned, sterile in the very place where he had lived his proud share of the century . . . But he finally told everything, or almost everything . . .

X. . .

The ship was empty now; the crew had less to do,
in the absence of the passengers; three days from
Port-Sudan, the men began to fish over the side or
stroll around the decks; discipline slackened. The
attendant often left to visit his friends in their
cabins; toward the end of the night, Rachid was
awakened by the old bandit; they went up on deck.
The sea was bad. The wind, at first, kept the two
shadows apart; then they discovered two deck
chairs in a sheltered place. Si Mokhtar sat down
facing the bulwark, digging into his tobacco
pouch, and began intoning; Rachid, sitting on his
left, listened and stared at the sea. He was about
to fall asleep when Si Mokhtar leaned toward him,
his turban unwound, in the sudden, rare gusts of
wind: ". . . Yes, the same tribe. Not a relative the
way the French understand it; as far as anyone
knows, our tribe must have come from the Middle
East through Spain and Morocco, under Keblout's
leadership. Someone told me that it's a Turkish
name: "broken rope," Keblout. Take the word

rope and translate: you get Hbel in Arabic. It's
only the K instead of the first H and the change in
the final syllable that makes the Turkish word different from the Arabic, supposing it is a Turkish
name . . . No trace of Keblout has ever been found.
He was the chief of our tribe at a date so remote
that it's hard to establish in the thirteen centuries
since the death of the Prophet. All I know I heard
from my father, who heard it from his, and so on.
But there's a probability Keblout lived in Algeria,
at least during the last part of his career, for he
was over a hundred years old when he died. Was
that the Keblout who founded the dowar, or just
one of the descendants named for him? According
to one of the few Ulémas who know our tribes'
history in detail, Keblout came from Spain with
the Sons of the Moon, first settled in Morocco,
then went to Algeria. But other details might suggest a different route: everyone knows that several
generations of Keblouti held specific offices down
to our own time: they were Tolbas, wandering students; they were musicians and poets from father
to son, possessing little wealth but setting up their
mosques and mausoleums everywhere, sometimes
medersas too, when there were enough disciples;
this would mean that the First Keblout was neither
a soldier nor a dignitary but a thinker and an
artist. In that case, he would not have been a chief
of an already powerful tribe, but an exile with
special ideas and talents, settling in Algeria by

pure chance, somehow elected or adopted by the natives who gradually entered his family and finally made him the elder of the community. That would be plausible enough, if other events following the French conquest didn't bring the hypothesis back to an authoritarian Keblout, chief of a nomad tribe or an armed clan in the province of Constantine since the Middle Ages, on Mount Nadhor, overlooking the eastern region of Cuelma. The situation of Mount Nadhor is already a clue —it's a sheltered site that makes it possible to hold a territory long coveted by the conquerors; the Romans had a garrison not far from there, near the Millesimo quarries; they had two other strongholds, Hippone on the Carthage littoral, and Cirta, seat of the Numidian province that then included all of North Africa. After the siege of Constantine, the French followed the old Roman tactics point by point; once their soldiers were garrisoned in the walls of ancient Cirta and ancient Hippone, they headed for the Millesimo region; they sent out patrols and reconnaissance missions, expecting to establish bases. The Nadhor inhabitants had remained unsubdued. They didn't attack, just pushed deeper into the forest, pretending to ignore the new conquerors; the decades passed without the French being able to extend their influence. It was then that the tribe was decimated."

xi. . .

"Everything happened in a few days, after they discovered the bodies, covered with knife-wounds, of a man and his wife left in the Keblout mosque. The bloody corpses were lying in a bundle of old clothes. The victims' identity is still a matter of uncertainty. According to some versions, the man was an officer of the expeditionary corps; others say he was only a European roadworker surprised with his mistress in a covered wagon . . . The Nadhor was put to fire and sword, military judges were appointed; a little later, the six chief males of the tribe had their heads cut off, all on the same day, one after the other . . . The old Keblout (not the first one, one of his direct descendants) had died around the same period. After the six executions, the tribe remained without a leader; but Keblout had so many offspring that other young men who had grown up in the terror and the confusion began to leave the Nadhor secretly so they could establish themselves incognito in other parts of the province; the decimated tribe tightened its

167

blood bonds, re-established the practice of intra-tribal marriage, took other names to escape reprisals, leaving a handful of old men, widows and orphans in the profaned patrimony, which was at least to keep the trace, the memory of the defunct tribe. They say one of the widows sacrificed on the Nadhor remained alone in the ruins to continue the teaching of Keblout . . . Meanwhile, the promoters of the punitive expedition had not succeeded in convincing the directors of the inquest; the fact that one of the corpses was a woman's could disqualify the hostile political attitude of the sons of Keblout; perhaps it was a crime of passion manipulated in order to destroy the tribe's resistance and prestige; the two initial victims might have been brought to the mosque; that might have been the work of the man's rival, a fellow officer or road-worker; the symbol of the bloodshed in the mosque seemed too eloquent, too apposite to the arousing of the conquerors and to the intrigues of the other subject tribes which were eager to discredit these poor, dangerous professors, these lifelong students, in the eyes of the French . . . The 'murder in the cathedral' could have been a theatrical gesture; did the investigators think so? They may have been frightened by the blind speed of the retaliatory massacre and the outburst of hatred that would react against them; probably some Native Affairs expert looked over the dossier, mounted his horse and rode off toward the East, questioning

168

the survivors, staying on the Nadhor during the brief trial which was ended by a sentence in the Cuelma barracks courtyard and by the fall of six heads, one after the other, while our tribe, deprived of its leaders, collapsed. The telegram arrived from the capital too late, a few days too late: the corpses in the barracks were pardoned. Reprisals continued surreptitiously while regrets and condolences arrived that no one could transmit or accept: the six condemned men's sons were still in their cradles when they were appointed acting caïds and cadis, thereby receiving patronymics corresponding to their future professions; hence the worst calculations triumphed even in the reparations that were made, for the name of Keblout was forever proscribed and remained a lamentable secret in the tribe, a rallying point for bad times.

Yes, the mosque remained in ruins; only the green standard of the mausoleum was still raised, cut out of the rags of widows and old men.

The men had escaped, and the orphans who benefited by the largesse were also to be moved away: the tribe's ruin was completed in the civil registers, the four registers in which the survivors were counted and divided; the new authorities completed their work of destruction by separating the Sons of Keblout into four branches, 'for administrative convenience'; the men in the first register were allotted lands at the other end of the province which were immediately expropriated; to this

branch belonged your father and Sidi Ahmed . . .
The men in the second register received jobs in the
magistracy and were sent to the different centers;
my father belonged to this branch. The men of the
third branch, although listed in a separate register,
received almost the same treatment, but moved
still farther away by contracting too many marriages with other less stricken families . . . As for
those of the fourth branch, they kept the destroyed
mosque, the mausoleum, the little bit of land, the
ancestral standard, and there was talk of con-
stituting a brotherhood to keep it in check, in case
a plot of vengeance should be brewing . . ."

xii. . .

And that day, in his deserter's cell, Rachid thought
he could hear on deck the passionate revelations of
Si Mokhtar, full of the tumult of the Red Sea, in
sight of Port Sudan . . . "You should remember
the destiny of this country we come from; it is not
a French province, and has neither bey nor sultan;
perhaps you are thinking of Algeria, still invaded,
of its inextricable past, for we are not a nation, not

yet, you know that: we are only decimated tribes. It is not a step backward to honor our tribe, the only link that remains to us by which we can unite and restore our people, even if we hope for more than that . . . I couldn't talk to you there, there on the site of the disaster. Here, between Egypt and Arabia, the Keblout fathers passed, tossed about on the sea like ourselves, on the morrow of a defeat. They lost an empire. We are losing only a tribe. And I shall tell you: I had a daughter, the daughter of a Frenchwoman. I began by leaving the woman in Marseilles, then I lost the girl (the photograph Si Mokhtar took out almost blew away; it was the unknown woman from the clinic) . . . The people I left her with—it was during the time of my friendship with your father, and they were our relatives,—have always kept her away from me; and now the adoptive mother has just married off my daughter. I can't do anything about that. All the sins are on my side. But I know that Nedjma was married off against her will; I know that much, now that she has found me again, has written me, visited me, that's why you saw her in Constantine, her husband brings her there with him from time to time . . . I knew the suitor long ago. I saw him grow up. His father belonged to my generation, the generation of your father and Sidi Ahmed. I've never been able to like that young man. Yet I had my reasons, good reasons . . . Actually, I was almost the tutor of the man who

171

was to take Nedjma without telling me . . . But
did he know it? And now here I am twice humiliated, twice betrayed in my own blood . . . It's you,
Rachid, you I'm thinking about . . . But you'll
never marry her. I've decided to take her away
myself, without your help, but I love you too, like
a son . . . We'll go to live on the Nadhor, she and
you, my two children, I'm an old tree that can no
longer bear fruit, but I'll cover you with my shade
. . . And the Keblout blood will recover its warmth,
regain its old thickness. And in the tribal secrecy
—like in a hothouse—all our defeats will bear their
fruits out of season. But you will never marry her!
If we die out in spite of everything, at least we will
barricade ourselves for the night, deep in our re-
conquered ruins . . . But hear what I say: You will
never marry her."

IV. . .

i. . .

The tribe remained without a leader; two of the
women died, named Zohra and Ouarda, the first repudiated, the second a widow with two daughters,
Mustapha's sisters, the two virgins of the Nadhor
who saw the beleaguered eagle bombard them from
above; stubbornly they climbed up toward the
wind-blown eyrie, and each time, as though to belie
its death before the decimated tribe that had found
it there, the ancient eagle long since abandoned by
its mate and its young, a victim of the virgins'
curiosity, dragged itself away from its nest, suddenly flapping off, its tragic efforts like those of
some hunted ancestor, circling high above the two
sisters like a blasé strategist fleeing the scene of a
victory within his grasp; then sudden rocks fell
from the bird's talons, unanswerable projectiles
whose fall consoled the tribe for its defeat, a sign
of aerial force unknown to the Elders. And one
sister vanished on a summer night; the older girl
said nothing to anyone; her body was found the
next day at the foot of the slope, a knife stuck in

175

her belt; and without a word, the tribe buried the
solitary virgin, the wild girl of fifteen who had
lost her little sister, supposed the eagle had taken
her, and left with a knife to lay siege to the inaccessible widower, killing herself in her fall. Had
she intended to attack the old bird? Did she foresee other encounters, or did she expect to use the
weapon against herself if she failed to find her
sister? And the little girl was never found; the
eagle itself didn't appear again; and the last
dotards of the leaderless tribe seized upon the
enigma: if the eagle had departed with its prey,
perhaps that was the sign that the malediction was
departing from them, thanks to the two virgins
sacrificed for Keblout's repose.

ii. . .

And in a dream the old legendary Keblout appeared to Rachid; in his deserter's cell, Rachid was
dreaming of anything but his trial; the tribunal
he feared was neither God's nor that of the French;
and the old legendary Keblout appeared in his cell
one night, with mustaches and tiger's eyes, a cud-

gel in his hand; the tribe gradually collected in the cell; the men linked elbows, but none dared approach Keblout; he, the ancestor with the wild-beast's face, his eyes dark and cunning, glanced around the cell, the cudgel within reach of his hand; merely by this ironic stare he laid bare each man's story, and it seemed to his descendants that he and he alone had actually lived out their own lives—making his way to the Nadhor where, already enduring their defeat, he died of it, still at the head of his tribe, on the terrain for which he had probably crossed the deserts of Egypt and Tripolitania, as his descendant Rachid was to cross them later, now reading his own story in Keblout's black and yellow eyes in a deserter's cell, in the twofold darkness of the prison twilight.

iii. . .

I was with Uncle Mokhtar and his daughter; I was playing them a tune of my own invention; Si Mokhtar was sick, and in the room where the three of us had been living for days and days there was an oil lamp he kept lighting and blowing out again,

looking for his tobacco-pouch that was perpetually
lost in the euphoria of the murderous weed . . . As
a group we scarcely deserved continuous lighting:
timid lovers in an ancestor's shadow—and Si
Mokhtar's unshaded lamp, reviving darkness, became with my lute an irresistible image, an abstraction of Nedjma's presence: her head buried in my
old companion's knees, she had revealed, during
childlike naps, the delicacy of her ankle under its
silver anklet, and the curve of her calf in that half-
darkness became an enticing danger of musical
chaos. After all the three of us were taking the rest
we had always longed for during the years of perpetual exile, of separation, of hard labor, or of idle-
ness and debauchery; finally we came back to the
last acres of the tribe, the last hearth (our relatives
were still living in tents and had isolated us here,
not without contempt, we whose fathers had let
themselves be deceived by the French, abandoning
the Twin Peaks for the cities of the conquerors);
still we had been greeted, received, and the ties of
blood gradually bound us close; in the heat of the
summer, we could live on fruits and coffee, even eating porcupine until it was time for the partridges
to lay. Nedjma, whose beauty and "family resem-
blance" had struck our relatives, now rode the
stable's last pony and did not seem dissatisfied with
her lot, though she had been snatched from her
adoptive mother and from the husband the latter
had given her to; besides, Nedjma's family was

178

more or less my own; the rape had made little or no
scandal . . . Now Si Mokhtar was looking for his
drum, while Nedjma seemed about to fall asleep;
I played all the more fiercely; hard, stupid notes
came from my hands, like tears bubbling up at the
sight of the inaccessible mistress and her father
whose madness seemed increasingly obvious to me:
he kept on gesturing for his drum while I was playing the lute, moving closer to Nedjma at the climax
. . . And just as I was about to lose my mind in the
racket the old fool made me constantly increase to
cover his stupid questions, the light suddenly burst
through the window opposite me and I closed my
eyes . . . It was no longer lamplight but storm
lightning; the downpour roused Nedjma from her
dream; then the sun appeared high in the sky and
Si Mokhtar fell asleep.

I found myself out in the desert beside
Nedjma; she was astonished at such boldness . . .
But I couldn't tell her I had felt I was betraying
Si Mokhtar . . . She asked me not to play the lute
any more in her presence; it reminded her of her
husband; then she ran off; under a fig-tree, she
prepared the huge copper cauldron that served
as both tub and laundry vat, filled it with water,
and let it warm in the sun. From the clearing where
Nedjma had left me, I saw the fig-tree swell in the
heat, huge, drunken wasps hovering over its leaves,
and though I had not lit my pipe again (how many
dead men, long before me, had been washed in that

cauldron handed down from father to son) I
thought I saw (two figs had just appeared upon
the tree's hump-backed trunk) a black man hidden
under another fig-tree (he was staring at Nedjma
frolicking in the cauldron) and it was too late to
yield to jealousy, too soon to begin struggling
with the black man who might claim to be not a
rival nor even an aesthete capable of appreciating
the scene, and perhaps, from where he was, he saw
more of the cauldron itself than the naked woman's
movements, although the fig-tree concealing him
was higher than the one that concealed my mistress'
body from me, so that my only possible choice was
not to think of the black man any more, to hope
that he wasn't seeing Nedjma and particularly
that she wouldn't move, that she wouldn't leave the
cauldron before the black man had left his fig-tree
or had fallen asleep, for if Nedjma saw the black
man . . . Either she would scream out and I would
have to intervene, taking action against a man
whose only crime consisted in enjoying the shade
of a fig-tree; or else, discovering the black man
and silently indicating his presence to me, she
would remain in her cauldron and even redouble
her flirtatiousness (that is always what the demon
of women suggests in such circumstances) and then
I would have to choose between the preventative
murder of the black man, or murder and suicide at
the very moment I was about to pluck the fruit of

the rape so long contemplated . . . But Nedjma was
leaving her bath! She appeared in all her splendor,
her hand gracefully resting on her sex, as a result
of the extraordinary modesty that kept me from
leaping toward the intruder whose imagination
must now be exceeding all limits . . . But how take
vengeance on an imaginary rival when I knew that
I myself was imagining still more than the black
man, I who was following the scene from three
perspectives, whereas neither Nedjma nor the black
man seemed to exist for each other, save by some
error on my part . . . I gazed at the two armpits
which all summer long are black and beaded with
sweat, a woman's vain secret dangerously exposed:
and Nedjma's breasts, their glowing thrust a revolution of the body that climaxed here under the
masculine sun, her breasts, revealed, owed all their
glamor to the modest movements of her arms, revealing beneath the shoulder that inextricable, that
rare variety of blazing weed whose sight alone is
enough to disturb, whose sublimated odor contains
the whole magical secret, all of Nedjma for any
man who has breathed it, any man to whom her
arms have opened . . . I knew that the black man
would be roused by such a sight. But I decided that
the essential thing was for the woman to notice
nothing. And innocence actually glistened on her
face. As for the black man, he was still lying under
the fig-tree from where I alone (I still think) perceived his hiding-place.

iv. . .

That splendid day, that incandescent corner of the sky!

I remembered my adventurous childhood; all true; I was free, I was happy in the Rhummel's bed; a lizard's childhood on the banks of a vanished river. During the hot hours, I went to sleep under the cedars, and sleep drove away sadness; I woke swollen with the heat. It was a joy like that one, under the fig-tree now, watching Nedjma leave her bath, remote but not out of sight, like irrepressible starlight.

Still haunted by the broken chants of my childhood, I wanted to translate this mad monologue for the girl the black man was devouring with his eyes: "Why not stay in the water? The bodies of desired women, like the cast-off skins of vipers, like volatile perfumes, are not made to waste away, rot and evaporate in our atmosphere: phials, jars and bath-tubs, that's where flowers should last, scales gleam, and women bloom, far from time and air, like a sunken continent or a scuttled ship, to be discovered later, a survival, an ultimate treasure.

182

And who has not imprisoned his mistress, dreamed of the woman who could wait for him, jailed in some ideal bath, unconscious and naked, in order to receive him unscarred after torment and exile? Bathe, Nedjma, I promise not to yield to melancholy when your charm is dissolved, for every attribute of your beauty has made the water a hundred times dearer to me; it is no whim that has compelled me to such love for merely a cauldron. Blindly I love the unconscious object where the last ghosts of my love contend . . . May it please heaven that you emerge washed of the gray ink my lizard nature inscribes so unjustly on your skin! What lover was ever so at bay as to desire the very dissolution of your charms? . . . And am I that lover? Ashamed to admit that my fiercest passion cannot survive the cauldron, the crude and symbolic crucible whose sides conceal the only human being my fate forbids me to approach and to embrace, to defend and to protect? Yet Nedjma was innocent. Did I have to lead her into temptation, speak to her of this black man and advise her to bathe in our room from now on, taking the risk of sending her father out at the sacred hour of the afternoon nap, but no longer exposing her beauty that has become mine now to the eyes of some stranger or even of a child, for the sight of a treasure is always dangerous, not only for the owner who would now prefer never having seen it, but for the thief and the mere *voyeur* who cannot rest in peace, who will lose the fruit of their theft or of their curiosity, all because they will never be able to conceal their treasure away from their own eyes and others'? Yes, Nedjma, hide yourself in your dress, in your cauldron or in your room, and be patient, wait until I send away everyone, down to the last rival, until I am invulnerable, until adversity has no further secrets for us; and even then, I shall look twice before running away with you; neither your husband nor your lovers nor even your father will ever give up trying to take you back, even if they momentarily entrust you to my care; that's why, rather than walk with you in the sun, I'd much rather join you in some dark room and leave it only with enough children to be sure of finding you again. And only a horde of alert and vigilant children can guarantee maternal virtue . . ."

But I couldn't say any of this in front of Nedjma, murmuring to myself the few words that might suggest the mystery of such thoughts . . . Moreover Nedjma had lain down beside me, wet still, and sleep invaded her relaxed body; I didn't know how to deal with my increasing anxiety, while the black man seemed to fall asleep too, exhausted by emotion, and the two brown figs, ripening, open to the first patrols of ants, made me chafe at my presence here in an overladen orchard where I vaguely felt myself the guardian, threatened from all sides, disputing Nedjma's problematical possession, I who merely wanted to help her remain alone as she was, waiting for the result of the struggle I knew had long since been joined, in my absence, when Si Mokhtar had not yet spoken to me of his daughter nor of the dramas of our tribe: I had already seen a part of the struggle, the elimination of Mourad, without being able to foretell the defeat of the two other lovers, ignorant of their exile; and there still remained Nedjma's adoptive mother who must have been looking for her, not to mention Kamel, Nedjma's legal husband, first victim of the kidnapping engineered by Si Mokhtar with my help; and now the black man who seemed unconcerned but who could also be aroused by Nedjma to contemplate another kidnapping here on our last territory, in the absence of all other males, save Si Mokhtar and myself, who could defend the honor of the tribe . . . Actually I saw that the black man lay motionless under his fig-tree as if nothing had happened, his face worn, deep in the sleep of some old animal, and I was about to attribute my fears to the hashish pipe that had gone out again when Nedjma wakened, stood up, walked, to my great relief, toward the fig-tree, the one in whose shade stood the cauldron which she lifted without waiting for me to help her and overturned, then walked back to her father's house with the empty cauldron, leaving me in an indefinable situation: was I to waken the black man now before the water (the water the fatal woman had bathed in) reached him? Wouldn't I then be like some lover saying to an intruder: "She's just bathed, get out of the way, this water contains all of her, blood and body alike, and I cannot endure its flowing over you"; even a black man, even a superstitious son of Africa might take such words badly and make them an excuse to hunt down the gazelle, damning himself with me; on the other hand, to leave the black man asleep was also to assure him the forbidden liquid that was now running in his direction; then he suddenly had the elegance to get up! Yet this black man was certainly a cunning creature: instead of leaving for good, he contented himself with a few jerks, like a lizard, giving ground only slightly to the advancing water, and obstinately lying down in the same tree's shade, to be dislodged once more by the stream from which a new jerk removed him again without putting an end to his strategy, as if he were confronting just any water, any stream which was not to invade his dreams and afford him a sense of swimming: I no longer doubted that Nedjma's charm would reach the imprudent man if this were not already the case, and I prayed that he would not go mad, that he would not contract some mental illness comparable to my passion, putting me under the obligation of interrupting his dream, me, a human being! I lit my pipe again with the intention of speaking to him: "Black man, leave this tree before nightfall, or else lose your way . . . Go home! The sun is sinking . . . While you are neither rival nor victim, we may talk, for though I am no easy wordmonger, it is long since my tongue has stirred, like a building infested with dragons!"

But I was not counting on the physical damages of the weed . . . My words crumbled with no further resonance, and as for the man addressed, supposing he vaguely heard me, he went right on with his nap and his jerks, so that I left my place, ashamed at having spoiled my day in this manner.

Si Mokhtar, whose face was incontestably red, stared at me, swearing he would rather spend his last days in solitude than watch our brains dissolve.

"Is it my fault?" I said, "and must I suffer for my least action, like some savage frightened by an airplane? If you hadn't brought me to Nedjma, you wouldn't tremble so at each of her disappearances . . ."

"I thought you were more energetic. If you weren't singing all the time . . . You've even lost my drum for me!"

"Here it is," I said. "Heaven! It's full of blood!"

"My toes were cut off by a thunderbolt while you were taking the sun," Si Mokhtar said. "But the blood is not wasted. Here, I'll drink it. Let's console ourselves by starting our music again. But be careful not to get excited. Our art requires tranquility, unflinching pacifism. Or else prepare to be tortured!"

"Your face . . ."

"It's nothing. Play."

There was nothing I could say. Obediently I picked up the lute as he added: "Play something I don't know, so that my drum has time to dry."

"You're badly hurt. And you still want to play your drum, even though your feet may be crushed?"

The door was pushed open.

"I knew I'd find you two here arguing," Nedjma said, "leaving me to the will of that black man out there . . ."

Heaven, I thought, my dreams are coming true!

"Ha! A black man is it?" Si Mokhtar said, suddenly laughing. "Well, you're in for it now! Never mind, my daughter! The black men are the friends of God, not to mention the fact that they play the drum so well."

V. . .

My left arm had grown considerably longer. The stream beside us rose above the pebbles, floating between earth and sky. I heard the insects making their way through the forest, and I even thought I heard the sap circulating by night. More, new streams and trees were about to be born deep in the earth, forcing me to cock my ears in the pleasures of insomnia. Dismissing a last-minute impulse to bathe, I stayed on my blanket. Soon my chaotic notions collapsed. I found I was greatly weakened. We would have to get back to the camp. Finally I took my place between my mistress and her father. It was too late for reflection. I felt coming to my lips the words of defiance I had suppressed for their sake. There was a long silence, each of us assuming an ironic expression to conceal his own perplexity. One of us would certainly have shouted bitter reproaches then if sudden thunderclaps hadn't restored our composure. Then Nedjma left us. Si Mokhtar, turning over on his blanket, made a long speech in the classical tongue of the Ulémas. I understood nothing. When I tried to wake him up, supposing he was having a nightmare, he made me keep still.

But the night was getting on. Suddenly Si Mokhtar stood up, despite his bandaged feet, seized by the demon of eloquence. His feet were bleeding. I couldn't endure the sight. The hashish fumes were leaving us through the window, but Si Mokhtar seemed stranger and stranger to me.

"I'm going to sleep, this time," he said. "I'm not ashamed of myself."

"You're so lucky," I answered.

The muezzin was already calling. He was obviously wrong about the time. Si Mokhtar, though punctilious on this point, did not get up for the morning ablutions. But the muezzin went on for a long time without stopping. At his last cry, it was really dawn, and I could overcome my insomnia.

vi. . .

We took supplies and a few belongings to spend a week in the forest. We walked a long way, without noticing ahead of us a dilapidated house that seemed to have no owner. Getting lost over and over again in the brambles, we finally found a field. The house wasn't far off. But none of us wanted to go there. We were tired. We pitched the tent for the night. A few hours after dinner, while father and daughter were sleeping, I heard a scream. I stood up, painfully. I listened carefully; nothing. The devil! What if it was just an accident? I raked some straw together to light the fire again. The northeast wind was still blowing across the field. It was cold. Only that scream kept me from going back to my blanket. But no one was screaming now; would I have to stay here until morning? But that's what I did, with a courage I'm proud of.

Heading straight for my campfire is a man wrapped in his burnoose, the hood pulled down over his face.

Without a word, he begins to warm his hands near me, then tells me his story in a tone so sincere, so afflicted, that I was glad I had waited all night long, and did the same for him; I had the impression that my own words did not please him, yet this didn't surprise me (on the contrary, I appreciated his lack of hypocrisy); as he talked I discovered he had a fine character; he stammered and swallowed too many consonants to be an Algerian, but he didn't sound like a foreigner either; did he have friends in the region? Perhaps he knew who had screamed before?

"Forgive this question, but did you happen to hear a scream during the night? Perhaps you were sleeping?"

"A scream!" the stranger said.

"Yes, that's why I stayed here with the fire, waiting to see if it would come again . . ."

"What an idea!" he said. "I heard nothing of the kind. God knows I have sharp enough ears! Maybe a bird . . ."

"No, it wasn't!" I exclaimed, red with anger. "Do you think I'm such a fool I'd leave my blanket for a bird? Look, I spend hours freezing over some

wretch and you think you can just make fun of
me?"

"Don't get excited . . ."

At this moment, Nedjma gave a terrible
scream. The man disappeared even more mysteri-
ously than he had come.

Trying to forget the faceless apparition,
promising myself to settle everything later, I
rushed in to find Nedjma trembling. As for Si
Mokhtar, I vainly tried to wake him, punching
him in the ribs, though he insisted on sleeping in
this cursed field, and I feared his sleep was the
sign of exhaustion. In order to lead us here, Si
Mokhtar had taken Nedjma on the crupper while
I walked behind, and I saw the blood dripping
through his bandages: this was after the obscure
accident that made Si Mokhtar's toes burst (when
we were both with him) without his having groaned
or screamed. Yet Si Mokhtar was sleeping, and I
would have to let him rest. So I put my head
against Nedjma's knees, before the dying fire.

How calm Nedjma's fears? Was she still
thinking about that black man? After all, the man
had shown rare politeness, had remained where he
was, gripped by some passion consisting of love
for Nedjma and adoration for the founder of the
tribe, the old Keblout whose descendant he too may
have been . . . For the history of our tribe is written nowhere, but no thread is ever broken for a man
who seeks out his origins. If the black man was

also a son of Keblout, his contempt for us was related to the distant attitude adopted by our relatives who had remained on the Nadhor, whereas Si Mokhtar and I belonged to the deserters' branch. And since all the men of the tribe were exiled or dead, this black man faithful to the Nadhor could even drive us off, since we were among those whose fathers had sold their share of the land and contributed to the ruin of the ancestral fabric.

But no. Si Mokhtar and I continued to enjoy the radiant weather which seems never to leave this country. Nedjma, jealous of the friendship which linked me to her father, had managed to make Si Mokhtar's presence burdensome to me, just as the old bandit himself now treated me distantly; and this is what made the attraction of this life *à trois* for me; this discord Nedjma unconsciously sowed everywhere was precisely the woman's weapon from which I hoped to receive a single wound before leaving, for separation seemed inevitable . . . Yet we kept silence about all these things, for we were not eager to disturb our existence . . . And then, before facing the future, we wanted to trace all the surviving members of the tribe, to confirm our origins in order to draw up a balance-sheet of bankruptcy, to attempt a reconciliation. For this, we would have to be admitted into the region, examine the vicinity . . . Which is what we did. But the halt in the field was prolonged by Si Mokhtar's sickness. He was delirious all day long . . . The next

193

day, we received a delegate from the tribe. An old man almost the same age as Si Mokhtar. He was soon joined by two more envoys. Nedjma was hiding under the tent, and when he saw her staring out at them, the first of the envoys burst out laughing:

"Tell that child to show her face. After all, she's one of us. She's a Keblout woman. It is our duty to keep her in the encampment. And besides, she's not made to live with fools . . ."

"We too are sons of Keblout . . ."

"That may be, but as men, what can you bring to the tribe? When your traitorous fathers left to work for the French, their purpose was presumably to return more powerful than they left. Where is your power? Is it the lute and the drum from the city? If you are sick and corrupt, that is your affair. But don't corrupt the women. They are not responsible for your betrayal. So we shall keep all our widows and all our daughters, though the tribe's last days have come. Let them go hungry under Keblout's tent, that is no disaster. We are still a few men with neither land nor money, guardians of the vanquished Smala. Leave us Nedjma and depart. I speak to you without anger . . ."

And the old messenger, after murmuring a few words with his followers, burst out laughing.

"You drive us away and you laugh?"

"We are laughing because, thank God, you are not the dangerous madmen we expected. Indeed, the French have taught you little enough . . .

They say that one of you, a Keblouti of the magistrates' branch, became a colonel. That one was dangerous. He served in the artillery. The French sent him to Morocco and Syria. He fought for them, married a Frenchwoman, made money. That one might have come as a traitor with his new power, buying back our land and dishonoring the tribe. We must believe he had forgotten the oath of his fathers. As for you, leave without fear. There is no hashish here, no wine, and no one will appreciate your music."

"Listen," I said, "we did not mean to upset you . . . You should at least respect the last philosopher of the tribe, the good Si Mokhtar who has lost his toes during a storm . . . He is about to die. You cannot take Nedjma away now. We ask you to let us live with you here a few days . . ."

"If he dies, we can admit him into the cemetery. But you must go immediately afterwards, and leave us the girl."

As a last shift, I agreed. Nedjma was sobbing at her feverish father's side; I lay down on the other side and this time went to sleep at once. I dreamed of Si Mokhtar in the ship sailing to Mecca, then in the Egyptian Sudan, on the Nile barge. When my dream was over, Si Mokhtar was dead. I was alone with the corpse. No sign of Nedjma. Finally the old messenger appeared, and behind him, hood raised, a man I immediately recognized: the black man from the fig-tree, the

one who was watching Nedjma bathe, the same man
who had come to warm himself at the campfire,
concealing his face.

"The girl is at the encampment," the old man
told me. "Go away now. We will wash the body."

Then the black man took me aside, with a
threatening look . . .

vii. . .

Great hunter, witch doctor, master of music and
physician to the poor, the black man had seen Si
Mokhtar coming; the black man was informed of
everything that went on in the *douar;* day and
night, from his early childhood, he had crossed the
Nadhor every which way; this season, he had seen
the old man come, had seen him encamped with the
girl, but had not noticed Rachid, had not heard
him speak until that day . . . And the black man
decided that Si Mokhtar and Nedjma were an
amoral couple, driven out of some city, come to
profane the ancestral earth. This was probably
what the black man thought. He was waiting for
the storm to begin, and stood in front of the open

door, his rifle in front of him. Taking advantage of a thunderclap followed by lightning and the loud hail, he fired through the opening where he saw the old Si Mokhtar's silhouette. The bullets riddled the old man's feet and he fainted. Thinking him asleep, not hearing the shot, not seeing the powder flash in the storm, nor the black man prowling around (with the help of the music, the two young people were in another world), Rachid and Nedjma had left too soon after the shower, taking advantage of the occasion. It was the first time they had been alone together since their meeting at the clinic years before . . . Meanwhile the black man had left his post, hidden the rifle in the brush, then hidden himself under the fig-tree . . . He had fallen asleep at once, without a thought for the shot he had just fired at the old man he didn't even know but whom he had judged, condemned and finally executed as he might have punished a child or slaughtered a marauding jackal.

And the black man had simply gone to sleep; Nedjma had not seen him; he had still not noticed Rachid. And the black man was simply sleeping when Nedjma surprised him under the fig-tree, soaked to the skin by the water from the cauldron she had just overturned, while Rachid went back to Si Mokhtar . . . The black man was sleeping in his own way. He sensed that Nedjma was looking at him. Slowly he opened his eyes, sneezed, jumped up, and Nedjma could not run away . . . The black man spoke to her, his large shining eyes fixed on her. He claimed he was sent by the Genies to guard the daughters of Keblout. He asked Nedjma what her connection was with old Si Mokhtar; he refused to believe he was her father; and Nedjma realized that the black man was mad. She ran away. Si Mokhtar was still lying down. Rachid could not calm her. She was convinced the black man would be spying on her from now on, contemplating some obscure sacrifice of which she believed herself the destined victim, without her companions' being aware of it . . . When the three of them left, the black man was still on the watch. He supposed that Si Mokhtar, having escaped murder by black magic, was now taking the offensive and would take Nedjma away from the tribe after trying to force himself upon it with her; but Rachid's presence intrigued the black man. He followed the three travelers as far as the field. He saw them pitch the tent and he waited for nightfall. Si Mokhtar screamed when he saw the black man creep close to him. Rachid and Nedjma had not noticed the figure at the tent opening. They thought Si Mokhtar had cried out in some bad dream. But the black man was still close by. He saw Rachid leave the tent, and light the fire. Then the black man wondered whether he had not fired at old Si Mokhtar unfairly, perhaps he really was Nedjma's father since he was not living alone with her and since a young man accompanied them. That was why the black man, after speaking to Rachid, visited the elders of the tribe who had sworn to live in the forest as ascetics . . . The black man told them about Rachid. Humbly he begged forgiveness for his rifle shot. The elders scarcely listened to him. They would hear of no reconciliation with kinsmen who had deserted the tribe, caused its ruin, leaving the mosque destroyed, the mausoleum without a standard, allying themselves to alien families—in short, betraying the tribe, which had sworn never to receive their descendants save as strangers scarcely deserving of charity . . . Finally the elders sent Rachid a delegate who demanded that he leave Nedjma behind on the Nadhor, taking the old man away with him . . . When Si Mokhtar died, Nedjma did not waken Rachid. She ran away alone, was found by the mad black man, and was led by main force to the women's camp.

Then the black man went to find Rachid and threatened him with death if he tried to see Nedjma again, without saying that he had kidnapped her . . . When Rachid grew angry, the black man took him by the arm:

"Keblout has said to protect only his daughters. As for the wandering males, the ancestor Keblout has said, let them live as savages, in the mountains and the valleys, those who have not defended their land . . ."

viii. . .

"*Ad'dahma Constantine*," the man standing at the window remarked; he had not slept all night long; Rachid did not stand up. He pulled his coat lapels over his old soldier's shirt, leaning forward, his forehead, nose and thick lip pressing against the glass, as if he were holding in his eyes the whole unaccountable suburb ·of Constantine which extended in slow motion, apparently inaccessible, leaping and petrified, with no hospitality nor mask of greatness—in the words of its returning citizens: *Ad'dahma*, the crushing . . . Rising gently toward the steep promontory that overhangs the wooded region of the High Plateau, its earth in turmoil since the Roman prospectors and the Genoese wheat caravans that rotted, unpaid for, in the Directory silos, Constantine was planted on its monumental site from which it still withheld itself by its paling lights, clustered together like wasps about to unfasten their alveoles from the rock without waiting for the solar order which guides their immediately scattered flight—unimaginable promontory in its vegetable haunt, a swarming desert wasps' nest thrust into the structure of the terrain, with its tiles, its catacombs, its aqueduct, its huts, its steps, its shadow of an arena open on all sides, barricaded—the rock, the enormous rock thrice gutted by the indefatigable river which flung itself upon it in sounding throbs, stubbornly hollowing out the triple hell with its wasted force, forever out of its still-unmade bed, too short-lived to reach its sepulcher of overturned blocks: the ruined cemetery the flood had never reached to surrender its soul, revived higher up in inextinguishable cascades, collapsing on the sides of the funnel, visible only from two bridges thrown over the Koudia, from the ravine where the wadi was no more than the sound of a waterfall echoed in a series of chasms, the noise of wild water that no cauldron, no basin contained, a muffled hiss without end or origin covering the stubborn hum of the machine whose speed was meanwhile diminishing, crossing the last traces of green, fields still forbidden to cattle, brilliant under the light crust of frost, dotted with naked, deformed fig-trees, carobs, overgrown mushrooms, upright orange-groves, troops of pomegranate-trees, acacias, walnuts, ravines of medlars and oaks leading to the approaches of the foggy, massive chaos—the rock, the solitude besieged by the brush, the enormous rock, and the winter petering out in its harsh and irritated folds . . . Sidi Mabrouk.

Wrapped in fog, the locomotive seemed lost at each loop and curve, each escapade, each trick of the sudden, persistent city—"crushing" close up as far away—Constantine with its stubborn camouflages, now the crevice of a hidden river, now a solitary skyscraper with its black helmet raised toward the abyss: a rock surprised by the invasion of iron, asphalt and concrete, specters linked to the peaks of silence, encircled by four bridges and two railroad stations, furrowed by the huge elevator between the gulf and the pool, assailed at the forest's edge, forced back, thrown down to the esplanade where the High Plateau is outlined— citadel of expectation and threat, forever tempted by decadence, shaken by age-old seizures—a site of earthquake and discord, open to the four winds, where the ground shudders and shows itself the master, making its own resistance eternal: Lamoricière succeeding the Turks after ten years' siege, and the reprisals of May 8, ten years after Benbadis and the Moslem Congress, and Rachid finally, ten years after his father's recall and murder, breathing again the smell of the rock, the essence of the cedars which he sensed behind the glass even before glimpsing the mountain's first spur. The train, reduced to a clatter of overdriven mares, crossed water for another day, screaming and jolting over old pastures—where once its horsepower was derived, Rachid mused, watching a stallion gallop alongside the train. The horse never glanced at the clattering engine that left it far behind, bearing off its usurped power.

Rachid had arrived . . . He was returning after a long absence. The station. The bridge. The cart blocking the way to the bus. It was the native rock Rachid had twice abandoned: first in uniform, then in the power of the woman he thought he was fleeing at the yards, on the scene of the crime, the second crime committed by a friend, and which brought Rachid back to the place where his father had fallen under the bullets of another friend Rachid knew intimately, one whom he suspected probably, but too late, for now he loved him more than the father struck down before he had ever seen the light of day. He had nothing to grieve over. It was only a surface sadness, a helmet like the rock that oppressed the deserter . . . He did not care about being pursued. Neither the medersa nor the army nor the yards had been able to hold him. Long before he had passed the lines, when he was organizing student strikes, the police had taught him inviolability. His hideout then was the lair of all outlaws: the Rimmis woods where he settled the night of his first return to Constantine; he had then just crossed Tripolitania on foot. But this time he headed straight for the house he had inherited from his father. Rachid pushed open the heavy wooden door without raising the knocker. The abandoned house overlooked the military tribunal through a dormer apparently the work of a

Turkish family eager to survey the Casbah's movements. Visible a hundred feet away, from the entrance of the alley, in the flood of garbage and mud the radical municipality preserved, supposedly by "popular tradition," Rachid's house, harshly whitewashed then daubed with methylene blue, made a frontier between the ghetto and the old city; to the left, two other partition structures closed off the alley; to the right, showing above the Commissariat wall—seat of the tribunal that judged deserters—a wild garden submerged the ruins of a fourth building razed by the Damrémont artillery during the second assault that ended with four days of shelling, all four rooms bursting into flame at pointblank range, and the heights of the Casbah answering shot for shot, as if the bullets had simply ricocheted along the wall and off the rock; then the powder magazine exploded, the last shot from the besieged; then it was conquest, house by house, to the height of the Koudia (today the civil prison where the conquered work off their sentences in other forms, for a crime much older than the one they were said to be guilty of, just as their bench of infamy actually rests on the silence of an abandoned powder magazine) which the besieging battery occupied, pulverizing the resistance nests one after the other; then, through the Place de la Brèche, where the modern city was to be built, and finally through the market gate, the entrance of Lamoricière himself, an axe in one hand, a saber in the other . . . "Near seven," Rachid thought . . . The hour when the French leader appeared in the ruins a century hasn't been enough to clear away; since Lamoricière's appearance this neighborhood hasn't changed its way of life: trade, bureaucracy, beggary. The great yards that were supposed to be opened had always excited the inhabitants like an exotic dream, worthy of the nuclear age, and which most of them were waiting for in order to start a home or buy a shirt . . . A few gigantic apartments, a few anarchic factories, and the persistent unemployment in the richest of the three departments, in the very city "where de Gaulle came to grant me citizenship . . . I hope no one saw me get off, alone and without luggage," Rachid grumbled, pulling the loose rail toward him, hoisting himself up the knee-high last step onto the terrace . . . "There's no one like rich boys to tell when a friend's had it, just by the way he walks . . . And who expected me back? They probably thought I struck it rich abroad, after driving my mother to despair . . . Strange no one approached me at the station . . . Not the moment to show up, for them or me." He knew each tenant of the huts that smelled of rancid oil, along the steep, mosaic-encrusted staircase. The oriental love of decoration devoured the infestations of light springing out of the alleys where modern urbanism seemed to turn away first. From the barracks ramparts, through the Place des Galettes and the

Place des Chameaux, Rachid had ventured since childhood as far as the ravines, to the once-sealed catacombs where the Dey's victims were hurled, sewn in sacks, over the overcrowded escarpments of Sidi Rached and El Kantara: the Rhummel devoured by the six arches of the Roman bridge, the only survivor of the seven bridges from Cirta, the Numidian capital—to the slums he examined at a distance among the gangs of children on the Perregaux footbridge: the slums of Bab El Djabia where a young spider by the name of Oum El Azz had lured him into her web . . . Not far from here Si Mokhtar had been born . . . Old Si Mokhtar, jailed by the prefect after the demonstrations of May 8, and who walked through the city alone, past the fascinated police officers, with a gag in his mouth showing two slogans of his own invention which crowds of people engraved in their memory:

> Vive la France
> Les Arabes silence!

Assassinated in circumstances never elucidated, Rachid's father had left his widows their jewels, his last property, debts of honor, and mortgages. The deceased had first taught Arabic at the medersa; suspended several times, then dismissed for not observing sanctions, he then lived off the pieces of land and the farm, debris of the ancestral wealth depreciated from generation to generation since the bloody fall of the fief, the now depopulated Nadhor . . . He had had four wives. Aïcha, the youngest, had not yet given birth to Rachid when they brought home her husband's body . . . It was Aïcha who was the guardian of her three older rivals until they remarried and left the house . . . Rachid, the last-born, was not to know his nine half-brothers and half-sisters for long; three women suckled him: Aïcha with her white breasts, the second wife, and the third wife holding out her black globes, showing all her teeth when she smiled, the Negress from Touggourt whose second wedding (blessed by Aïcha, the youngest of the four widows, the one who never remarried) was celebrated the first year Rachid went to school. Only his mother remained in the house. The other three women had left for other households, with their offspring . . . And Rachid had begun to loathe the place of sadness and abandon inherited from a father cut down in the prime of life, still well-known in Constantine and not only on account of his polygamy, another heritage which fated Rachid to feminine dictatorship; at ten, he adored two idols: the mother whom he refused to consider a widow, and the schoolteacher, Madame Clément, whom he refused to consider married . . . She would caress his cheek sometimes; the day he was promoted to the elementary course, he waited for the recreation period to rush into Madame Clément's courtyard . . . It was Monsieur Clément who found him. This time he received a rather rough smack on the cheek and was sent back to his new class from which he was quickly expelled: timidity became despondency, then playful savagery, finally hostility pure and simple. Then the other emotional bond with his mother broke . . . Rachid's father had taught in the medersa a long time before being discharged (polygamy, *folie des grandeurs*, trips abroad, impudence, intermittent alcoholism were preposterous grievances: he was actually accused of supporting a student committee that had just been formed under the banner of the Moslem Congress then being constituted) . . . It took three or four years to prepare for the medersa entrance examinations; Rachid had just found out the circumstances of his father's disappearance; some said that he died in an ambush, that there had been foul play. Rachid began studying fiercely, forced into the paternal tragedy by Aïcha's rare accounts and the thousand other rumors the murder inspired; after eight months of preparation he was accepted . . . And Rachid reconstituted the committee supported by his father . . . The scholarship provided two hundred and eight francs. He had to live on chick peas. Wearing the fez and wide trousers was obligatory.

At the year's end Rachid was elected president by an overwhelming majority. In his absence, the police seized the cash box and the papers. But the students of two other medersas had joined the movement. At Tlemcen there was a strike, followed by expulsions. Then the governor was forced to sign an agreement recognizing the student committees. Summoned first by the Intelligence Officers, then by the Cadi who pleaded with him, in the name of the deceased he had known so well, to devote himself to his studies, "the only way of working for the country," Rachid could only fail the examinations.

Old Si Mokhtar, another friend of the deceased, was waiting for nothing better than this extremity to intervene. He made Rachid enter a free medersa as a schoolmaster. The prefecture dislodged him during the course of the school year. Then Si Mokhtar put him in a pharmacy. He was forced to leave at the end of the month: he had refused to wear a fez, as well as the white shirt which was supposed to make him "presentable to the clientele." At eighteen, with a diploma in pharmacy, Rachid pocketed the one remaining gold piece which his mother unsewed from her own belt, and took Aïcha to stay with relatives; his mother was thus cared for to the end of her days while Rachid, unemployed, applied himself to dramatic art.

Three months later, he received at home a creature ruined by her impresario; the Arab theater was in terrible need of actresses. Rachid took Oum-El-Azz out of a life of prostitution to present her as the star of his new troupe. The girl's apprenticeship took several successive nights. Si Mokhtar brought a second-hand phonograph and lavished his advice. They lost no time winning the public's favor . . . The ordinary spectator couldn't know he was contributing to the livelihood of the mistress of the defaulter, an insubordinate (Rachid had not presented himself before the examination board), and the police grew quite civil when the gleaming brown Oum-El-Azz appeared on the boards without making them creak; they baptized her Kaltoum like most actresses and dancers of the period, after a famous singer of this name then celebrated in Egypt . . . When Oum-El-Azz bent over backwards, her waist a perfect arch, many turbans bent even quicker, and the savings of the future pilgrims were extended in convulsive fists, to Rachid's annoyance, for he had decided to go back into uniform and after fifteen days in jail headed for Tunisia; during the first days of the Ramadhan he deserted, made his way through Tripolitania and left Oum-El-Azz, for good this time, after a decisive scene: an Agha had ordered him to buy a bottle of anisette while he was entertaining the star, who then had all her favorite records hurled at her head, while the dignitary fled . . . Old Si Mokhtar came to his protégé's rescue. Cured of the theater, Rachid was thinking of going to France when he met the strange woman at the clinic. Rachid had merely come and gone, from city to city. Once more, he collapsed on the Rock. He found himself back in his house, alone, without news of Si Mokhtar's mother whom he had not seen since he had come back from the Red Sea trip with the old man, who had suddenly left him in Bône, without rhyme or reason, without saying he was going to disappear, like the three friends Rachid had just left behind at the yards . . .

ix. . . .

Slumped forward against the open window, Rachid found himself nose to nose with a cockroach that was also on its way home after the night . . . Rachid gave a faint groan, and the cockroach crossed its feelers, a sign of submission; the sky remained dark. "Maybe I could make a little money out of the house, but where will I find a broker who won't ruin me with the excuse of avenging my mother? . . ." The fifth day, he refused all invitations, wouldn't answer any more questions or let himself be drawn out by all the gossips who fell into his arms, embracing him as if he were returning from a war or some triumphant election tour.

He turned under the footbridge; the establishment that stopped him opened off a paved alley, a few steps from the medersa. It was a shed divided in half by a wood partition separating the drinkers from the smokers. Through the fetid cloud rising to the ceiling, Rachid caught sight of another deserter, a student over his books, some players holding their cards far from their eyes, feigning indifference and fatigue . . . At the door of the *fondouk*, a low counter forced a decision; the man holding the sachets was sitting behind it, an Olympian of twenty, his forehead bulbous. Rachid had thought the man was in the psychiatric ward.

"You got away from them again, brother Abdallah!"

Rachid embraced the master of the *fondouk* who left his counter and accompanied him behind the partition, catching the attention of the players long enough to allow for a false deal. The sun caught the tail of a cat creeping into the smokers' corner. Exhausted, the cat stretched out opposite Abdallah's pointed slipper. Rachid was pushed between three men in overalls. The one with a broken nose held out the pipe whose stem was a green reed. Abdallah and the cat purred louder. Abdallah smiled to himself; he dropped a brown pellet that made a dull sound as it fell onto the table between a paper spread out under the olives and a lily in a soda bottle, swaying with the smoke from the pipe.

Traditionally it was the owner who opened the session and introduced the visitors. He was somewhere between his fortieth and fiftieth puff. Huge and solemn, Abdallah contemplated the wet reed for a moment and wiped it off with the back of his sleeve, but did not light up before emptying the teapot and helping himself to the date box, while the man with the broken nose unsheathed his knife, sliced off a piece of greenish substance the size of half a date pit, and reduced it to sticky bits with a patience, a sad, insistent forbearance that made Rachid tremble (though he could not, properly speaking, pass for a novice). Finally Abdallah joined in, mixing the pale tobacco with the greenish fragments that looked grey in the sun that had come out again.

"Fix the parachutes," the man with the broken nose said, while the master of the *fondouk* made the mixture, prodding the grains of chopped concentrated hashish heated on a brick being worked into one-gram tablets wrapped in cellophane.

"Real scorpion juice, good for our black hearts."

The man with a broken nose held out a glass half full of water which Abdallah had set on the edge of the bench; the pipe filled, he plunged the reed into the water, under Rachid's bewildered eyes, for he had smoked only rolled cigarettes, "shells" the initiates called them, back at the medersa; but this was the canon itself. The man with a broken nose applied his lips between the edge of the glass and his fingers that pressed against the bowl of the pipe which he held out to the match Abdallah moved over the whole surface of the tobacco; the latter was immediately covered with glowing points; Rachid took the first puff, according to the custom. He smoked confidently making the little points glow again and the water bubble noisily as it yellowed. Abdallah took the pipe next, then the man with the broken nose, then the two other men who, from their metallic dentures, their striped shirts and the amount of smoke they consumed, seemed to Rachid like knights of some order founded on the renunciation of the human carcass. The one who looked oldest, considering his white hair, despite his white teeth, hugged his banjo and released a toneless voice:

> With her slipper, with her slipper.
> She left the baths with her slipper.

The singer skillfully disengaged himself from his song about a city girl in clogs, and Abdallah imagined himself far from his crowd of bums, manager of the Casino of Constantine after the proclamation of Independence. He waited until the song was over to reveal the ideas obviously inspired by the shepherd he had worked for in his childhood: ". . . I'm getting thinner from my wrists to my shoulders even though my body stays healthy. It's neither wine nor *kief*. Besides, I eat like four men and I'm losing weight. To get fresh air, I go the tourist way, early in the morning . . . What's worst of all about all my exercise is that they show how my bones are wasting away. The doctor says, your lungs are all right. But I know I'll die of suffocation, like fish . . . I'm growing old, and I have more and more ideas; and each time I get back up I fall down further . . ."

"Me," Rachid interrupted, "what I remember are the fights from when I was a kid."

Rachid was interrupted in his turn; the old singer bawled out, talking about something altogether different.

"Besides, if I counted my years, I'd be dead long ago, and since I was registered one war after I was born, when the government started to call us citizens, for better or for worse . . . Officially, I had four children in my family papers, they said I was a farmer. All I've ever farmed in my life is a hemp field. They turned me in. I sold the field, I turned into a chick-pea vendor, I went back to the hemp on account of my troubles, but now I have neither field nor children: There's my divorced daughter who makes a little here and there, and my other daughter who brings up the kids of a caïd who can't even get me a hunting license, there's my boy who works in a restaurant in Tunis, passing himself off as a Neapolitan. The older boy,

215

my only support, died of typhoid. So I took a second wife, but the first one died in her prime . . ."

X. . .

At the school in my neighborhood Madame Clément, the teacher, hit Mouloud on the head with a ruler. Our leader Bozambo took out his knife and offered it to Mouloud who tossed it at the teacher's feet without taking revenge.

Mouloud was crying.

The whole school was loyal to Bozambo, who had to repeat every class.

Mouloud was crying. Mario, Marc and Henri's brother, each in turn in love with Madame Clément's niece, hit Mouloud on the neck with his umbrella. I wasn't afraid of Mouloud any more and I threw my slate in his face.

Monsieur Clément came running into the classroom. He took Zoubir, Mouloud's older brother, by the ears and lifted him like a rabbit. Out of respect for Monsieur Clément, we rolled on the ground laughing. Monsieur Clément laughed. Mouloud was crying. Bozambo took back his knife under Monsieur Clément's nose, and Monsieur Clément got angry.

Bozambo's cousin Chérif took out his grammar:

général   généraux
amical   amicaux

"Rachid, to the blackboard!" Madame Clément said. "Mouloud, take your things! . . ."

Rachid no longer heard her voice; he was swimming in the deep calm of his memory, jeering, indifferent. The words escaped in fireworks he was the first to be astonished by, but he no longer heard them to the end, speaking quickly, stumbling through as best he could, unthinking, with a dazzling facility that swept him still further, though he was pursuing a series of chaotic dreams whose vanished substance did not rush in upon him with the words, but propelled them, impregnated them, gave them color and form. Occasionally, taking off his dark glasses pausing, he suddenly started in again, glancing around half-triumphant, half-persecuted, without answering the looks, the smiles, the outraged silence of the man with the broken nose—talking faster in his overcharged voice which he seemed to intend for some inaccessible contradictor, himself perhaps, although he still did not hear his own voice:

"Bozambo had a brother even stronger than he was, the glory of Constantine . . ."

Abdallah nodded and added: "Killed during the war . . ."

"The two brothers used to fight all the time. It was fate. One of them had to die in the war . . . They lived near the rich part of town. One day, their mother caught them with a crazy woman that hung around the neighborhood . . ."

"Not so crazy as all that," Abdallah said. "It was her way of keeping away from the pimps. I know some who used to work for her . . ."

"Well," Rachid went on, "the mother must have known what her tricks were. She saw what had come over her two children. She began watching them even closer. Ferhat (Bozambo to his friends) and Aïssa are my eyes, she used to tell everyone, while they laid ambushes for each other. The crazy woman had disappeared, but the two brothers went on threatening each other, picking fights and finally actually fighting, because Bozambo wouldn't admit he was beaten, and Aïssa was a little bigger than he was. . . . But the mother watched over them. She did everything in her power to make them forget the crazy woman, found them shoes, even let Bozambo go to Algiers to play the tambourine with a truckload of musicians . . . Nothing did any good. The two brothers terrorized the whole neighborhood. They sold the anisette their father hid for the Jewish holidays, and they fought over the money. Finally the father gave up his business and went back somewhere where his mother-in-law soon joined him . . . But the poor woman stayed with her children, bandits or not. Then she began to go a little crazy . . . She wanted to marry them off, apparently, to a neighbor's daughter, without even choosing between the two fruits of her womb, for both were out of reach, and not even old enough to marry, since Bozambo had just left school . . . The mother certainly lost her head. . . . And then the two brothers met . . . Actually, they began quarrelling as if they were both to be left for dead. They started from a distance, a stone's throw, in the whorehouse hallway—started! Even at the "Rose de Blida"—one of the most popular. Aïssa had only one hole in his forehead, and the blood ran down into his nose. Bozambo had several holes, in his face too, but he wasn't bleeding much more. He drove forward, his eyes closed. He picked up old scraps of tile and threw them as hard as he could, taking just enough time to aim, and the blows followed each other thick and fast, like a repeating rifle, two or three, one after the other. Aïssa stopped throwing stones; he picked up the projectiles Bozambo was throwing at him and tossed them back. The two brothers ran around like gadflies. At each throw, they covered their face or their head. Blood flowed into the whores' slippers, the beggars' bowls and over the illegally sold packs of cigarettes . . . Then the two brothers started crying; they cried over their interminable fight, lectured by the madams in light dresses; the passers-by castigated them with proverbs. Hordes of children holding each other by the hand passed tiles to the belligerents, ready to follow their example, and then the mother came. She screamed, elbowing the women out of the way. A good number of the spectators had rushed into a bar. Bozambo and his brother beat a retreat, still continuing the battle, while their mother concealed all the pieces of tile she could find under her dress, slipping in the puddles of blood. . . . What a story! she didn't want to go back home, saying that she was sure to find the body of one of her children on the doorstep . . . No one had the courage to look for the antagonists: it was funny to know that they were around somewhere, covered with blood, fighting or spying on each other. And that same evening, the relatives used all their powers of persuasion on each boy. My mother kept me home, but that night I jumped over the wall and fell on the two brothers . . . They were playing cards near the place where they had been fighting, not trying to cheat, but ready to spring at each others' throats if there was the slightest excuse for it . . .

xi. . .

The old singer was already talking about entirely
different things, leaning toward Abdallah; the man
with the broken nose lowered his head, calm, jubi-
lant, and Rachid felt again as if he were traveling
underground, or perhaps across prairies of plenti-
tude and unconsciousness, where he could live with
the insects, the water of the fountain, the stones,
the shadows outside, when his thought barely rose
above the simplicity of beasts . . . Since childhood,
he had been able to catch only increasingly fragmentary snatches—disparate, intense: flashes of
the paradise ravaged by the combustion of the
hours, a rosary of delayed-action bombs which
the heavens held suspended over the always clandestine joys, reduced to taking refuge in the sub-
soil of the frailest being, the child still perching
on his skylight, still curious about the day's brilliance followed by the encroaching shadows, the
fear of remaining the world's prisoner, when other
universes were raining night and day upon Rachid,
whether he was asleep in the poplar-wood cradle

with the little windows to breathe through, or
whether he was taking his first steps in the rain. . . .
Rachid hadn't traveled during his childhood; he
had travel in his blood; a nomad's son conceived
in a drunken fit, with the sense of freedom, of
contemplative heights; the mysteries rained down,
and Rachid had always known the earth would pass
like a dream once people could live in airplanes:
his nose in the air, at four or five, he had conceived
his aeronautics, despite the fall of the mysteries
he was still hunting for alone without anything
being explained, swallowing his mother's stories
like agreeable but uninteresting sleeping-pills . . .
He wore no hat, his slippers usually stayed on the
doorstep, and the word God itself, which preoccupied Aïcha's widowhood, lay with the balls lost on
the roof . . . Rachid the adolescent did not remember his early childhood; he only felt the immediate
consciousness of the early years; like a scar. Rachid
of today seemed to him only a thick layer of lichen
stifling the other one, the Paradisiac and frail
Rachid lost in the prime of life . . . Even at thirty,
nomad as he was, he believed only in his shadow,
and it seemed to him that the surplus of the years
would eventually be reabsorbed, sucked into the
void, would channel his past as it rose in spate as
if he had been conscious of drawing a circle without
leaving the point of departure which he vaguely
situated between the moment he left his cradle and
his roamings around the Rock, so that the circle

was only a grudging promenade that had almost
ruined him, from which he groped his way back,
not only himself—the adolescent returning to the
cradle, no, his ghost consigned to this pathetic
blind man's bluff, stumbling over the fabulous
past, the dawn, the first childhood where he lay
prostrate, repeating the words and gestures of the
human race with a fluidity that left him inwardly
intact, like a seed about to germinate under other
skies, a stray lump endowed with imperturbable
recollections, still materially experiencing his existence in flight, like a weed or like water, and, at
around five or six, he recalled adopting the dark
brilliance of a stucco wall he embraced, addressing
his orphan monologues to it—the wall was part of
the alley; to reach it, he had to run through the
terrible heat and straighten up in tears—but the
wall was there. Rachid bit the clay provoking the
bypassers to an outburst of inaccessible laughter,
but they could neither laugh nor bite the clay nor
run after the lizards on hands and knees, without
giving up hope of catching them . . . But as the
years passed, the vile canvases of the child's illusions split open; he had only the daily degrada-
tions, catnaps and oblivion . . . He emerged incognito and severe: school was sadder, poorer than the
wall; his childhood was lost. The world would grow
no larger, reduced to a cruel vision of its limits;
his dream lost its obscurity, his brain shrank at
the discovery of so many refuges gone, his tongue

223

refused to pulverize the ideas Rachid had grown
so furiously conscious of, as if the world's final
forms now weighed heavy as horns on his head.

xii. . .

Rachid didn't leave the *fondouk* balcony any more;
the stretch of mosaic, of wrought iron; he didn't
leave the savage collectivity, the Divan, the intimate revery of the horde anymore: ten or twenty
men of all ages—silent dreamers who scarcely
knew each other—scattered along the balcony,
deeply intoxicated, at the cliff top; in one of the
Rock's honeycombs, the refuge where they met
night and day, with the odor of basil and mint,
the taste of mouldy tea, the cedars, the storks, the
crickets' timid Morse, the unconcluded shrilling of
their calm agony. Rachid had long since discovered
the *fondouk* of which he had become the master,
after losing himself from city to city; he would
not leave Constantine again; he would probably
die on the balcony, in a cloud of the forbidden
weed; as a child, he had noticed the severe heads
of the troglodytes; he had heard the music, and

without seeming to had stopped in front of the *fondouk*, where the rare pedestrians bent like trees beneath the spellbinding echo of the tambourine whose violence was as rousing as a domestic thunder, covering the warm hail, the crescendo of the lute, the weight and speed of the inner tears whose flow Rachid furtively felt like some attentive plant, while there rose from another part of the abyss a flute melody, a breath of virile summer, of vibrant night drunk off like a fly in the coffee; as a child, Rachid had guessed that this melody came from a secret society, half-necropolis, half-prison, although he had never heard anyone speak of the sect of the Assassins. He knew, like every child, that the music-lovers of the *fondouk* smoked something besides tobacco, something that made them crazy, but not like drunkards . . . Later, through the half-open door he had seen a corner of the balcony, the aviary . . . Now, he knew he was caught, like the nightingale and the canaries you could hear at the doorway of the *fondouk*, and he no longer dreamed of leaving. It had happened to him when he came back from Bône, after the murder; questioning him at the time, people had supposed and spread around Constantine that Rachid had his story to tell, without being exactly an accomplice, and everyone had tried to find out what it was. "It's nothing. Just an accident," he answered; a *crime of passion*, the newspapers said. Rachid no longer mentioned it, didn't want to talk about it anymore; as he grew used to the *fondouk*, his language grew rarefied, just as his dark gaze grew misty and vague, and his ribs stood out under his old soldier's shirt, as if his body, desiccating, had to reveal the skeleton, just the skeleton of the powerful man he might have been in other circumstances. . . .

i. . .

The murderer, who was usually called "Rachid's friend," was condemned to twenty years of hard labor; some thought, without saying much about it: "A third crime hangs over Rachid's head. Wasn't his father killed before he was born? And now one of his friends commits another murder . . . At the third incident, Rachid will talk." That's how the sleuths of Constantine put it, a city where more detective stories are read than anywhere else in the world. The citizens who thought about Rachid's case were, moreover, the last to bother with it; even when he gave evidence—when they surrounded him outside the court—he was not particularly bothered. They had watched him exchange signals with the accused, send him cigarettes through the lawyer: nothing extraordinary. The friend was in prison. Rachid wasn't looking for any more work, wasn't leaving the *fondouk* where he had stopped in after an interval of isolation, which he considered salutary, in his mother's house, the latter having died without his knowing it while he was working "at the scene of the tragedy" as the reporters called it, which made Rachid laugh.

Two nights after the crime, he had come back to Constantine by train alone, and had shut himself up in his mother's house, leaving after the fifth day and going to Abdallah's . . .

People were furious . . . They disapproved of Rachid's renouncing his family, burying himself in a *fondouk*, he who had been able to do nothing to avenge the honorable deceased who had once made such a scandal but whose fame, thanks to his tragic death, had acquired the salt of legend; he was talked about like a knight struck down in the prime of life by a lesser rival . . . Not only had Rachid never sought out the murderer—"his father was killed with a rifle in a cave"—but had made friends with another murderer, slipping into debauchery, reduced to the status of a day-laborer, then of an idler living on nothing but hemp, master of the *fondouk* now, the triumphant pariah on the scene of his own collapse and downfall. People were indignant at seeing Rachid with old offenders, men without profession, without domicile, without papers, half-mad, like Abdallah who was always just out of the asylum; it was he who first renewed his intimacy with Rachid, the fifth day after his return from the "scene of the crime," as the reporters called it.

ii. . .

One of these scribblers, haggard and badly dressed, looked like a public scribe. He had discovered Abdallah's *fondouk,* and Abdallah had offered to take him to the other *fondouk,* where he had just put Rachid in charge. Even now, Rachid never left the *fondouk.* Abdallah had put him in charge of it. The work was simple; all he had to do was prepare the pipes, pour the tea, take in the money, and the journalist found Rachid spellbound in the tavern on the side of the abyss; now there were mosaics inlaid along the walls, all around the room. The important smokers, and Rachid, the inaccessible manager, rarely had access to the wrought-iron balcony recently painted green, in the luminous haze of the abyss, among the doves, the storks, the wild olive-trees; this was the city's heart, a honeycomb in the rock, an arachnean retreat above the abyss, and the balcony seemed a hammock filled with figures gathered from the river's deathbed in a bubbling-up of tombstones surfaced by the infrequent surges of the Rhummel whose strength was always in suspension, receiving only rare, unpromising rains, like a blood transfusion for an old man whose bones are already dried out . . . Rachid no longer left the *fondouk*, the wrought-iron prow, the deep atmosphere of basil, cedar and twilight on the brink of the precipice—his nostrils were filled with mint, and the reporter (the scribe) bent over the one lily, near the aviary; the mint and the lily—the green tea brewed slowly, blackened as it cooled, the sugar at the bottom never dissolved, for it was time for mint-tea day and night on the balcony lately fastened like a challenge above the abyss where Constantine broods over its exhausted river.

iii. . .

"Two cities," Rachid murmured, "all I know is two: the city where I was born (he needed only lower his head over the pot of basil and lean down;

229

between the plant's thick foliage and the railing of the balcony, merely by sitting still, turning away from this reporter more wretched than any public scribe, Rachid could breathe the strong odor of the cedars among which his father's body had fallen, shot with his own hunting rifle) . . . The city where I was born, here, above the woods where the criminal . . ." "But the other crime . . . Not so far back," the scribe said. "I love two cities: the city where I was born . . ." The scribe took the pipe.

"And the city where I lost my sleep, on the banks of the other river, over there on the plain, with the old pirate who was looking for his daughter and was shot . . ."

"Shot?"

"Yes, by the black man of our tribe. Old Si Mokhtar had just carried off his daughter, his own daughter, but the black man wouldn't believe it, and he stood in front of the door with his rifle . . ."

"A third crime?"

"One stormy night out in the brush, a region almost as wild as this one . . . And the black man shot at the old bandit, but there was thunder, and the shot sounded like a dream . . . I never heard a thing . . ."

"But Mourad?"

iv. . .

Rachid had turned a little further. He was cleaning the pipe, knocking the ashes into the void. He
handed the glass to the scribe and went on after
another pause, his forehead leaning against the
cold rail of the balcony, letting his eyes fall on the
calm, shadowy bank, at the foot of the Rock . . .
"The same destiny has willed the two cities to have
their ruins near them. But nowhere else could the
two matchless cities be neighbors, both sacked,
deserted, rebuilt, one after the other, mirroring
each other without seeing each other: two riders
at the end of the race, disputing the province where
they meant to renew their youth despite the past,
by the ebb and flow that restored like an inad-
missible hope, a dream beyond memory, the caval-
cade from Numidian times supplanted by the
heavy cohorts of the Roman descendants rising out
of the depths of the night . . . For cities besieged
too often have no taste for sleep any more, still
await defeat, can never be surprised, nor vanquished . . ."

231

V. . .

Rachid could no longer tell what he was thinking
from what he was saying. Perhaps he was talking
too much? Perhaps he was only expressing the
froth of his thoughts, his forehead pressed against
the cold, moist rail, as though to contain the cata-
ract . . . He filled the pipe and began again, slowly,
distinctly, his eyes fixed on the foot of the Rock:
". . . Not the remains of the Romans. Not that kind
of ruins, where the soul of the multitudes has only
time to waste away, engraving their farewell in the
rock, but the ruins watermarked from all time,
the ruins steeped in the blood of our veins, the
ruins we carry in secret, without ever finding the
place or the time suitable for seeing them: the
inestimable ruins of the present . . . I have lived in
both places, the rock, then the plain where Cirta
and Hippone knew greatness and afterwards the
decline for which the citadels and the women wear
their sempiternal mourning, in their cruel longev-
ity of city-mothers; the architects have nothing
left to do there, and the vagabonds have not the

232

courage to seek refuge longer than a single night; thus glory and defeat have founded the eternity of ruins upon the growth of new cities, more alive yet severed from their history, deprived of the charm of childhood to the benefit of their ennobled specters, like pictures of dead brides that make their living replicas grow pale; what has perished flourishes to the detriment of all that is yet to be born . . . Constantine and Bône, the two cities that dominated ancient Numidia, today reduced to a French department . . . Two souls struggling for the power abdicated by the Numidians. Constantine struggling for Cirta, and Bône for Hippone, as if the stake of the past, petrified in a region apparently lost, constituted the only ordeal for the future champions: it is enough to set the Ancestors forward to discover the triumphal phase, the key of the victory refused to Jugurtha, the indestructible germ of the nation spread between two continents, from the Sublime Porte to the Arc de Triomphe, the Old Numidia where the Roman descendants have succeeded each other, the Numidia whose cavaliers have never returned from the slaughter house, any more than the corsairs have returned who blockaded Charles the Fifth . . . In their country neither the Numidians nor the Barbary pirates conceived in peace. They leave it to us virgin in a hostile desert, while the colonists follow one another, pretenders without law and without love . . ."

vi. . .

And it's up to me, Rachid, a nomad in forced residence, to glimpse the irresistible form of the virgin at bay, my blood and my country; up to me to see appearing under its first Arab name (El Djezair) the Numidia Jugurtha had left for dead; and I, the old orphan, I was to relive the obscure martyrology for some Salammbô of my obscure lineage; I too had to accept the same challenge, lost so many times, in order to assume the end of the disaster, to lose my Salammbô and to abandon hope in my turn, certain of having emptied the cup of bitterness for the relief of the unknown man who will supplant me . . . Nomad of a prematurely exhausted blood, I had to be born in Cirta, the capital of the vanished Numidians, in the shadow of a father murdered before I ever saw the light of day; I who was not protected by a father and who seemed to live at his expense the time he might have yielded to me gradually—I felt like a piece of broken pottery, an insignificant fragment from an age-old architecture. I thought

234

of Cirta; I found ancestors there nearer than my father to the blood shed at my feet like a threat of drowning at each step I might make to escape his vengeance.

"You knew the murderer?"

"He was older than my father, and his close relative . . . I didn't know it when I followed the old bandit to another city that seduced me immediately . . . And at Bône I discovered the unknown woman had deceived me . . . It was his daughter. And I didn't know she was my evil star, the Salammbô who would give a meaning to the sacrifice . . . Under the palm trees of Bône other ruins were waiting for me, where I was to run like a lizard driven out of his burrow . . . She lived far away from her father whom she recognized too late; strangers had married her to a man who may have been her brother; and I dreamed day and night under the harbor palms, experiencing my fragile life like an unsuspected break in the stem toward the root . . . The ray of light with which she had blinded me made my pains all the worse; yes, I smoked like paper under a magnifying glass, sickened by the evil chimera . . . She was merely the sign of my ruin, a vain hope of escape. I could neither resign myself to the light of day, nor recover my star, for it had lost its virginal luster . . . The twilight of a star: that was all its dim beauty . . . A deflowered Salammbô who had already lived her tragedy, a vestal who had already shed her blood . . . A married woman. I know no one who has approached her without losing her, and that is how the rivals multiplied . . . Mourad, first of all."

The scribe gave a start and almost fell off his chair, suddenly dizzy. But he fell silent, his throat dry, after asking one question:

"And then?"

Rachid did not react. He let the match blacken his thumb, until it was burnt up. Then he remarked, in a puff of smoke:

"Wait a minute, don't get me wrong."

But the scribe was in Nirvana. He was dozing, his head ringing, pulling his jacket around him. Rachid continued in a low voice, as though to convince himself of something long recognized, but still incredible:

"Mourad's crime wasn't a crime. He didn't love Suzy."

vii. . .

The scribe was prepared to take notes from the moment he came in, but he did no such thing, swept into a column of harsh light and smoke, hanging from Rachid's lips—Rachid impassive, clenching the pipe between his teeth, leaning over the balcony, the evening wind in his shirt. And Rachid stared at the river deep in the chasm: the Rhummel that flows only a few weeks out of the year, dissipated in the rock, with neither lake nor delta, a pseudo-stream vanquished by the riddles of the terrain, like Rachid, an only son inopportunely born of a father assassinated before his birth; it was the father who was carrying the hunting rifle, and it was his body that was found in the cave; Rachid's mother gave birth shortly after the removal of the body, never having counted the hours or the days, for she was the fourth wife, overburdened with cares, as astonished by her pregnancy as by her widowhood, so that Rachid, losing his mother twenty years later, was still to know nothing of the two dead beings who left him facing the abyss—the man and the wadi confronted by the abyss—Rachid having never heard a divulging word, and the Rhummel having never received the storm's wealth under the rock where its birth had so cruelly dashed it, keeping it at a distance from its natal Atlas to the sea, modifying its course. For the escaped wadi is only a false Rhummel that has become the Great River, the Wadi El Kebir, in memory of the other lost river: the Guadalquivir, the river the Moors driven out of Spain could not take with them; Guadalquivir, Wadi El Kebir, the river abandoned in Spain was recovered beyond the Strait, but this time vanquished, tracked down under the Rock like the Moors driven from Andalusia, Rachid's fathers, and Rachid himself, he too returned from a futile escape to the harbor where adversity in the form of a woman waited for him—Nedjma the Andalusian—the daughter of the Frenchwoman who had set the four suitors against each other, three from the same tribe, the three descendants of Keblout, for it was Nedjma's mother, the Frenchwoman, who had caused the tribe's downfall by seducing the last three males none of whom was worthy to survive the ruin of the Nadhor . . . And the last, the oldest of the three, had waited too long! More than twenty years. Not mentioning that Nedjma was probably his daughter, not mentioning how he had left his accomplice in the cave, the close relative, one of the other two males, the one whose victimized blood now flowed only in Rachid's veins—that accomplice, his rival, the man who never went out without his rifle, whose side he never left until the day the two of them carried off Nedjma's mother, imagining they were avenging the other relative, the third man, Sidi Ahmed, from whom the Frenchwoman had already been kidnaped in a resort town by the puritan, the fourth suitor, the one whose name Kamel bore, and Kamel married Nedjma . . . And Si Mokhtar had just died too, after carrying off Nedjma. Had Rachid's father seduced the French-

woman before being killed, had he replaced Si
Mokhtar before being killed in the cave where the
Frenchwoman had been left by the two ravishers?
Rachid's father or Si Mokhtar, dead in confusion:
which of the two engendered Nedjma there in the
cave? It was to find this out that Rachid had
spared his father's murderer, and Si Mokhtar had
died without knowing it himself, and Rachid would
never know to what degree Nedjma, the woman
made adversity, was a tributary of the blood shed
in the cave: for men were to dispute not only
Nedjma's favors but even her paternity, as if her
French mother, in a shameless forgetfulness, or in
order not to have to choose between four men, two
by two, had not even separated the last two, her
ravishers thus condemning the girl to her destiny
as a forbidden flower, threatened to the depth and
the fragility of her roots . . . Just as the Rhummel
betrayed in its torrential violence, delivered to
another course than its own, just as the betrayed
Rhummel hurls itself into the sea through the
Wadi El Kebir, the recollection of the river lost
in Spain, the pseudo-Rhummel escaped from its
destiny and from its dried bed, just as Rachid's
father, murdered in the nuptial cave, was torn
from the warm body of his mistress by Si Mokhtar,
his rival and near relative who married the woman
in secret, and it was then that Nedjma was conceived, a star of blood sprung from the murder to

obstruct vengeance, Nedjma whom no husband could win over, Nedjma the ogress of obscure blood, like that of the black man who killed Si Mokhtar, the ogress who died of hunger after eating her three brothers (for Mourad, to whom she was secretly engaged, then Lakhdar whom she loved, were the two sons of Sidi Ahmed, the first ravisher supplanted by the puritan, Kamel's father, and Kamel married to Nedjma who left him without a divorce in order to end her days sequestered on the Nadhor after Si Mokhtar's death, Si Mokhtar having taken her there with Rachid after the false pilgrimage to Mecca, during the ultimate rape from which Rachid alone had returned), Nedjma the trembling drop of water that swept Rachid off his Rock, drawing him toward the sea, in Bône, where she had just been married . . . Just as his father had died when Rachid came into the world, so when Rachid reached the port, Nedjma was already Kamel's wife . . . And that evening, on the balcony, leaning over the abyss with the scribe who had been listening to him since noon, Rachid was nothing more than a shadow without a rifle, without a wife, knowing only how to hold onto his pipe, a pseudo-Rachid issuing too late from his father's death, like the Wadi El Kebir prolonging only the Rhummel's shadow and its dryness, without restoring its vanquished violence, not far from the nuptial cave where the Frenchwoman entangled her lovers.

viii. . .

Between the *fondouk's* open door—the continual
uproar of the profane could not be heard, only an
ivory clicking of dominos—and the railing of the
balcony with its freshly watered tiles, the summer
twilight comes on. The miasmas of June days
growing warmer persist no matter how often the
tiles are watered, but they are miasmas of mint
and lily, a place on the balcony being the privilege
of only the smokers who, before Rachid, have taken
up residence in the tavern, moving closer day by
day to the aviary and the pot of basil, having
finally conquered the space of mosaic and wrought
iron, the bright tiles, the long alfa-grass matting,
the evenings on the balcony with the tribe in the
huge aviary which wakens at the sound of the lute
(the canaries singing at almost the same rhythm
as the fanatics above the chaotic abyss slowly
crossed by the soaring flight of the storks; once
one of Rachid's means of subsistence had been selling storks' eggs to a Jewish witch, the eggs stolen
from the top of the poplar that seemed, seen from

the balcony, to rise far above the cedars planted in a star by the besieged city's first municipality), and the litanies of the doves nesting in the side of the rock, never perching in the streets, furtive and irritable, knowing that the smallest child can strike them with a slingshot, "and even the doves know we're hungry" Rachid thinks, no longer taking off his dark glasses, no longer hoping to leave Constantine or even the *fondouk;* the wrinkles, the short hair, the dry lips, the thin and swollen torso, the short legs are like a cinder statuette, a man burned alive who has only been able to escape the fire to be carried from river to river, to the port where he did not believe he could join his widow of one night, nor the kindly ghost who waited for him on the quay, nor Lakhdar, nor Mourad: all projected like the sparks of one and the same brazier, but the Rachid bereft of his passion, speaking to the scribe, has no longer the least consistency, and his words dissolve far from the initial thoughts of which he is now merely the collapsed receptacle, his heart and face in ashes, devoured by too sudden a flare of time. ". . . No, not Suzy. Not the kind of woman you can believe crimes were committed for, it was the other one, the unknown woman; the old bandit had introduced me to her; later I followed him instinctively to Bône without knowing that Nedjma (not Suzy, Nedjma) was his daughter. It's true we went further, toward the Holy Land . . . We were supposed to come back together, linked by the secret of which he had revealed only a tiny fragment, the part that concerned me the least; we were supposed to come back to Bône long before the rape, the intervention of the black man, the second crime that once again reduced me to impotence . . . And it's at Bône that I saw Nedjma again, having taken her at Bône only to lose her after the rape organized by her father. Yes, I only saw her again a year after taking her, the unknown woman in the clinic, the daughter of my own tribe whom I instinctively pursued from city to city, in ignorance and resignation.

ix. . .

Providence had willed it that the two cities of my passion should have ruins nearby, in the same summer twilight, so near Carthage; nowhere are there two such cities, sisters in splendor and desolation, that saw Carthage sacked and my Salammbô disappear, between Constantine, the June night, the collar of jasmine blackened under my shirt, and Bône where I lost my sleep for sacrificing the abyss

243

of the Rhummel to another city and another river,
on the track of the strayed gazelle who alone could
tear me from the shade of the cedars, of the father
killed the eve of my birth, in the cave that I alone
could see from this balcony, beyond the fragrant
peaks, and with the unknown woman's father I left
the ruins of Cirta for the ruins of Hippone. What
does it matter that Hippone is disgraced, Carthage
buried, Cirta ruined and Nedjma deflowered . . .
The city flourishes, the blood dissolves, appeased,
only at the moment of the fall: Carthage vanished,
Hippone resuscitated, Cirta between heaven and
earth, the triple wreck restored to the setting sun,
the land of the Maghreb.

X. . .

From Constantine to Bône, from Bône to Constantine a woman travels . . . It is as if she no longer
existed; as if she were seen only in a train or a car-
riage, and those who know her no longer distinguish her from the other women passing by; she is
no longer anything but a final gleam of autumn, a
besieged city fending off disaster; she is veiled in

black. A black man accompanies her, apparently her guardian, for he is almost as old as the old pirate whose life he cut short, unless he has married the presumed daughter of his victim, after having kept her by force on the Nadhor and watched night and day around the women's camp . . . Sometimes she travels under guard, veiled in black now, from Bône to Constantine, from Constantine to Bône. There are cities like fatal women, the polyandrous widows whose names are lost . . . Glory to the conquered cities; they have not yielded the salt of their tears, any more than the warriors have shed our blood: the rewards go to the wives, the eruptive widows who populate every death, the conserving widows who transform defeat into peace, never having despaired of the sowing, for the lost terrain smiles at the sepulchers, just as the night is only odor and fragrance, enemy of color and noise, for this country has not yet come into the world: too many fathers to be born by broad daylight, too many ambitious races disappointed, mingled, confused, constrained to creep upon the ruins . . . What does it matter that Cirta is forgotten . . . Let the tide's ebb and the flow play with this country until its origins are blurred by the stormy languor of a people in agony, the immemorial continent lying like a watchdog between the old world and the new . . . There are few cities like those that lie near each other at the heart of North Africa, the one bearing the name of the vine and the jujube, the other a name older perhaps, perhaps Byzantine; a name perhaps older than Cirta. . . . Here some wild horde had built its fort upon the rock, imitated by unknown tribes, unknown colonies, until the arrival of the Romans, then the Janissaries—the two cities growing under the mistral and the sirocco, on the edge of the desert, so near Carthage; Bône, the gulf where our wealth begins, where our ruin is consummated—Bône growing along the beaches, at the climax of abundance, plantations of vines and tobacco (neither Constantine nor Algiers has such a railroad station, shaped like a minaret, with wide glass doors, the belt of palms, the carriages from another century carrying off the taxi clientele) ; Bône growing from the plain, from the endless beaches of the gulf, from the steep path of the Place d'Armes, the Turkish terraces and the mosque to the side of the steep mountain plunging into the water, the brush where Bugeaud's men could dominate the city, but its wine intoxicated them, its tobacco drew them to the harbor . . . Neither the soldiers nor the colonists who followed them could leave the city—neither leave it nor keep it from growing. . . . The scribe passed the pipe; they were not in the *fondouk* anymore, but in the narrow street sloping down toward the Place des Chameaux. They were sitting with other smokers in front of the window of a sweetshop; the owner took the pipe (the stem was a reed that

Rachid cut with his knife as he spoke) and sat perfectly still. He sucked gently, with an expression of intense irony, facing the vendors crouching around the square who pretended not to notice him.

"That's enough for tonight," Rachid said as he stood up. "It's all a pure malediction of God or of the old pirate . . . I cannot trace the causes further. For I am entangled in too many deaths, too many deaths . . ."

xi. . .

MUSTAPHA'S NOTEBOOK (*continued*)

. . . Incontestably, Nedjma's fatality derived from the atmosphere she was surrounded by as a little girl, when the already devastating games of the sacrificed Vestal glowed in her rarest adornments: the raw splendor, the streaming weapons it is incredible that a woman uses consciously, as if Lella Fatma's flatteries and the weaknesses of her husband had made the little girl into a quasi-religious object, washed clean of her childish filth, polished, inlaid, perfumed with no fear of spoiling her. The true Nedjma was wild; and her educators gradually agreed to raise all barriers before her; but this gratuitous freedom, beyond her world and her time, became the cruellest barrier of all . . . The adoptive mother was sterile, and her husband bigoted. The eunuch and the shrew, prostrate in adoration before the virgin, could harvest only hatred by their poisonous cult. Nedjma's charms, filtered by solitude, had bound her, reduced her to the contemplation of her captive beauty, to skepticism and cruelty before the dejected adoration of her guardians, having only her taciturn play, her love of darkness and jealous dreams, a batrachian full of nocturnal cries that vanished at the first ray of heat, a frog on the brink of the equation, a principle of electricity igniting every ill, after having gleamed, cried, leaped in the face of the world and crazed the male army that woman follows like a shadow it would be enough merely to cross in order to reach the zenith, far from the prolific counterpart whose product man expects only after shedding his vigor engulfed in endless experiment: the male army has embraced only a form; there remains only a collapse at the foot of the old order: male and female ready to unite at dawn, but it is a route at sunrise—the frog in the warmth of the mud, wounded in the first season and deformed for the other three, fatally bleeding at each moon, and the experimenter still virgin, still ignorant, in the despair of the vanished formula—the man and the woman mystified, deprived of their cruel substance, while outside their bodies roars the hermaphroditic horde procreating its own adversity, its males, its females, its night-long couples, from the tragic meeting on the same planet, the contradictory tribe continually emigrating for fear of other worlds too vast, too remote for human promiscuity, since watchful nature abandons us along the way; nature proceeds by errors, by crimes, to awaken the geniuses at the stake and punish those her blindness favors in some impulse of maternal naïveté, revoking all her senses and dispensing them only at random, unknown to the spawn whose stumbles she imitates, for the ingenuous mother educates best by her errors; our destinies must fall with the free leaves, once the jig-saw puzzle begins: their number condemns them to a preconceived elimination, accumulating their influence in increasingly rare champions who alone will experience, without witnesses, without memory, the confrontation with adversity; even as the nations, the tribes, the families, the operation tables, the serried cemeteries where the arrows of fate begin; even as Mourad, Nedjma, Rachid and I; our ruined tribe refuses to change color; we have always married each other; incest is our bond, our principle of cohesion since the first ancestor's exile; the same blood irresistibly bears us to the delta of the passional stream, near the siren who drowns all her suitors rather than choose among the sons of her tribe—Nedjma concluding her stratagem, a queen fugitive and without hope until the husband's appearance, the black man forearmed against the social incest, and this at last will be the nation's tree taking root in the tribal sepulcher, under the cloud, pierced at last, of a blood too often skimmed . . . Who knows with what hereditary ardor Mourad thought he had saved himself when, far from Nedjma, in the presence of some completely different woman, he made that gesture of madness—and all of us belonged to the sacrificed patrol creeping forward to discover the lines, assuming the error and the risk like pawns swept away in the fumblings, so that another should resume the battle . . . As for Mourad, he has murdered in the shadows. Perhaps in the prisoner's impotent rage he foresees the moment when the force that impelled him to the crime will bring him back among us, unaware that he must return under a sky whose signs he has not been able to decipher; he might seize the meaning of our defeat, and it is then that he would vaguely recall, like an exorcising irony, the memory of the lost game and the fatal woman, sterile and fatal, a woman worth nothing, ravaging in the darkness of passion all we had of blood, not to drink it and liberate us like so many empty bottles, not to drink it instead of shedding it, but only to stir it up, fatal, recently married, disgraced in her solitude of doomed beauty, supported only by invisible protectors: yesterday's lovers and today's, mostly yesterday's, from that sumptuous past where she had scattered her charms in even dryer places; they saw her fall and prepared their defection in the dark, mostly senile or else so young that they could still flee and deny the presumptuous combat they seemed to join for her, linking in friendship, uniting their rivalries the better to circumscribe her—mostly senile; they all had vengeance in mind, politely yielding to each other, wary dogs calculating with their pack reason that the victim is too frail, that she cannot endure the halloo, re-placing each other beside her, seeing her fall and thus consoling themselves for her loss. She wore still the richest finery, but too many elegant women, offended, pushed her back into the shadows with the three or four unveiled native women, not the richest, daughters of officials or businessmen whom the European women ignored, and whom their former companions pointed at out of windows, who could not remain secluded nor expose themselves in the other world, condemned and tolerated as if their turpitude deserved consideration merely for emphasizing the virtue of those who remained in their own camp, accepting custom and orthodoxy, loyal to the veil and to the traditions—that virtue of elderly virgins which is the honor of the city, giving free rein to the prettiest or the wildest woman, provided the clan's old modesty subsists, the blood savagely accumulated by the leaders and the nomads separated from their caravan, seeking refuge in these cities of the littoral where the escaped men recognize each other and associate, in trade and in bureaucracy with an age-old patience, and marry only one another's women, each family keeping its sons and daughters inexorably paired off, like an Egyptian yoke bearing the vanished arms and principles of some ancestor, one of those noble vagabonds separated from his caravan during those *periploi* the Arab geographers report and which from the Middle East and from Asia proceed to North Africa, the land of the setting sun where, sterile and fatal, Nedjma was born, Nedjma our loss and our ruin, the evil star of our clan.

xii. . .

"He'll be going to the court of appeals."
"Drink," Rachid says.
"You say he's your friend . . ."
"Nothing better than cold tea."
"What if I wrote to the court?"

Rachid leaned out a little further over the narrow promontory. The summer wind swelled out his old shirt that was open at the neck, and he continued without turning around, as if the scribe were not there; his voice grew faint—neither monologue nor narrative—merely a release deep in the void, and Rachid went on, remotely, like a storyteller swept on by his material before an invisible audience; at the climax of his curiosity the scribe dozed off in his chair like a child endlessly insisting on the verisimilitude that soothes him. "... Mourad has not committed any crime. He inadvertently killed the father of a woman he didn't love. It was the wedding night . . . The circumstances . . . A switchyards error, with other causes than those the court will mention. Everything starts with the thoughtlessness of a Frenchwoman probably dead now who couldn't decide among her lovers; so that the incest is problematical . . . What court? Don't write. Listen to my story: I've lived a long time as a deserter without even taking off my soldier's shirt, and I haven't been caught. Not only have I wandered from city to city, but I've accumulated many official irregularities, always without punishment, then one night I throw a stone at a car that almost ran over me on the Boulevard de l'Abîme. The driver gets out and I find myself in prison. They look at my record. 'So you're the deserter?' And there you are. Leave the court alone. Time passes. Let sleeping dogs lie. As the saying goes."

The scribe was dozing, his closed notebook in his hand; he had just crossed out the one page he had written. Keep still or say the unspeakable. He was dozing. The lily. The mint. The basil. The birds reeling in their light sleep, artists' sleep. The cold tea. Rachid cleaned out the pipe, leaning over the dark abyss, gaining altitude like a balloon unballasted, harmless and vulnerable, caught on the wing between the ground and target, between the murdered father and the black man who had avenged him, keeping Nedjma as a hostage.

V. . .

i. . .

Two years have passed since Zohra, Mourad's mother and Lakhdar's, was abandoned by Sidi Ahmed, when a new character appears; an old farmer from around Sétif, who happens to be staying in the Aurès at the time, makes friends with Zohra's father, a sixty-year-old woodcutter with three other daughters on his hands; the old farmer, Mahmoud, takes an interest in the repudiated wife; he has an only son, a bad boy named Tahar, for whom he has just bought a grocery-store in X . . . The woman, along with the grocery, might quiet my son down, Mahmoud thinks. At the time of his mother's second marriage, Lakhdar is still not weaned.

The time comes to leave the giant pumpkin, the cradle hung in the corner of the conjugal bedroom, half way between the bed and the hearth; the baby shows his strength with sooty kisses; the smells are of ashes, dry linen, mother's milk; often Lakhdar is banished to a sheepskin of incommensurable size.

Lakhdar is bored in the hut; four uneven walls and the thatched roof form the inaccessible space to which he aspires; hunger, impotence, isolation have him helpless; his only object of pilgrimage is a chest (too high) in which his mother keeps things; one day Lakhdar sees the lamp burning on the chest. He rebels; he invents a new, contemptible way of crying, lurches out of the swaddlings Zohra still wraps him in like some noble Egyptian; Lakhdar sees himself powerful and paralyzed.

Torn to pieces, the sheepskin is replaced by blankets of woven wool, Tahar's monopoly; Lakhdar is not allowed under them; in the hot season, the bugs pull him out of his prison on all fours; he butts through the curtain that serves as a door; the kingdoms of the field appear where he forces Zohra to give suck; he doesn't bite the breast once! Mahmoud takes him in his arms; Lakhdar is aware of peeing on something bigger than he is . . .

Finally they leave him outdoors.

The neighborhood children don't take kindly to the newcomer.

Rival infants sniffing each other out.

He tries other people's mothers.

In the course of time Lakhdar is taken from farm to farm. Beaten. Exposed to every thorn. Scraped against trees. Overweighted by huge bones destined to consolidate his jaw; he walks secretly; reverts to crawling; gets into everything; lacking education he trains himself; he is provided with a blue canvas tunic, and after many struggles he is weaned; henceforth his mother, once his accomplice, corrects him harshly; Sidi Tahar confines himself to acts of virile tenderness; he gives the child coins and publicly exhibits his testicles.

Mahmoud conceals the fact that the orphan is not his own son's child; he takes Lakhdar to the café to defy his old rivals; Zohra never dreamed so much; Lakhdar hangs from her finger during the summer housekeeping and in wintertime is horrified to be accompanied by so ugly a mother; the illiterate heroine and the handsome baby are mother and son and lovers, in both the barbarous and platonic sense; then come struggle and independence; the shadow of his arms lying across the clods of earth, the old man, his chest still white, crosses the furrows covered with crows. The sudden splendor of sunbeams in the pear-tree! Lakhdar picks up his sling and, lying on the moss, alone under the poplars, gaily kills the birds stupid with sleep; he is too young even to count his corpses . . . Intoxication of space—the goats cry, smaller than Lakhdar under the poplars . . . Dresses ragged, feet bare in the thistles and the sunshine, there are girls at the fountain with shawls and captivating glances, but Lakhdar, a shepherd-to-be, runs after only goats, almost as intent as the presumed grandfather who smokes, dreaming, with the absurd ferocity of a mahout on his donkey's sharp back; the child joins the animal and the man: they cross the fields, looking for cool places; a trace of sunlight on the red beard closes Lakhdar's eyes; they land in a thicket they deflower only for its coolness, for the grandfather's repose and the animal's; they listen to the workers sing from another world.

When the laborers have disappeared among the trees, Zohra looses her dress in magnificent soap bubbles; in her bride's chest, the mother stirs delightful things; a pot full of dead cloves, a necklace of heavy yellow and blue glass; the censer is used on the brows, to drown out the Sudan dust. Lakhdar comes back to the hut only for meals; at dawn he leaves with the men, but heads for the other side of the village, where the tombstones of his false ancestors are . . . What does the orphan care if it is not exactly his family that perished here, transforming the slope into an olive-grove, far from the village, between the cemetery and the slaughter-house?

ii. . .

Zohra gives Lakhdar five eggs for the principal of the native school: *"M'sieu, the new boy is spitting*

in the inkwell"; the principal knocks him down;
Lakhdar's hand swells from fingertips to forearm:
he walks back and forth in front of the school, outraged at being the only one expelled; he aims his
slingshot at the window; the schoolmaster doesn't
see him; pitiful village!

Lakhdar lays traps; he digs up roots for the
two-mouthed stove Mahmoud has transformed into
a furnace.

Mahmoud lives in two rooms built out of paving stones at the edge of a swampy field; filled,
levelled, the swamp is part garden, part pasture,
stable, and construction yard where a third room
is being built, with the help, this time, of un-
matched bondstone; old Mahmoud intends to retire
here; he intends to leave the two rooms to Tahar
and his wife, who live for the moment in only one
corner of the hut, which will become Lakhdar's
room; besides the hut and the olive grove, Mahmoud owns a donkey, an exhausted mule that he
will soon have to replace, eight sheep and a goat
whose kids depart this life for various reasons,
under Lakhdar's care.

Seventy or eighty, Mahmoud's age doesn't
matter: he has lost too many children; he has saved
these two acres behind the clearing; his fathers
had sixty; the ancestral soil seems to melt away
under the feet of the new-born; Mahmoud has
lived here since the founding of the village; he has
lost land but acquired the grocery his son runs to-

day; the grocer runs after women with the chauffeur of the mixed commune, Monsieur Bruno, who came from France no one knows how.

When Lakhdar is transferred from the Aurès to the olive grove, his stepfather is in the process of selling the grocery to run away with an Alsatian laundress Monsieur Bruno is after too, even while he is encouraging Tahar: *"She's ready to fall in your arms. I tell you: the woman's a widow, she has no one; she likes always seeing you with an administration man."* Madame Odile's establishment is on the largest artery of Sétif; the two villagers drive a hundred kilometers each way to see her, in the truck that belongs to the administrator, supreme authority in X . . . Monsieur Bruno stresses the secrecy of the trips: Tahar gives him packages of food, jars of oil, chickens and other valuable things likely to please the laundress and neutralize Monsieur Bruno's superiors concerning the admissibility of an Arabo-Berber grocer in a vehicle where only the head of the commune and his assistants belong; it should be added that Tahar borrows a mule to leave the village; Monsieur Bruno picks up his friend opposite the cemetery; they reach the city by taking a rarely used road; Tahar would go all the way to Sétif by mule provided he is in the truck when the driver stops in front of the Alsatian woman's window; she invites them to her apartment with other women, reserving the right to dismiss her company around midnight—all circumstances which, including the nocturnal returns interrupted by the stops Monsieur Bruno suggested, give Zohra's husband back to her stammering and vague; the autumn of her second marriage, she is no more than twenty; it is no use pleading; Tahar takes out of his hood no fewer of those cursed white bottles that make Zohra mistrust even water.

Grandfather's herd brings Lakhdar, in the middle of his whooping-cough, three dresses, as well as a pair of trousers and a shirt for holidays; from now on Lakhdar will look at the countryside on donkeyback; he also receives a wool cap, goatskin sandals, and an olive-wood cane; there is no Spring; until April, a strong wind clusters the clouds on the side of the Taffat, a place where the shepherds gather; more than once Lakhdar gets stuck in the mud there; today the sky is low; the rain lashes at the soggy oaks hour after hour; Lakhdar wants to run; the sheep come back to the wet grass; he hits one on the muzzle, so violently that he has to load it on the donkey: *"You're not made out of paper, you don't have to be afraid of the rain,"* Mahmoud says; Lakhdar is beaten with his own cane; the sheep is dead; the donkey sleeps with the goats and the sheep; a lot of hay, branches, carbos are needed. One night, the kid of a newly acquired goat seriously provokes the donkey, passing under its belly to steal its daily allowance of food; the donkey kills it with a kick between the eyes; Mahmoud is away at the market; Zohra helps Lakhdar carry the kid to the Bousel-

lem ravine; on the way back they find Mahmoud
with the herd.

"The kid?"

"Dead."

"Who?"

"The donkey."

"Which donkey? You or me?"

Lakhdar doesn't snivel; it is Mahmoud's first
injustice; Lakhdar has a precedent to avoid blows;
a little later he is comforted by the death of another
shepherd's goat; a famous nanny-goat; she had
three kids each year; they had decided to race,
Lakhdar on his goat, the other boy on his; the
latter fell on her belly; her progeniture died with
her; there were four kids that time; Lakhdar tells
Mahmoud the story; he is beaten on account of the
racing.

The river road is easy, wide, solid; it is the
Roman road, still shows the tracks of their chariots,
has seen the village born; but the donkey is a sabo-
teur. It follows the road for a while, never for the
same amount of time; the donkey seems to be used
to the road; Lakhdar loosens the bridle; he holds
onto his little brother's back; the animal walks
along slowly, regularly, with something like pride;
the pride of a slave under a perpetual fetter, of a
professional soldier, meditative and watchful; its
impassivity assumes the significance of an ordeal:
for the guide's precocity, for the rider's infancy;
if Lakhdar dozes, he lets go of the bridle, letting

himself be ensnared by the donkey's prodigious unconcern, its one idea, the idea of freedom, the loss of the rider; Lakhdar's little brother doesn't know; if he knew, he would hold on better, would cling to the saddle horns, wouldn't laugh up at the sky.

Lakhdar's little brother is not heavy; he pounds harder and harder; the donkey avoids most of the blows.

Lakhdar maintains the guide's apparent neutrality.

The donkey remains deaf to the conventions.

Nothing affects the heavy anger . . .

iii. . .

Nothing affects the heavy anger of the oppressed creature; he doesn't count the years; he doesn't distinguish men, or roads; for him there is only one road; the Roman road; the one that leads to the river, to rest, to death. How control the donkey? He is doomed to business. He remains neutral and malevolent; he doesn't follow the guide; he neutralizes him, communicates his slave's forebearance.

Impossible to come to terms with the donkey.

He scrapes the rider off against the tree, tenderly.

Lakhdar's little brother has fallen on his nose.

The river has turned red.

Lakhdar puts his brother back on the saddle.

He has forgotten the belly-band at the house; he holds the bridle.

Lakhdar watches the goats drink; they belong to another class; their lightness makes them lovable; but you have to keep an eye on them; they can strip a garden, provoke a scuffle in this old man's country: the young people are exiled: this earth is too thankless, too precious: the goats can be the cause of it all if the shepherd is asleep.

Lakhdar knows he is going into the water; he has been up since three; at nine he will milk, then pretend to sleep in front of the courtyard, waiting for bread; he will eat, listen to the calls, go back to the river without the herd. His friends will be in the water. There will be a wedding in the village; he will have to sleep with his ears open; if Lakhdar falls asleep during the night or even afterwards, he might miss something; wakened at three all summer long, the season of weddings, he will nap leading the animals; some creature will take advantage of him.

No.

He has to fight against his dreams.

Lakhdar pays the price for the swim and the night lying awake.

The donkey drinks.

Lakhdar holds the bridle.

The little brother is happy.

Lakhdar is dreaming.

The donkey drinks a long time.

Lakhdar turns away from his brother to eat a fig.

The donkey drinks.

The sun rises.

The donkey steps aside.

"Those are the horseflies," Lakhdar dreams.

The donkey takes a step. He slips, as though willfully, on the pebbles.

The little brother falls into the river.

He falls sick in the house.

Mahmoud comes back from his trip. He is riding a new young mule.

"No one move," Mahmoud says, distant and impressive, to Lakhdar sitting hangdog on the doorstep.

Mahmoud wants to get down.

The mule heads for the door, as if it were at home.

Mahmoud knocks his turban against the wall.

He falls sick in the house.

Mahmoud and Lakhdar's little brother are in bed together.

The donkey and the mule eat with their heads together.

"No one rides my mule," Mahmoud says.

"No one rides my donkey," Lakhdar says.

It is harvest time.

Mahmoud gets up before dawn.

Lakhdar loads the sheaves.

The donkey eats them on his way.

Lakhdar beats him with his cane.

The donkey eats.

Lakhdar gets off on the sidewalk.

The donkey falls sick, on the way.

He closes his eyes.

Lakhdar cries.

The donkey wheezes.

Mahmoud catches up with them.

"Why hit the donkey?"

"He was eating the wheat."

"Where are the other sheaves?"

"I couldn't load them all."

"The goats will eat the rest. You should have put them all on and let the donkey eat."

"The wheat's not for donkeys."

"Go get the other sheaves."

Lakhdar rides off on the restored donkey.

The sheaves are near a ruined wall.

The sun is sinking.

The serpent is happy.

He comes out of the wall.

The donkey pulls away.

Lakhdar gets off.

He wants to loosen the wall.

The serpent coils up.

The donkey gallops away.

Lakhdar throws stones at him.

"And the wheat?" Mahmoud asks.

The goats have eaten it all; Lakhdar runs away too. He sleeps on the church steps. The Oukil's son teaches him how to smoke.

Maître Charib is a badly dressed oukil.

The *oukil* drinks anisette at Madame Nora's.

Mademoiselle Dubac is a pretty schoolteacher.

The schoolteacher has neither family nor village.

Mademoiselle Dubac eats at Madame Nora's restaurant.

"Lakhdar has no father," the oukil's son thinks.

"The oukil's *son has never ridden a donkey,"* Lakhdar thinks, handing Mustapha the cigarette.

iv. . .

Madame Nora, proprietress of the only hotel-restaurant in X . . . serves *Maître* Charib his eighth anisette; he won an important trial last Wednesday, with the help of Habous provisos and quotations from Sidi Khelil; his clients have brought him a sack of partridges which he offers to Madame Nora; she replies by pouring a round for the house.

"To *Maître* Charib's health!"

"Bravo *Maître* Charib!" the chorus of habitués replies.

"Excuse me," Tahar the grocer says, leaning on the *oukil's* arm, "do me the honor of accepting a glass."

"No, please God! Today is my day."

". . . I've always admired you, *Maître* Charib.
If we were all as smart as you . . ."

"What we haven't had, our children will. You
have a son?"

"I have two," the grocer says. "One of my
wife's and one of my own."

The *oukil* leans on the counter.

". . . What could I do, *Maître* Charib. My
wife had this orphan, he was still nursing!"

"And what did the grandfather say?"

"My father's fond of him. He's the one who
named him Lakhdar."

"Just between us, you have the means to send
him off to school . . ."

"He'll have to manage with his grandfather!
We sent him to the native school, but he's back to
being a shepherd now. A bad lot."

"He's over school age?"

"Going on nine! Running after girls
already."

"My son Mustapha's age! I sent him to the
mixed school. We're French! That's the law."

The schoolteacher walks down the restaurant
stairs.

Maître Charib raises his voice.

"Bring him, that boy of yours, I'll see that
he gets accepted. *Mademoiselle Dubac has no
prejudices!*"

Only the prominent Moslems in X . . . put

their children in the mixed school. Tahar is only a grocer.

And Mademoiselle Dubac . . . Tahar can't look at her; he smacks his fat hand against the zinc counter.

"Hakim, may god keep you, let's drink a last glass!"

"It's easy, come downstairs with me. It's all in knowing how to talk!"

Maître Charib leaves his cane on the counter. He entrusts his burnoose to Madame Nora. Tahar dares not follow the oukil downstairs.

"Mademoiselle, my respects . . ."

The schoolteacher simpers, a wing between her teeth.

The magistrate's presence restores the orator's confidence; the judge is cheerful; he embraces his favorite attorney; in order not to lose their balance, the two men of law take seats beside the Beauty; Madame Nora automatically brings them the menu; she repeats her thanks for the partridges; Mademoiselle Dubac, her lips shiny, is eating one right now; this creates a link; one thing leads to another, and it is the judge who pleads for Lakhdar.

V. . .

As for our schoolteacher, the families can laugh in front of her. She comes from far away.

Mademoiselle Dubac.

The chime of the perfect name.

"Silence. All right, my little friends."

There are big ones and little ones! School is supposed to mix us up, yes or no? She has a cold. Doesn't use her fingers. Never has a spot of ink. Her handkerchief or a snowball. Bleeds with a smile. Maybe she spits poppies in the thousand-and-one-nights! No, roses. If she let me feel her nails. If we had different sweat. She doesn't dirty her knitting needles. The sweater's for me? She always watches the others. Dubac Paule. Her name goes down like air. Say it again. Toss it up. Paule. Terrible to be named Mustapha. Frenchwoman. France. She has a car? But she eats pork. First of all she's not hungry! Nobody says anything if she breaks the chalk. She has a hundred new notebooks. She can write letters. Her family has a fort? It's far away. She came in a car. With her fiancé. Fi

an cé. The fiancé plays football. Shoots. Fiancé.
French. I'm an Arab. My father is a learned man.
He has a cane. My mother's name is Ouarda. Rose
in French. She doesn't go out. She doesn't read.
She has wooden shoes. Rose. France. Some words
change. And clothes. And houses. And places in
the bus. When I'm grown up, I'll sit in front. With
the schoolmistress. Summer vacation. She'll take
me. Student to encourage. She wrote that. I'll give
her something back. I'll correct the homework for
her. She'll buy me trousers. She'll give me a name.
"Mustapha, page 17."
Ooh, she called me the other name!
"Next!"
Anyway, she went past me. She's thinking
about me. I read badly. I'm the strongest. I set the
tone. And I don't even want to! If the others
weren't there. I'd learn the whole book by heart.
No need for school. I'd go to her house. She has
electricity.
"Mustapha, you aren't following!"
Am I the only one?
Fall of an angel.
Recess.

vi. . .

Lakhdar pulls Mustapha toward the hencoop.

"You see this broom. We'll put it on top of the door and we won't go back in; it opens from inside. It'll fall on *her*."

"I dare you!"

"You're scared."

"In your seats!"

The hens revel in the deserted courtyard.

Lakhdar and Mustapha, alone with the dung.

The smells, and their beating hearts.

Lakhdar: Now they're all inside!

Mustapha: You think anyone saw us?

Lakhdar: Shit on them!

They scale the chatter of good children. No longer afraid of hearing the ruler smash down. The school is out in the country. The hencoop smells friendly. Like the men in the Arab café.

"Ready?"

Mustapha puts the broom in position! Lakhdar selects a piece of scorched tile. Aims slowly. Bang! right in the middle of the door! *The school is engulfed in sacrilegious silence.* Mademoiselle Dubac walks off the dais to open the door, hoping to spread a little of her perfume under the principal's nose, but it is the teacher's pretty nose that acknowledges the falling broom signed Lakhdar and Mustapha! Is it likely she will investigate further? She doesn't scream the way they expected her to. A broom's not heavy. *The art of committing only half-sins.* Her hand on the latch, will she decide to investigate for form's sake, or simply go back to her chair? The classmates laugh, a way of denouncing the sharpshooters.

The years pass.

Drawing today. Obedient, the girls suck their colored pencils; they'll do anything to please, and their work is always poor.

The boys make banknotes for recess.

Lakhdar permits no accumulation of capital.

"Your money or your life!"

Albert lets himself be robbed.

Cunning Ferhat lays his traps.

Will Lakhdar break the pact and ask Mustapha to give his back? Monique, leader of the girls, keeps her green eyes on them.

"Aren't you going to give anything?" Lakhdar asks.

Mustapha says nothing.

Lakhdar hits him.

Mustapha spits. His hatred appears in a tiny puddle. Both of them are on the ground. Frenzy.

The classmates count the blows.

Torture of the combatants when the judges make mistakes.

Bites: cheat the judges.

The girls scream. Mademoiselle, they're fighting!

Fix their titties with a good kick! *Unfortunately, it's the fighters who are lying on the girls' feet.*

Too exhausted to separate.

Brutal and glamorous nap.

"Ruffians!"

Mademoiselle's iron ruler. "*Strike, ma jolie,*" Lakhdar says, and holds out his hands.

vii. . .

At the fence, the former shepherds lay their plans. Mademoiselle Dubac's residence stands at the foot of Mount Taffat. Blue eyes, the princess dreamed of by many a barbarian of ten who, denied access to the splendid school-habitation, creeps through the forest where he enjoys the mistress's charms and then, emerging all gooseflesh from a pool, re-

turns to meet with his army . . . The schoolboys
show the shepherds the wide-open gate, but they
must climb the fence, for the girls are on guard
there . . . The perpetrators of this raid are children
expelled from school by a painful and hidden law;
yet Paule Dubac has nothing against the little
savages; she knows all their names, but cannot
endure the sight of torn clothes . . . She knows
that after the students leave, the school does not
remain empty: the inhabitants of the ponds move
into the deserted courtyard; they frolic with the
swallows in this cage for spoiled children, and
without toys, without electric trains that keep going round and round, the children of the Taffet
learn to play with overturned beetles, and the
muddy arms of the bad boys catch Monique's eyes,
though she is soon driven away by a shower of
stones, for war can break out again from one minute to the next.

viii. . .

Four wrinkles intersect the parallel lines of the
last blood-letting on his forehead; father is sleep-

ing, you can ask me any question you want about the participle. It's the barber who bleeds my father. He lowers his forehead coldly slit open with the razor. That's what happens when you have too much blood! This time, father has the back of his neck cut; next time, it will be his forehead again; about one blood-letting a month; that's what happens when you're too strong! You turn to alcohol and that means sickly children. When I was born, I was fat, the tourists picked me up in their arms. "He doesn't look like an Arab baby! How pretty he is!" But I soon became just like my mother, thin, thin as a rail, it's good in fights; only Lakhdar is as thin as I am; at least we have bones and nerves! And we can run. We have fists hard as stones. Father's asleep. It's the blood-letting that's tired him out. I'd like to kiss him when he's asleep, quietly, without the girls' seeing me. It's not fair having two sisters and only one father . . . He's sleeping. Doesn't want me to go out while he's asleep. A good student like me. Father's asleep and I'm not sleepy; some people get stupefied by the sun; but it just makes Lakhdar and me want to run, like the cows during the Tikouk; Lakhdar's waiting for me down at the river; he doesn't even have a father; his grandfather's in charge; Lakhdar was a shepherd before coming to school; he's used to the sun; and besides, he doesn't have a father; he has one they call Si Tahar, but it's not his real father; Lakhdar's real father's dead;

279

Lakhdar's never seen him; *he was born alone* with his mother Zohra, a nice lady who married that Si Tahar. Lakhdar's father's dead; my father's snoring; there's a boy from Paris in our class; "papa's snoring"; he's the one who earns a living; today he brought home two chickens from the market; Mother cut their throats over the same basin the barber Si Khelifa uses to bleed my father once a month; Mother will stretch the chicken's neck over the basin, and Father will recite a proverb from the Koran, working the knife like a saw under the chicken's suspicious eye; some of them are tough; the dance of the chicken with its throat cut is a family show; humanity has a narrow escape! Father turns over on his left side. He's still asleep! A father's foot has a lot to say about the past; the deformity of a nail tells the story of a military campaign; if my father weren't an Arab, he would have been a field marshal; oh yes, I can use the subjunctive; I'm an excellent student, I do better than all the French boys in my class, and I answer the inspector; the teacher gave me a portrait of Marshal Pétain; I sold it to Monique for a pencil sharpener; today I was chosen to raise the colors, and Roland got up and left because he's a Jew. Father thinks he has to sleep on his left side. Hard to bear. Does he notice I kiss him when he's asleep, always on the left side, the same side where his shirt pocket is, where he keeps his change? He doesn't care about money. He's been

through the war, that's why he sleeps with his
clothes on. Father didn't make anything out of
the war; he thought he was coming home rich, but
he had to go back to court; still, we save up to
kill the fatted calf; on public days, Mother hides
the money in a biscuit tin, the only one in the
house, and she puts it up on the highest shelf in
the wardrobe; a good thing we have chairs! I still
haven't seen a wardrobe with a mirror on the door.
They say there was one in Guelma ten years ago,
I wasn't born yet; once I came into the world it
disappeared; my father broke it with his cane because the woman in childbed refused to go back
to work if she didn't get a velvet dress to celebrate
the seventh day of my birth; the mirror of the
wardrobe was broken, my mother's bone was
cracked, the tibia (I get A's in natural science),
my mother got her red velvet dress, and the judge
came to the house to scold papa, who ordered
champagne and invited home all the local magistrates: all that for a whack with a cane! My mother
forgave him without any nagging; the same night
she fixed a monster *couscous*, standing propped on
her broken tibia; the whole village talked about
that dinner for a long time. Father's asleep: that's
his nature: break everything and sleep. A good
man. Why doesn't he breathe faster? If you don't
breathe, you die: Lakhdar's father . . . Go on
breathing! Father's asleep. He's snoring. He's
not dead. No one like him. He's never lifted his

cane against me. Only once. The pack of "Bastos"
I stuck in my sock to take to Lakhdar. I don't
smoke very well. Lakhdar inhales. Father opened
the door just when I was pulling my sock up over
the pack. One stroke of his cane. Hardly touched
me. I started crying. I exaggerated my sufferings:
actually there was nothing to cry about. But father's as sensitive as he is violent. He gave me ten
francs and a kiss. Father congratulated me on my
French composition. I was so moved that I thought
I saw my mother gasping in triumph; her name
is Ouarda, Rose, there's a song about her, a funny
song where she turns young and shameless. But
that's not the way things are; she spent her life
dreaming she's going out with my father, just
when she hears his cane tapping away; even when
she cries, her eyes are dry, and she works. Mother
sleeps on the floor with the two girls; I hate seeing
girls snore, especially my sisters. The prophet's
right. Men and women should be kept apart. But
I feel full of affection and sympathy and courage
when I see *Maître* Mohamed Gharib's powerful
body stretched out for a nap: that's my father,
and I'm the only one who knows his secrets . . .
*"Maître Mohamed Gharib requests your presence
in his office to discuss the question of expenses and
fees,"* that's father's style. My father's office is a
hallway with a clay floor, a black bench, a fine
chair dating from his wedding in Guelma, a table
and bookshelf knocked together by a carpenter to

282

pay his fees to my procreator, *Maître* Gharib, lawyer to the poor and the criminal. My father's poverty is a way of fighting the war. He was in Tunisia until the armistice. He drank the whole section's wine. A handsome man, *Maître* Gharib, with his particolored eyes, "Partridge eyes," my mother calls them. Short and full-blooded. I already come up to his chin. He's asleep. A good man, hard-working and noisy, brutal and meddlesome. He sleeps with all his clothes on, and with his cane. If he didn't have Arab slippers, he'd sleep with them on: you can take off Arab slippers just by moving your feet; my father's slippers and his cane make a noise Mother teaches me to reconstruct when he's not here at night . . . Father stays out. He says it's his work; we wait for him patiently, and I taught my mother the French alphabet, on the little table with cushions around it, in front of the fig-tree that almost died in the slops of dirty water (there's no plumbing in our house; mother does the laundry and the dishes in huge kettles) from the eternally simmering pots on the fire; when I start falling asleep, mother sticks a pinch of snuff up my nose, or else she gets the ladle to tell my fortune: if the ladle handle sways to the right, I'll get my diploma, but I took the first Economics course—I just got over a spell of malaria with bronchitis, that's why I'm so thin; Mademoiselle Dubac came to see me; my father kept her on the doorstep while my mother made me get off her mattress and climb into papa's bed; the school mistress kissed me! I smelled the tobacco. But the kiss drove off the fever; Mademoiselle Dubac came with me to Sétif. My mother got rid of the bad luck by throwing a bucket of water on our heels; the school mistress had wet stockings. My father smelled of eau de Cologne. I left cursing my family, and I succeeded! I even read Mustapha Gharib in the *Dépêche de Constantine*. Lakhdar's name came ahead of mine, because of the alphabet.

ix. . .

Mustapha's first recollections go back to a court-yard whose uneven tiles have all kinds of plants growing between them; the three adjoining rooms are used by the *oukil,* his three brothers, two of their wives, and the children; they form the left wing of a huge one-story house in the center of Guelma; the clan's liabilities (widows, grandmothers, the unemployed, the sick) are always kept here; Mohamed Gharib is the supreme commander; he marries off his brothers before taking a wife himself; he is the most learned man of the clan:

after seven years of Medersa in Constantine, he
was named interpreter to the Guelma tribunal,
then finished his military service; in 1919 he obtained his *oukil's* diploma; at first he did a splendid
business, bought property which he resold in order
to marry; the day after his wedding, he found
himself in debt: the whole clan had sent its dele-
gates to the feast; according to tradition, the
bride and groom were second cousins; the *oukil*
could not face his creditors; he took advantage of
the first judiciary upheaval and had himself appointed to Sétif where business is not so frequent
or so good as at Guelma; the *oukil* sold his wife's
jewelry; he rented two rooms near the station and
an office two steps away; the household was never
so comfortable; the *oukil* had only European
neighbors, uninterested in his affairs; they didn't
know that Ouarda lived on dry bread (she was
nursing Mustapha), and that the *oukil* drank wine
on credit; after a year, a few poor but regular
clients kept the family alive; Mustapha was still
the only son; he dressed in European clothes lined
with fleece, he gorged on delicacies; some evenings,
the *oukil* was so affectionate that the spoiled child
was asked to pee in a sugar can: *Maître* Gharib
is noble which means naïve; he hopes by these
ostentatious attentions to preserve his son from
the all-too-familiar marks of poverty . . . But
Mustapha need only open his eyes to change his
tune: his mother has one cotton dress which she

discards only to make rags out of it for scrubbing the floor . . . The handsome floor! . . . *Maître* Gharib has only one red burnoose, a canvas jacket, a pair of baggy trousers, two shirts; his sweaters all have holes; his fez is filthy inside, misshapen, with a hanging tassle which Mustapha, two years after the move to Sétif, still bites at furiously, without being able to tear it off; on the other hand *Maître* Gharib owns a lawyer's gown on which the academic palms are sewn (*services rendered to the educational establishments*). . . . One summer night, Ouarda shakes Mustapha awake; he is six; without a word the *oukil* stuffs them into a taxi that takes them to X . . . , deposits them in a huge damp room; the carpenter comes to fix the door; the wall around the courtyard is raised so that Ouarda can go about her business without being seen from outside; a brick partition divides the room in two; the carpenter comes back to put in another door; the fireplace side becomes storeroom, kitchen, and dining-room; Ouarda brings in her trunks, the utensils, and Mustapha's trophies; the window side becomes the bedroom reserved for the *oukil*; he buys a secondhand bed and a large cupboard which he uses as both bookshelf and wardrobe; the hallway from the courtyard to the street is transformed into an office; after these first arrangements are made, Mustapha goes to spend three months with his mother and her relatives in

286

Guelma; on January 1, 1937, *Maître* Gharib spends a thousand francs on champagne: a third of his savings; he goes to get his wife, who has just given birth to a daughter; Mustapha frets in the train and wants to throw his little sister Farida out the window; his mother is delighted to be back at home; the *oukil* has had electricity installed and the whole house whitewashed.

X. . .

The spotless lady has forced Mustapha to sit down, without any more smiles, and now she stands motionless, drawing on a blackboard. Mustapha leaves despite himself, pushed between two rows of tables as impressive as those in court; in the street, a girl in rags touches his apron.

"Listen, son of the *oukil*!"

She is wearing a pleated dress that she rolls up around her hips to be able to lift the buckets more easily; they call her Dhehbia, the water-carrier.

"She works for her old father," *Maître* Gharib said.

"Small and quiet and wide-awake!" Ouarda added.

The water-carrier has long black eyes that squint a little; her eyebrows are arched; she has the shiny bronze skin of a pomegranate; she rouges her gums with walnut husks; she is nine years old.

Dhehbia thrusts her hand into her dress and pulls out a badly wrapped package.

"Don't stay out here in the street," she says.

Mustapha instinctively runs to the playground; the others have stopped eating and are chasing each other.

Opposite the school, in the blacksmith's shop, Dhehbia is trying to help a farmer tie up his mule; chased away, she presses against the fence of the courtyard swarming with children; she calls again:

"O son of the *oukil*!"

Mustapha dares not go near her nor open the *secret package*: he is convinced it will be dry bread, broken by hand. He runs to give it to Dhehbia; she hesitates, then gobbles it down; Mustapha turns pale; he hears the chocolate crackle.

Among the girls there is a tremendous silence.

They are playing hopscotch with empty boxes.

Huddled in a corner of the playground, Mustapha cannot stop admiring the clean blouses, the collars, the braids . . . They have a sublime way of blowing their noses. What delicacy! Back from the fountain, a red-haired girl bumps into

Mustapha; a cool cheek brushes his forehead; the overpowering scent of candy makes Mustapha weak, but three boys have appeared in the playground, on all fours! Mustapha doesn't know which of the three digs him out of his corner, in one leap; when they leave, Mustapha sits down again, calm. Two long painful lines run across his nose.

"*In your seats!*"

At four o'clock *Maître* Gharib is waiting for his son outside the school.

Mustapha sees nothing but the baggy trousers and the fez. He blushes.

The schoolboys flock past the *oukil.*

Their fathers must have hats and straight trousers; Mustapha feels the tears coming; the others stand clustered around father; curiosity or contempt? *The same uniform for all fathers*; that is what Mustapha's wet eyes plead for; *Maître* Gharib's face grows severe.

"Who scratched you?"

"He did!"

"No, M'sieu, he did!"

The schoolboys denounce each other as if it were a game; they don't seem to take the Arab lawyer seriously; *Maître* Gharib grabs the biggest.

"What's your name?"

"Albert Giovanni."

The boy doesn't look frightened; the *oukil* holds him with one hand and pulls his son and heir

289

with the other; the cane leaps on the cobbles; Albert has blue eyes; his face is covered with little pus-filled pimples; his yellow corduroy trousers are too short; he wears shiny boots that have scowling faces in their bulging tips; Mustapha often sees faces in people's shoes; these terrify him; but he is not sure it was Albert who scratched him; impossible to say anything to the *oukil,* who pokes at every pebble in sight, furious, his mustache grim; Albert's black apron (Mustapha's hasn't been pressed) has a red border, and the collar of his white shirt falls over a brown cable-stiched sweater; Albert walks almost as fast as the *oukil* and doesn't look at Mustapha.

The prison guard is reading the paper in his front garden.

"*Porca madona*! Hey Gharib! God be good to you!"

Albert vanishes in the house.

"The boys have been fighting," the *oukil* smiles.

The prison guard slaps his knees; a cloud of ashes flies out of his pipe.

"Wait, I'll go get the whip."

"No," *Maître* Gharib says. "They're going to make up."

A huge woman with blue eyes appears. Albert is hidden behind her.

"Please leave your hat on. Is this your boy?"

Madame Giovanni embraces Mustapha.

She goes inside to get the anisette bottle.

"Come play in the garden," she says.

Visiting Albert's sister, Monique is crouching on her haunches, juggling with clods of peat, and in the trembling shadows reveals a pink slit whose sight and emanations can be enjoyed only in the burning torment of abstraction: a slit of flesh innocently revealed to the precocious eyes of the smitten Barbarian!

Furiously Albert pulls around the cart General Mustapha is sitting in.

"All right. You can stop."

Albert pushes his cap onto the back of his skull; he runs over and fills the gourd in the fountain; the general takes off his kepi; he turns his field glasses toward the slaughter-house.

Albert has come back with Sergeant Luigi, who stands at attention:

"Mission accomplished, *Mon Général.*"

"Is the enemy still under cover?"

"I've looked everywhere," Luigi says.

"Where is Corporal Max?"

"With Monique."

General Mustapha blushes.

"Officer, my car!"

Albert hitches himself to the cart; he pulls his leader to the uncultivated part of the garden; a hole a yard deep and two yards wide is half full of water.

"I told you to put the lid over it. If Lakhdar's

gang attacks, how can we get into the trench?"

"They won't attack."

Luigi has picked up the bucket; he bails out the water. He adds as he works:

"Lakhdar's in our school now. He's not with the shepherds anymore."

"Why don't we ask him to join our army?"

"My father wouldn't let him," Albert whispers.

"Why?"

"*No gangsters, no Arabs in the garden*, Papa says. He won't let us," Albert says.

Luigi stops bailing.

"But since our general's an Arab anyway?"

"Yes," Albert says, "he's an Arab, but his father's a lawyer."

Mustapha merely blushes.

"I've got an idea," Luigi exclaims. "Lakhdar won't come to the garden, but we'll tell him to come to the maneuvers on the Taffat."

"Good idea, sergeant! I'm promoting you to a lieutenant. Take my bayonette and find Lakhdar!"

"Be careful," Albert says, "my father doesn't want us to play with his military stuff."

During the maneuvers on the Taffat, Lakhdar loses the prison guard's bayonette and refuses to call Mustapha *"Mon Général."* They improvise a ring. The whole army immediately starts fighting each other. Mustapha is the final victor. Weapons

292

are abandoned for games. The general drops his own rank. Lakhdar and Mustapha becomes organizers, arbiters, and leaders of the gang, which admits a few shepherds. Lakhdar and Mustapha fight two more times. Lakhdar takes his revenge; the two leaders are of the same strength; Mademoiselle Dubac cannot separate them; they never copy or cheat; Mustapha is always first, but Lakhdar, after skipping two classes, gradually catches up. As for girls: Lakhdar terrorizes Monique's suitors and Mustapha mounts guard when Lakhdar kisses Dhehbia in the *oukil's* office.

xi. . .

"You have three quarters of an hour to finish."

Monsieur Temple blows on his fingers.

He takes off his glasses and sits down again.

The natural science room is the best equipped; it has three long wooden platforms to which the desks are attached; each class has its own place; third-year "classics" students stay in the same row the whole year.

Monsieur Temple is the dean of the school.

He is a member of the discipline committee.
He has a powerful voice.
He is very strict in class.
He never repeats what he says.
He never forgets a penalty.
He never talks to the other professors.
He is never seen in the streets of Sétif.

Mustapha changes his seat and his row! That's not all. This autumn morning (1944) is distinguished by an unusual number of absentees. Mustapha is alone in the left row. It is composition day.

Monsieur Temple doesn't say a word.

Perhaps he is waiting for the absentee register.

He leaves his office a moment, enters the laboratory.

One girl, then another turns toward Mustapha.

He stares at them, lips trembling.

They whisper to each other.

Charles, the effeminate boy, hums.

S . . . and T . . . begin a nasty palaver full of allusions.

"In God's name!" thunders Monsieur Temple.

His mouth stays open.

A white lock dances over the wrinkles in his forehead.

He slams down the skeleton Casimir.

Everyone bends over his desk, all heads down, including Mustapha's.

"Mademoiselle Duo, report to the principal!"

The daughter of the biggest baker in Sétif leaves the room, shaking her heavy black hair. Mustapha inhales the thread of wind she makes as she closes the door.

In comes the attendance-taker with his green book.

Charley gives the names of the absentees.

He emphasizes the gutturals.

Everyone absent is Moslem.

The attendance-taker leaves a paper on the stand.

Monsieur Temple, his face impassive, reads it.

Mustapha pretends to be examining the skeleton.

He feels the professor's eyes on him.

". . . Dear Teacher, I will not be handing in my theme . . . today is the anniversary of the prophet Mohamed, the Mouloud . . . Our holidays are not provided for in your calendars. My schoolmates were right not to come . . . I was sure of being first in composition . . . I am a false brother! . . . I like natural science. Lakhdar doesn't understand it that way. I came alone. I'll hand in a blank page . . . I simply came to learn the subject . . . To go through with the formalities of composition day. I like natural science. I'll hand in a blank sheet."

"Mustapha Gharib . . ."

The skeleton dances.

. . . To the principal's office.

The heads rise again, still terrified and triumphant.

xii. . .

The principal is bent double in his chair.

No chest; his belly rises to the assault of his wrecked skull. Mustapha remains standing.

"I don't have much to tell you. You have undoubted gifts. Almost all your grades are good . . ."

Mustapha feels the thick carpet through the hole in his shoe.

". . . One can hardly say as much for your associates . . ."

Mustapha respectfully peers at his swollen lids, sly and watchful, but meets no answering glance; the principal gestures and speaks from a distance, turning to one side; he does not seem to be talking to Mustapha.

". . . Now listen carefully to what I'm going to

read you. I'm quoting at random: *Out of the thousands of children swarming in the streets, we are only a few students, surrounded with suspicion. Are we to work as flunkeys, or content ourselves with 'liberal professions' in order to become the 'privileged few' ourselves? Can we have any other ambition? Everyone knows that a Moslem accepted in the air force sweeps up the pilots' cigarettes, and if he's an officer, even from the Polytechnic, he can only reach the rank of colonel in order to send his compatriots to the recruiting office . . .* Do you recognize this text?"

Mustapha hasn't time to answer.

"I'll go on: *Do you know what I read in Tacitus? These lines, which occur in the translation from Agricola: 'The Bretons were living like savages, always ready to make war; in order to accustom them, by the pleasures of life, to peace and tranquility, he (Agricola) had the children of the leaders educated, and suggested that he preferred to the acquired talents of the Gauls the natural spirit of the Bretons, so that these peoples, lately disdaining the Roman language, now prided themselves on speaking it gracefully; our very costume was given a place of honor, and the toga became fashionable; gradually, they yielded to the seductions of our vices; they sought our porticos, our baths, our elegant banquets; and these inexperienced men gave the name of civilization to what comprised part of their servitude . . .' That is*

297

what you can read in Tacitus. That is how it is that we, descendants of the Numidians, now undergo the colonization of the Gauls!"

Mustapha stops listening. Expelled for eight days.

VI. . .

i. . .

Fanatic.

Nothing to do but fight and keep still.

Make a place for himself in the gang of poverty-stricken students.

They are pitiless.

Acrocephalic, a piece of cigarette paper sticking to his thick lip every morning, his eye vague as a caged bear's: Lakhdar. He learns he is scorned by the seamstress.

He has sold most of his school clothes.

If you don't have your books you can't attend courses.

Old Mahmoud has sent back the list with an enclosure of a hundred francs and a letter: "When you've finished the first book, I'll send you enough to buy the second." Lakhdar does not insist. He has blatantly omitted Tahar's name in his registration; at the moment of introducing Lakhdar to Mademoiselle Dubac, Tahar's remorse had given way to indifference.

"He can take over the grocery without going through school."

Zohra, recalling Lella Ouarda's confidences, had agreed:

"Haven't you noticed how many educated men there are in the cafés?"

Mahmoud controlled all expenditures.

The old man had the list of Lakhdar's school clothes read over to him in Gaston's shop.

"You see what they ask for the child's education?"

". . . Two pajamas and two nightshirts . . . Of course, you wouldn't understand . . . That's for the dormitory. There may be a hundred boys sleeping together, with a monitor paid by the state, just to watch over them while they sleep. You can't think that's easy . . ."

Gaston hoped Mahmoud would stop there, he hoped that a good-for-nothing like Lakhdar would never achieve a secondary education, or even bookkeeping.

Mahmoud was relentless.

". . . They have a special way of making them sleep? Costumes for bed? And you have to pay for that?"

Gaston agreed that the sacrifice was enough to give a good man pause; he agreed that his yellow cottons were selling badly, although, if anything was really bad, it was these bastards in X . . . , incapable of wearing cloth that cost three hundred francs a yard.

"Look at this workmanship. Feel it. I swear

on my son's head, and he's in the army. The bailiff's
wife came herself. She took six yards."

Cunning is repaid in kind, with cunning three
times over.

Mahmoud pressed the package to his breast.
He asked questions about Gaston's son.

The horn signalling the arrival of the Sétif
bus allowed him to leave the shop unnoticed: no
villager could resist his curiosity when the powerful vehicle pulled into sight; Gaston had looked
up; Mahmoud had taken one step, then another
. . . He would take his time about paying.

ii. . .

In his yellow cotton pajamas, Lakhdar attracts a
number of jeering boarders; they have the same
effect as his striped shirts, his two pairs of mat-
tress-ticking trousers, his box, with its enormous
lock, filled with dried figs, while his neighbors in
the dormitory swallow their glazed chestnuts without even tasting them, and Mustapha furiously
tears off the silver paper Lakhdar wants to save.

Lakhdar carves *Independence for Algeria* on
desks and doors.

Lakhdar and Mustapha leave the club to look for pennants.

The farmers are ready for the parade.

"Why the devil have they brought their cattle?"

Field workers, factory workers, businessmen. Sun. A big crowd. *Germany has surrendered.*

Couples. Bars crowded.

The bells.

Official ceremony: monument to the dead.

The police keep their distance.

Popular counter-demonstration.

Enough promises. 1870. 1918. 1945.

Today, May 8, is it victory this time?

The scouts march past first, then the students.

Lakhdar and Mustapha march side by side.

The crowd swells.

Four abreast.

No one in the streets can resist the pennants.

The Cadres are broken.

The anthem begins on the children's lips:

> *De nos montagnes s'élève*
> *La voix des hommes libres.*

Mustapha sees himself at the heart of an impregnable centipede.

With the strength of so many mustaches, so many hard feet, they can stare down the *colons*, the police, the fleeing rabble.

A member of the secret police, hidden in the shadow of an arcade, shoots at the flag.

Machine-guns.

The Cadres dissolve.

They have let the demonstrators be disarmed at the mosque by the commissioner, with the mufti's help.

Chairs.

Bottles.

Branches cut on the way.

The Cadres are vanquished.

Defeat the people in their first mass demonstration?

The standard-bearer collapses.

A former combatant seizes his bugle.

Reveille or Holy War?

With his sword a farmer slices open the shoulder of a student whose short hair makes him look like a European.

Mustapha throws away his tie.

The French mayor is struck down by a policeman.

A restaurant-owner rolls in his reddened burnoose.

Lakhdar and Mustapha are separated in the confusion.

There are only three students left around Mustapha; an old Jewess throws her flowerpot at one of them, more to get it off her windowsill than to hit anyone; the last groups give way before the nests of machine-gunners; the army blocks the central avenue, firing at the tatters; the police and the *colons* range through the poor districts; not one door is left open.

Ten o'clock.

It has all happened in a few minutes.

The bus for X . . . , half empty.

Mustapha pulls himself in.

The childhood dream is realized: Mustapha is beside the driver; a Moslem policeman gets in beside him:

"Sit next to the window," the policeman smiles.

Mustapha is delighted.

He doesn't see the policeman's hair is parted by a bullet. *It's dangerous to lean out the window,* the driver says; but the countryside is deserted; the bus remains empty all the way to the village. The telephone lines are cut. *The farmers have risen.* Machine-guns. The first men shot are Ferhat Abbas' partisans: a court stenographer, a scribe; the treasurer, a merchant, has committed suicide; the Senegalese have broken through north of the village; women have been raped; machine-guns were suggested by the *colons,* organized into armed militias, as soon as they heard about what happened in Sétif.

The administrator insists on maintaining order. The *colons* and their suppliant wives want to put an end to it.

The administrator yields to the commander of the Senegalese.

The farmers are machine-gunned.

Two fugitives are shot just outside the village.

The militia publishes the list of hostages.

Maître Gharib is indicated as one of the leaders.

The sun is still high.

May 13.

Mustapha goes to look at the two men who were shot.

Curfew.

Cries of the crickets and the police escorting the suspects with kicks.

The bodies are exposed in the sunlight.

iii. . .

MUSTAPHA'S DIARY (*continued*)

I climbed up on a hill where Monique used to come and sit with the policemen's daughters.

There on the road, examining the men who were shot, was the ranger and his inseparable wife

Madame N . . . , both of whom every Moslem was ordered to salute ever since May 8. With them was B . . . , the prison guard, R . . . , one of my classmates, F . . . the electrician and his wife, Monique's parents.

I could hear everything they said.

F . . .: My God they stink!

Mme. F . . .: Please! I feel like being sick as it is!

F . . .: Of course, you women . . . I've seen bodies before. Even at the Marne, the ground was covered with Boches and Frenchmen . . .

Mme. N . . .: But not Arabs. When these men were alive, they stank to high heaven. But now that they're dead, it's even worse . . .

B . . .: They think the army's for dogs.

F . . .: This time they'll understand.

N . . .: You think so? I tell you they'll start all over. We didn't do enough.

Mme. N . . .: My God, if France didn't take care of us, we couldn't even protect ourselves!

F . . .: France is rotten. They should give us arms and leave us alone. No need for laws here. They don't recognize anything but force. What they need is a Hitler.

Mme. F . . . (caressing R . . .): And they even go to school with you, my child! Of course now they know everything . . .

R . . .: Oh, it'll be different. Before, we were afraid. There were a lot of them in my class; only five French boys, not counting Italians and Jews.

Mme. F . . .: You be careful, my child, they're savages!

Mme. N . . .: If you knew how I wept for these innocents. If I had a son, I'd be out of my mind!

I left the hill, so exalted that I found myself running down the middle of the road without taking any precautions.

My father was "taking the sun" in front of the door. He kept saluting invisible soldiers . . . All evening, he nagged at me: I was crazy, I thought I was so much smarter than the rest, I'd get my parents massacred, etc. My mother was crying. It got worse after curfew, when the village idiot was shot, a starved, solitary girl . . . She was shot down near our house on her way to the fountain.

I was arrested the next morning (May 13).

I came back from Si Khelifa's where I had gone before my father woke up.

Si Khelifa taught us—my friends and me—to learn the village secrets, to smoke, to enjoy girls, to send them messages. At sixty, the barber played dominoes with us, shared all our diversions, even the most childish, answered all our questions. The bourgeois of X . . . hated the barber. They said he was a corrupter of youth. They whispered that he was a political agitator, without being able to accuse him of belonging to any party whatsoever. He had fought in every campaign, been awarded the Croix de Guerre; in spite of his poverty, he sent both his children to the school. Whom else could I trust but a man as precise and complicated as this one, with his enormous belly, his discretion and his audacity, his wisdom and his whims—they all went so well together! Barber, thinker, organizer, sexagenarian! I felt a growing admiration for Si Khelifa. Each time I came home on vacation I brought him books, newspapers, cigarettes. A curtain divided the room, concealing the corner where Si Khelifa received his customers. His friends came in one after the other. Lakhdar picked up a mandolin made out of a turtle shell and with the help of a blind beggar composed satiric songs dedicated to the "swell heads." Everyone spoke Arabic and French fluently, although our group included one Jew who was assassinated on May 9 by a merchant, and one Italian who had just left school for his father's construction yards.

Luigi was funny and abusive, timid with girls, good at games, knew the country path by path. Brought up among his father's workmen (his father was a public works contractor), Luigi spoke Arabic better than I did and as well as the barber. One thing distinguished him: his assiduous presence at mass, among his six brothers and sisters . . . He listened thoughtfully to our arguments. When anyone asked what he thought, he always answered: *Politics is hot air. It gives me a headache.*

The morning I was arrested, I was waiting

for Luigi at the barber's. Events had obliged our Italian friend to barricade himself in the police station with the European population until the arrival of the gunmen. After the army was billeted in the village, I lost all hope of seeing him, when I recognized his voice coming into the room.

Holding his beret, sweating, Luigi:

"They asked me if you were spreading propaganda. They say you were at the Sétif parade, and that you brought the password for the uprising here."

"Who says?"

"The administrator's assistant and the inspectors. They came for me at home early this morning. They use their whips pretty hard!"

The barber groaned.

"Now they're turning on the Italians."

"Did you tell them?"

"I played dead."

"What proof do they have?"

"A huge dossier, on the assistant's desk."

I left without another word, not even saying goodbye to my friends.

On our doorstep, I noticed two Europeans. Machine-guns in their arms. Police. They were talking to my father.

He gestured me to follow them.

They didn't say a word all the way to the police station. Once inside the door, someone gave me a smack under one eye that felt as if it had

311

fallen from the ceiling. There were an impressive number of police, village men, and some from other barracks called in as a reinforcement.

"Ah! It's you," the corporal screamed. He was the one who had hit me.

"Your name!" said a policeman I had never seen before, hitting me in the chest with his crop.

"I'll take care of this one," the corporal said.

He ran his hands over my pockets without noticing the half-empty pack of cigarettes, pulled off my belt, then pushed me through the door.

I received other blows that were harder and more carefully aimed. I stumbled over a step and bumped my head against the corridor wall. I was bleeding. When he grabbed my sweater, the corporal got blood on his hand and a strange fit came over him. He started shaking me. He slapped me with the back of his hand, kicking me upright when I lost my balance.

When I came to again, the corporal was gone.

I thought I was free.

I was lying between two barrels in the police station courtyard.

The corporal's daughter, who used to come play with my sisters, was jumping around the barrels. She smiled at me. I could see the corporal's wife behind her curtain.

I turned around and saw two men chained up facing the watering-trough. Their arms were fastened by handcuffs to the rings where the police usually tied their horses. The position of the rings made it impossible for the prisoners either to lie on the ground or stand up.

I recognized the house-painter Tayeb, with whom I used to go fishing during Easter vacation, and an old blacksmith, the same one who had chased Dhehbia out of his shop the day I was admitted to Mademoiselle Dubac's class . . .

Tayeb was a joker. All the kids loved him, but no one dreamed he could have been a militant. He was sickly, although no one could walk as far : sometimes he covered fifty kilometers in a day, barefoot, visiting outlying farms and markets, where friends and relatives helped him when he was out of work.

In the village, he always found someone to offer him a cup of coffee or a cigarette. His nights were usually spent in fierce domino matches. When everyone had gone and the police drove the last prowlers off the streets, he went off into the woods.

His mud hut contained so extraordinary a family that he generally abjured facing it: besides his wife and five children, a huge troupe of relatives succeeded each other, even worse than the "useless mouths" that once lived at my father's, in Guelma.

Tayeb rarely worked. He had a competitor in Sétif, and his own supplies were quite inadequate. Still, when he had a job, he put on an important look, made fun of everyone, and became touchy. The whole village echoed to the rattle of buckets he kicked along the ground. According to general opinion, these buckets were merely a front. Perhaps there was something inside, but no one knew what. And everyone was afraid to ask because his tongue was so sharp . . .

At nightfall, I still didn't know what fate the corporal had in store for me. I had wakened Tayeb from his stupor and learned that he had been there for five days.

Would we be shot or sent to Sétif with the "leaders"? The blacksmith protested his innocence, raising his forefinger to heaven as a sign of resignation.

I remembered that I had cigarettes, but no matches. The little girl was still in the courtyard. I showed her the pack and made the gesture of striking a light. I waited a long time before the corporal's wife raised the curtain and threw out a box.

"It's too bad for children like you," she whispered.

Then she ducked back inside.

Tayeb smoked eagerly. I saw that he was disfigured by the beating he had received. Since his hands couldn't move, I had to hold the cigarette in his mouth for him.

The corporal's wife came back with some bread and a cup of coffee.

"Here, quick. My husband . . ."

"A policeman's a policeman, but a mother's a mother," Tayeb said.

The blacksmith stopped complaining.

Before taking us to prison, our guards organized a Roman banquet before our eyes. We watched them butcher the lambs stolen from the farmers. The corporal, now in civilian clothes, spattered Tayeb's face with the blood, throwing the hot guts at me, without reaching me.

Skewered on spits, in the center of the circle formed by the guests—Monsieur Bruno acted as chief cook—the lambs gave off an aroma of garlic that made the wind unbearable.

Disturbed by the atmosphere, by having to sit on an island surrounded by blood, the women released a torrent of gossip with which we had to console ourselves.

The banquet was over; the corporal threw the contents of his glass at us. Like a bird pressed against the bars of its cage, the blacksmith could only wiggle his mustache . . . As they left, the guests passed close to us. The corporal's daughter pulled at my chain out of curiosity. The wind blew twice as hard on our bodies soaked with alcohol.

It was a triumph to find myself in jail with Lakhdar and about a dozen others! Triumph is the word. We could walk, sit down, sleep on the cool cement! Above all, we were among friends . . . Si Khelifa was with us, calm and comforting.

The old Corsican who acts as guard pretends

not to know anything about what will happen to us. He hands out a bucket of colorless soup and a loaf of bread for four men, twice a day.

The important thing is that from now on we are worth a prison room. The moment of summary executions must be over . . .

As we crossed the prison threshold, surrounded by police, we looked up at the horizon.

There was no one in the streets. The gunmen were patrolling in all directions. The guard said nothing as he locked us up.

iv. . .

Our courtyard is empty. No one to meet me. Mother has let the rosebush die. She used to come quickly once, and there was always a cup of coffee, miraculously hot. Why don't I hear my father's cane? My sisters aren't hiding behind the door, don't look to see if my mustache has grown, if my suitcase is heavy with presents. In his bed, my father holds back his groans. He recognizes my step. Silent embrace. Face burning, beard, dirty shirt, piece of dry bread.

In the other room, my sisters, without their

Aïd dresses. Long hair down . . . They're playing knucklebones. They kiss me, in tears, as if they didn't believe in my return. Near them, a prone shape. Tangle of white hair.

"Mother keeps waking up and going back to sleep."

A letter came after my arrest, telling about the death of most of our relatives in Guelma during the first hours of the repression: my maternal uncle, his pregnant wife, his ten year old son, shot.

"Uncle Hassan didn't want to turn traitor," Farida said (aged 11). They killed him because he wouldn't take up arms. Mother can't talk any more without tearing her face. She speaks to the birds and curses her children. She's been chanting the prayers for the dead for me. Despair is followed by melancholy, then torpor. The courage to embrace her . . .

Another judiciary *oukil* arrived after my father (he hasn't stopped drinking since May 13) vomited up the cyst on his lung.

I have had to borrow enough money from the village elders to take him to the hospital in Constantine; in the taxi, my youngest sister, who hasn't all her teeth yet, sings a little song to herself:

> *My brother's in prison,*
> *My mother's crazy*
> *And my father's gone to bed.*

We have one uncle left, a farmer near Constantine. I take my mother and my sisters to him. I'll be sixteen this fall.

Work and bread.

Those are my dreams of youth.

I'll go to a port.

A ticket for the Constantine-Bône express, please.

V. . .

Lakhdar walked slowly toward Mustapha's table.

"You came by train . . ."

"Same way you did."

"Last summer, I heard that a foreigner had come by the train from Constantine. Because of the clothes, I thought of you right away. You have a foreign suit."

"It's not mine," Lakhdar smiled. "It belongs to a brother I never knew."

"From Bône?"

"We have an aunt in common . . ."

". . . In Beauséjour."

"You know as much as I do about it! Do you know my brother?"

"No."

"You don't know Mourad?"

"Mourad!"

They daydreamed.

Then Mustapha continued:

"Mourad never talked about me?"

"He told me he had two friends, and that one came from around Sétif . . ."

"I know someone who . . ."

"I don't want to see anyone," Lakhdar interrupts.

"You're making a mistake. The vendor's a good guy, he's a widower with time on his hands, he can't read so I read him the papers. I'm sure he'll take you in. He likes discussions . . ."

"All right, I'll come later. Now I'm staying at my cousin's."

vi. . .

"Let's telephone Tahar," Nedjma says. "After all, he is your father, in a manner of speaking."

She walks in proudly; without a veil, she looks like a gypsy.

Tahar: "You say you're in Bône?"

Lakhdar: "I expect to be working for a notary. Wait a minute, I'll put my cousin on the line! . . ."

Tahar (drinking a glass of water so the telephone won't betray the smell of anisette) : "Write your mother!"

Lakhdar (to Nedjma) : "Tell him I mean what I say. Explain what a notary is."

vii. . .

On the mattress Lella Fatma has put in the living room for him, Lakhdar examines his ticking trousers. Kamel has already broken the charm by putting his wardrobe at the newcomer's disposal, though the latter has temporarily abstained.

Nedjma delicately pushes open the door; she is still in pajamas; the silk clings to her spreading breasts; she approaches Lakhdar!

"*A woman like that has left her bed for me*" exults a skeleton in a dirty sweater: Casanova or Lakhdar?

It is the first living room he has ever seen: a room with scarlet hangings, brass vessels that should go in the kitchen, framed photographs: living room, museum, boudoir, casino? The chairs have a little dust on the green cushions; the chandelier bristles with bulbs: the temptation to light them all.

"Get up whenever you want. I'll turn off the lights now . . ."

"I must be crazy. Money and beauty. If I had a jewel like that, I'd chain her to the bed. He must have a hundred neckties . . . What's the matter with me, ranting on like some Spaniard! Boor, coward! The notary will finish me off; I'd rather sell sea urchins . . ."

viii . . .

"He's awake! Your breakfast, Monsieur agitator . . ."

Nedjma speaks in French. Lakhdar makes his muscles outside the covers ripple. The coquetry is not overlooked. Blast those damned trousers!

"Aren't you going to tell how they arrested you?"

"Apparently I'm a rioter."

Lakhdar immediately decides that his answer is presumptuous; the lover decides on a painful strategy: to keep his mouth shut.

ix. . .

I've seen Lakhdar again, at the café. As if we were back at the club, as if the eighth day of May had never happened. The conversation was cheerful; our separation might have dissolved the past, might have given it divergent meanings . . .

Rachid and Mourad are meeting us for dinner tonight in the shop.

Overcome by the virulence of a pepper, Mourad showed his teeth, his eyes filled with tears; when the vendor made a bad joke, Mourad left the plate of gnaouia alone, took a paper out of his pocket, and immediately monopolized the conversation: "Soccer players and spectators, have you never asked yourselves this troublesome question: what has happened to our referees? Once upon a time, our sports-loving city swarmed with referees who inspired not only our own department with confidence but were unanimously appreciated by the neighboring leagues and by the F.F.F. Unfortunately it appears that many have been discouraged by the attitude of recalcitrant spectators, or have resigned to work for local clubs, or are generally disappointed. So that now the Bône captains are appealing to referees from Philippeville or even from Constantine, with the inevitable travel and lodging expenses, as well as supplementary fees! On the other hand, Philippeville or Constantine would certainly not use a Bône referee in any friendly match . . ."

The tears of the pepper eaters grew heavy with indignation.

"As a citizen of Constantine, I go along with that," Rachid says.

"I knew Bône would get taken," the vendor says.

X. . .

MUSTAPHA'S DIARY (*continued*)
We follow Lakhdar unwillingly.
What's the use of complaining?

"Why get all excited about the villas and the women lying around in them?" Rachid complains.

Lakhdar, shaggy, walks faster. As a matter of fact, I suspect him of leading us secretly toward Beauséjour . . . He's still living in the same house with Nedjma . . . Does he know I know her?

We're climbing the hill!

Have they quarreled? Concealed by dint of difficult acrobatics (inspired by Lakhdar), we see Nedjma in her garden. She is leaning against the lemon-tree.

Rachid stiffens. "That's the one. The same one. The woman from the clinic."

Nedjma, unconscious, turns toward him, and Lakhdar hides behind a cactus.

"You know her?" Rachid asks.

Nedjma turns a little further, intrigued, as though to kill a fly on her glowing shoulder.

Lakhdar!

Rachid and Mustapha run down the hill with the humility of two foxes leaving a third at the hencoop door to deal with a rare bird that would have driven them to fatal conflict had they not withdrawn.

xii. . .

It was a winter night brightened by the sum of
five thousand francs Mourad unexpectedly acquired as he was wandering around the harbor,
piloting a Norwegian sailor through the sale of
twelve Swiss chronometers. Mourad ran for a long
time; he wakened Lakhdar, suggesting that they
make a night of it, and Nedjma who had not left
her bed in Kamel's absence . . .

Nedjma's cousins Mourad and Lakhdar were
related to her in the same way, but Mourad had
been born in the villa, while Lakhdar, suddenly revealed to the family's eyes this spring, could only
be embarrassed by his brother's comings and goings; Mourad went into Nedjma's room, sat down
on a corner of the bed, sometimes in her husband's
presence, and fell headlong into the woman's
games, her laughter nailing Lakhdar to the living
room floor and leaving a mournful legend in his
mind . . . *"I can't be everyone's brother and
cousin,"* the wanderer groaned, the day after his
installation in Beauséjour; as a son of the High

Plateaus Lakhdar could not admit that a man (for after all, Lakhdar regarded his brother as a man) could have such blatantly familiar relations with a cousin.

Mustapha was invited, but they couldn't find Rachid.

i. . .

The party took place in the room Lakhdar was living in; Lakhdar took down the framed photographs of Nedjma, who had gone away with Lella Fatma and some other women, loaded with candles and pastry they were going to offer to a famous saint on his tomb in a nearby *douar*. Mourad found Mustapha in the café; Lakhdar had prepared a soup filled with oily, sputtering potatoes; the dry mint drowned the emanations of the stewed tomatoes; the parsley wilted on the spiced chick peas (they had to soak them the day before), and the lamb had been cut into tiny squares, giving a flavor of quantity as well as of youth . . . Mourad and Mustapha mastered their hunger, broke into the third thousand-franc note, and came back clutch-

326

ing a bottle; Lakhdar discovered the roast lamb's head in the oven; the smoking cheeks were quickly torn away; the brains sprinkled with pepper, and the thick tongue seemed to whisper for a long time between the jaws; all this caused the unregarded loss of the bottle, for the trio feared Nedjma's unlikely return; she rang eagerly, while Mustapha went off for a second bottle.

The storm raging outside permitted no deliberation; Lakhdar went to open the door.

"I left my mother at the mausolem; I was bored . . ."

Nedjma walked past the door Mourad and Mustapha kept closed only with their eyes . . .

She did not go in, danced off toward the nuptial chamber, gaily leading Lakhdar by the hand; he followed her against his will, thinking of Mustapha who had been invited by two cousins of no influence in the family, and whom they couldn't introduce . . . He would have had to warn Mourad, make Mustapha vanish, hide the remains of their banquet, the bottle first of all . . .

But Nedjma kept Lakhdar in her room. She had brought him cigarettes; Lakhdar found himself speechless on the bed where he could not forgive Mourad for sitting; he no longer tried to escape.

At this moment, Kamel was on his way to Constantine, where his probably dead mother was waiting for him; Lakhdar asked about the absent husband; Nedjma pouted; she always scolded Lakhdar for bringing up the disgraced Kamel.

The embrace had an unheard of intensity; Nedjma cried. The electric light flowed over her body still wet with rain.

Lakhdar saw the crocodile bag; the soldier's portrait was stuck to the powdery mirror Nedjma had just taken out without noticing it.

Lakhdar tore off the portrait. He said nothing.

In tears, Nedjma spoke of Kamel's delicacy —Kamel who had just sat down at his mother's bedside to speak of his precious wife Nedjma and his handsomely furnished living room, where Mourad and Mustapha dared not comment on Lakhdar's desertion since the bell had rung; Mustapha decided to wait. Mourad left in silence.

ii. . .

Mourad visited the bars of the old city one by one; his drunkenness vanished after the first cup of coffee; he began drinking again, and in the darkness went on puzzling over Sidi Boumerouene's allegory: *I swear that the house of God is full of mystery, it is a great monument shining with light, the sublime stars seem less sublime, and thanks to God the stars of happiness rise in Bône.*

iii. . .

Lakhdar lit a cigarette and burned the portrait; his silence succeeded in hurrying Nedjma, red and sullen, out of the room, as he ran after her, he heard her open the living-room door where, pressed against it, he now heard only the wind's insistent breathing. He turned the key from outside and went back to the empty bedroom.

Locked in Nedjma and Mourad locked in, the wind whistled in light gusts, drowning the electric light, driving its odorous immensities astray, stumbling against the shutters, scattering the forest in rainy resin and the sea in decapitated eddies. Lakhdar put the key down on a book. "Love's Catechism." The wind had razed the living room, proscribed all vision, and the whirling blood permitted no idea to settle, as if the city, on account of the storm, were suddenly freed of its leaves, as if Nedjma herself whirled somewhere, suddenly swept away.

The bell rang again.

iv. . .

Dead drunk, Mourad was back.

Lakhdar started to push his brother away, but suddenly grabbed his shoulder instead. Lakhdar did not seem to see Mourad, and remained lost in thought standing in front of him, like some sage who has met a ghost. Calmly, Lakhdar realized that Mustapha was alone with Nedjma. *"It was Mourad I was thinking about when I locked her in; it was to bring Mourad and Nedjma face to face that I risked sounding my passion, not foreseeing I was making Nedjma innocent by delivering her, unawares, to Mustapha; I thought he had gone out for wine. He must have come back; but why did Mourad go? Out of jealousy, because I didn't come back to the living room after the bell . . ."*

Images pierced him like nails.

Lakhdar walked, holding the key, listening to the wind and to his hatred. He was singing.

"When I locked them in, Mustapha didn't exist, he had remained in the shadow, reality's secret weapon; but when I broke moorings, I knew that a friendly wind would bring back the inevitable wreck. That wind was Mustapha and the wreck brought me closer to my love as much as it took me from her; my love is a woman perpetually in flight, beyond the paralyses of an already perverse Nedjma, already imbued with my strength, cloudy like a spring I have had to vomit in after having drunk from it; Nedjma is the tangible form of the mistress who waits for me, the thorn, the flesh, the seed, but not the soul, not the living unity where I could blend myself without fear of dissolution . . ."

Lakhdar heard someone kicking the living room door; he decided it was Nedjma's little foot. He leaned once more against the living room door, put the key back in the lock, turned around and left the house.

V. . .

They did not leave the shop of the fritter vendor. For two days, rain and hail had poured down on the city; they waited.

Rachid tapped the sole of one shoe as he nudged Mustapha with his elbow, and Mourad, his rainy-day beard gnawed by the calmly endured itching, followed the evolutions of the Rue Sadi-Carnot, inhaling the odor of a woman's umbrella with all his strength.

They did not leave the shop of the fritter vendor, who thought he had won a victory over their impatience to find work, exulting in his fatherly soul, a peasant proud of receiving (after a long celibacy) four students; he had used as wrapping paper a whole carton full of letters returned or unanswered: Rachid re-read them furtively, in hopes of sooner or later possessing a weapon:

"Monsieur le Directeur:

"I have the honor . . .

"May I add that I have had an education consisting of more than twelve years of studies . . .

"Relying on your sense of equity . . .

"Monsieur le Directeur:

". . . My conduct has always been . . . Honorable family . . . Despite my youth . . .

"Monsieur le Directeur:

". . . employment in your services as bookkeeper, secretary, receptionist or turnkey.

". . . support of a family of four . . .

". . . the director of the Institut Pasteur has forwarded your letter in which you proposed the sale of your eyes . . ."

vi. . .

Lakhdar came back as Mustapha was standing up to stretch.

"Smile, apes!"

Rachid swore without offending the vendor's meditative posture, and Lakhdar caught his breath, shaking his dripping clothes.

"It's over. Tomorrow we work."

". . . If it was true, we'd be princes; with work like that, no need to think; once we eat and drink, no more worries!"

"I'm just afraid you'll faint the first time you lift a shovel."

"I was a gravedigger in the European cemetery in Constantine, to pay the debts of my beloved . . ."

"That dancer?"

"She never knew where the money came from . . ."

"Look how pleased Rachid is," Lakhdar says. "He's never talked so much before! Tell us the story of your life, don't be embarrassed."

Rachid swore again, his voice low, and this time disturbed the speculations of the vendor, who was waiting for nothing better than an opportunity to cool his protégés' enthusiasm:

"Hey, Lakhdar, are you serious?"

Mustapha was sure Lakhdar was telling the truth, and he began prodding his muscles, nonplussed at the idea of becoming a laborer, nonplussed, repentant, and proud.

"What's the name of the place?"

"Every village is the same, if you have enough to live on . . ."

"Let him tell about it," the vendor said.

"I went into a shed to avoid that ex-J.B.A.C. player who gave Mourad a thousand francs . . ."

"Now I can give them back!"

"Maybe he didn't know Mourad was your brother . . ."

"Anyway, I wanted to get out of his way, and that's why I went into the shed; I went in, and I read on the sign, *Reinforced Concrete*. I went on toward the courtyard, it was full of bricks. Office on the left. I found a bald man cleaning his nails. He signed us up almost without looking at me. He was married; I always thought married men were bald, I imagined that his wife had pulled out his hair during their honeymoon, and I laughed to myself, maybe so he would look at me too; I must have seemed to be several people bothering him at once; he had his eyes all over the place, slowly turning toward someone, but I couldn't manage to get him to look at me, even though I was the only one there! I'm telling you this because I was afraid right up to the end that I wouldn't be hired, and I think that when I was trying to catch his eyes I wanted to be sure it was really me he was taking on and not someone else . . . Well, he read back our names and I felt relieved; I even got to like him a little when he was reading back our names . . . That's what it means to be out of work! You get to thinking of a boss as if he were God the father . . . When I told him again that there were four of us, he didn't make a move: "*The same age?*" I said yes. He didn't make any mistake with our names. So he must be an old Algerian. "*Tomorrow, at five o'clock. The truck will be here. The foreman of the yards will talk to you. Bring something to eat.*" I even said yes again, I was so happy!"

"The boss thinks we have wives, or mothers?"

"Two hundred francs a day."

"You asked him the name of the village?"

"What difference does it make?"

The vendor pointed his index finger toward the Creator, as a sign of annoyance and resignation.

"You'll be back; why should they keep you?"

vii. . .

While his two acolytes walk along on either side, Beaver, the bearded man they encountered in a bar, leads the four newcomers to the rooms they have rented from an old Italian woman along the edge of the road, where the houses are few and badly built, not even whitewashed; the Italian woman lives at the other end of the village; she never visits her tenants, according to Beaver. He claims the old woman's afraid of going out, just brave enough to collect the rent; despite her avarice, a visitor's shadow is enough to terrify her. *"She's never been able to get used to the idea of living among us, and her husband was a ranger . . . She may have savings."*

Mustapha does not conceal his disappointment.

"Let her stay where she is."

"We'll send her the rent by mail."

"Or in a suitcase."

"Why not a coffin?"

Beaver is pleased to have drunk with young

men; he has white hair, red eyes, yellow skin, black teeth, and his hands are blue with cold; the night is getting on; the church bells rang ten; the night watchmen are blowing their whistles for the curfew.

"They've kept you in since the eighth of May?"

"There's always been a curfew," Beaver says. "After ten the watchmen can fire at strangers if they don't stop at the whistles."

Rachid turns around.

"And who's that kid playing the harmonica?"

"The postmaster's son? One day the old Italian woman saw him breaking off branches from her cherry-tree. He saw she was watching him out the window. He fell out of the tree and his pants got caught when he climbed over the fence. I don't know how long they ogled each other like that, him hanging by his ass, she standing terrified at her window. Later she was running along the road screaming: "There's a German parachutist in my garden!" The war was over. Too big for his age, that boy . . ."

Lakhdar laughs: "Good for her!"

"If that isn't a shame," Mourad says, "a hundred francs a day for cells full of drafts!"

viii. . .

Lakhdar is in prison; the fight has scandalized the whole of the administrative staff, as well as the entire population, without distinction of race or religion; the general opinion is that outsiders go too far; a story like this on his first day of work is enough to condemn Lakhdar in every villager's conscience; one could say a lot about this condemnation . . . A judgment so summary and so generalized cannot be explained *a priori*, since Monsieur Ernest is famous for his villainy; everyone in the village frankly loathes him, yet it is Lakhdar's behavior that is frowned on . . . The most plausible hypothesis is that the people, including the workers who have more than once been victimized by the foreman, are annoyed to see a stranger from the city settle straight off an old dissension that was getting juicier every day and becoming everyone's business.

ix. . .

Will the new men be sacked?

x. . .

They decide not to show themselves in the village for several days; at twilight a boy brings them a bottle of wine.

"Just in time."

"We'll drown our sorrows."

Around nine at night, the three are visited by two men who come in after a thousand precautions: Beaver, accompanied by a long-eared, timid, stoop-shouldered friend who unwraps an anis-seed cake and a package of boiled lamb-fat; another bottle of wine sways in Beaver's hood as he walks back and forth to warm himself.

339

"Just in time," Mourad repeats.

Mustapha puts an old newspaper on one of the doubled-over mattresses: *"one table's as good as another,"* he smiles at the man whose long ears are growing purpler by the minute; Rachid carries over the second mattress, stretches it out, and Mourad crouches on it beside Mustapha, who sniffs the cake with great dignity; his detachment does not seem likely to last; Rachid hands him the package of fat, forcing a smile.

"Eat, my son. There's just enough for you."

Beaver, having brought the food, finds the joke somewhat savorless; his friend's ears are burning, as if he were afraid of seeing them fall under the trio's teeth along with the lamb.

Mustapha breaks the ice and the cake, beginning to eat.

Beaver tries to change the subject.

"I knew you wouldn't go out. What a business! . . ."

The workmen eat and drink determined to talk as little as possible; *"Filthy villagers! They bring us an anis-seed cake to impress us when three kilos of bread would have been enough,"* Mourad thinks, just about through with his share. Beaver tells how after leaving them last night he was pursued by the husband of one of his mistresses.

"You were armed, that's what counts," his friend whispers.

"Half-way down the street, I stopped to light

a cigarette, and I saw him turn around, worse than a coward."

"You weren't scared?" Mourad asks, respectfully considering his white hair.

"I'm used to it."

"You never know," Rachid whispers.

"I usually go out armed . . ."

"That's the way it is when you fool around with women . . ."

"You die a violent death."

Beaver's friend shows a photograph and his eyes darken.

"He's a fool," Beaver says, "he's going after one of the girls!"

"She makes him jealous?" Mourad asks, extraordinarily interested in the photograph.

"He wants the Cadi's daughter. You think that's easy! All he does is send messages . . . Only she's never seen him . . . He keeps walking back and forth under her window, she says she can't see his face. It's enough to drive you crazy! . . . One day we found out she was going to the baths with her old servant-woman. We watched for them. At the right moment, he went straight toward them, almost knocked the old woman down. Luckily there were only kids around . . . Besides, the girl didn't expect us to speak to her. No one saw anything. The next day we sent the girl a picture postcard showing a couple separated by the war saying goodbye, to remind her that the writer was the same man who almost knocked her servant over without daring to speak to her . . . Well, the message was complicated, but we didn't have any luck . . . After reading it—not without pleasure, according to our messenger (a well-brought-up boy who has access to honorable families)—she answered (on the back of a calendar), saying she still didn't see who could be writing her like that; she added that she remembered the clumsy man all right, but not his face."

"Terrible!"

"But what about this photo?" Mourad insists.

Beaver shrugs, amused by his own story. *"That's the singer Osmahan . . ."*

The watchmen's first night whistle is heard, followed by a long, smoke-filled silence.

"He'll get tired soon . . ."

The long purple ears go out with the candle.

"She'll end up seeing me," the unhappy man says, suddenly growing bolder in the dark calm of the evening.

xi. . .

Lakhdar has escaped from his cell.

At dawn, when his shadow appears on the landing, everyone looks up, indifferently.

Mourad stares at the fugitive.

"So what? They'll get you later."

"They know your name."

"I don't have any papers."

"They'll look for you here."

"Shut up. Don't nag."

No question of sleep now. Lakhdar notices the empty bottle.

"How did you get that?"

"From Beaver. He just left."

"Don't I get any?"

"Listen," Mourad suggests. "We'll sell my knife."

xii. . .

"Don't light a fire," the elder suggested.

Lakhdar groans, his head buried in the straw.

The stars swarm.

It is bitter cold.

Mustapha hums, both to fight off the cold and to fall asleep; the stars swarm.

At sunrise, they follow the bad forest paths.

They don't talk to each other.

It is the moment to separate.

They don't look at each other.

If Mourad were here, they could each take one of the cardinal points; they could each stick to a specific direction. But Mourad is not here. They think about Mourad.

"Beaver gave me some money," Lakhdar says suddenly. "We'll share it."

"I'm going to Constantine," Rachid says.

"Let's get started," Lakhdar says. "I'll go with you as far as Bône. What about you, Mustapha?"

"I'm going a different way."

The two shadows fade on the road.

CPSIA information can be obtained at www.ICGtesting.com
Printed in the USA
LVOW11s0236121113

360873LV00008B/189/P